Jamie Raintree

Perfectly Undone

GRAYDON
HOUSE

**GRAYDON
HOUSE**

Recycling programs
for this product may
not exist in your area.

ISBN-13: 978-1-525-81137-1

Perfectly Undone

To my husband,
the hero of my story

Perfectly Undone

1

Some things can never be forgiven.

This thought flashes down my spine like lightning. The rain thunders overhead with the same rhythm as my heartbeat as I sit at the dining room table I bought together with the man I love, in the house we've shared for the last two years.

Can they? I ask myself, consuming every last inch of him with my eyes, as if it will be my last chance.

Cooper.

On one knee.

His blue eyes tense, waiting for my answer.

Those stubborn strands of blond hair fallen over his forehead.

"Dylan?" he presses.

I shake my head—not an answer, a try at clarity. It comes. *We can't start a marriage based on secrets.*

"I can't give you an answer," I whisper in a voice that isn't mine. His eyebrows furrow, unsure of whether or not he heard me correctly. I can't stick around to watch understanding take over his features. He can't push me into this one. I place the fork in my hand back on the table with forced precision, then attempt to pull my fingers from Cooper's grasp. "I'm so sorry. I love you, but I can't."

Still he won't let me go. The fact that he knows he isn't going to get the answer he wants and he still doesn't want me to leave pushes a sob from my lips.

"Cooper," I cry, but I pull myself free, stand and cross the living room. I wrench open the front door, no shoes, and walk out into the rain without looking back.

The storm hits me with a force that shocks me, making me feel more awake than I've been in years. I don't know what I'm walking toward or what I'm running away from, I just feel the wet earth against the soles of my feet, holding me up, pushing me on. My breath comes quickly, and the spring air is so new, it forms a cloud in front of my face with every exhalation. I rush forward, rain and tears mixing together on the palette of my cheeks. I reach the road, follow it with my eyes until it disappears in both directions and realize I'm in the middle of nowhere with nowhere to go and not a single person I can turn to.

My hair sticks to my face, the mud to my clothes.

With no one to hear, I ask myself what I'm doing, how I got here. Don't I have everything I'm supposed to want?

With no one to notice, I wonder if I'm wasting the life Abby never got to live.

2

Six weeks earlier...

I stand at the edge of the terrace outside the Women's Clinic and grasp the cold metal railing. I watch the orange rays of sunset spray across the downtown high-rises, Portland's never-ending rush-hour traffic and the landscape of trees as they soak up the last offerings of winter moisture. My white coat is draped over the back of the metal chair next to me, and a cool breeze sweeps over my arms.

This is my midday ritual, when my first round of patient consultations is finished, before the bustle of the day is replaced by stacks of charts to be filled out. I escape to this terrace, this place of solitude, and hold tight to a few moments of perspective. I breathe in the busy silence, and once a day, I pretend I could go somewhere no one knows my name, where absolution is easy and truth isn't so hard to come by.

A bird flies overhead, past the parking lot below me and the still street entrance beyond that. My gaze follows it to the path of the Willamette River, a wide divide of sleepless water that cuts Portland in half. The break in the scenery means nothing to the bird, but I often wonder why they bothered to build the foundation of a city on land that would always be split. No matter how close to the water they plant offices, or how many bridges traverse one shore to the other, the two sides will never connect. It will never be whole.

But I am up here, seven floors high, and if I close my eyes and raise my face to the sky, I can almost pretend that I, too, am flying above it. Untouchable.

"Dr. Michels." I turn to see Enrique, a nurse intern, leaning against the open glass door to the clinic. His dry sarcasm and the way his brown eyes squint almost closed when he smiles has made him one of my favorite nurses.

"You ready for another delivery?" he asks, his Puerto Rican accent pulling down his vowels.

"Of course," I say. I pick up my coat, feed my arms back into it and follow him inside.

Sunlight shines through the towering glass walls of the clinic and glints off the modern furniture tucked in alcoves and lining the walls around the check-in desk. Enrique and I weave through women at various stages of pregnancy, with their families, nurses and doctors, and back into the halls of the clinic—a beehive that from the terrace is a low hum; inside, a violent roar. Between my four-year residency and my year as a licensed OB/GYN, this is my fifth year at this clinic, and it still surprises me how many patients we fit into a day.

Once we hit our stride in the hallway, Enrique passes me the chart of the laboring mother.

"Eight centimeters," he says. "She's been laboring for six hours and progressing at a steady rate."

I quickly flip through the pages of Mrs. Forrest's chart, then let the pages flutter back to their place.

"Have you seen Vanessa around today?" I ask him. Vanessa Lu is the chief of the OB/GYN department and the woman who holds my fate in her email inbox. Vanessa agreed to be my mentor for my first clinical trial, one of a dozen hoops I have to jump through to get my research grant approved. A place to conduct my trial is the final piece of the puzzle. Once Vanessa gets the okay on lab space, I can finalize my grant application.

"Does anyone ever actually see Dr. Lu?" he asks, and I have to laugh. It's true that although everyone knows she hardly ever leaves the hospital, no one ever runs into her in the halls. She appears as if out of nowhere when she needs something and disappears just as quickly when she's done with you. "The clinic nurses have a pool going as to who her secret lover is."

"Secret lover?" I say through stifled laughter.

He shrugs, as if to say, *Why not?* She is a beautiful woman if you can look past her tough exterior. Of course, more than a few people have said the same thing about me.

"It could explain where she's always hiding." He waggles his eyebrows mischievously.

We reach the labor and delivery wing and Enrique leans on the entrance button. When the nurse on the other end of the line picks up, he rattles off something in Spanish. The doors swing open as if of their own volition. Our patient, Mrs. Forrest, is on the bed, her feet in the stirrups, her brown hair splayed around her head like a mermaid underwater. The woman standing next to her is clearly her sister—they both have dark freckles smattered across their noses and catlike green eyes. I smile at the two other nurses in the room and walk over to Mrs. Forrest. Her eyes are closed in concentration, the epidural taking away most, but not all, of the pain. She's focusing in on it. Meditating. I place my hand lightly on her hair to let her know I'm there.

"Mr. Forrest still deployed?" I ask her sister softly.

"Three more weeks," she says.

Fingers curl around mine, and I look down to see Mrs. Forrest staring up at me with tears in her eyes. I squeeze.

"We've got this," I say.

She nods, and I run my fingers over her hair one more time before I make my way to my seat.

"How are we doing?" I ask the nurse monitoring her dilation.

"Ten centimeters," she says. "She's ready."

Enrique appears at my shoulder with a gown, and I take off my jacket to feed my arms through. He snaps gloves on my hands as the nurses flutter around me, unpacking instruments, setting the lights and preparing for the new life about to take over the room. I sit down and confirm Mrs. Forrest's progress for myself. When the shuffling stops and everyone is in position, I look up with a smile and say, "It's time."

Mrs. Forrest nods, and with an ear-shattering screech, she begins to push.

An hour later, once I've helped deliver a healthy, red-haired baby girl, Enrique brings me a cup of the strongest hospital coffee he can find, and I drink it around the corner from the emergency entrance as Enrique smokes a cigarette—our celebratory routine.

"You're always so cool in there," Enrique says between drags. "Cool. Calm. Collected," he muses, almost to himself.

I swallow down the dregs of my coffee and toss the cup into a nearby trash can.

"I have to be," I say. "It's when emotions get involved that things get messy. I follow procedure, do what needs to be done, and everyone comes out safely." I trained under a few doctors during my residency who were scattered in the delivery room, and I could sense that their patients didn't fully trust them. Since practicing solo, I've been able to approach deliveries with my own style, and even in that short time, I've noticed the difference in patient rapport.

"Literally."

I snort a laugh.

Afterward, I walk the halls back to the clinic, with an unapologetic smile on my face, high on another successful delivery. I can't imagine it ever getting old.

When I walk through the doors of the clinic, Vanessa is standing with her arms hugged around a chart, waiting for me. My breath hitches, as it does every time she asks to speak to me privately these days, wondering if today I find out that everything I've been working for is finally coming to fruition.

"A word?" she asks.

I nod.

When we enter Vanessa's office, she closes the door behind me and breezes around her desk. She perches on the edge of her chair but doesn't offer me a seat. She's succinct enough to have rendered the visitors' chairs useless.

"You got it," she says. "You're on the clinic schedule."

I got it. A chance at absolution.

After a long moment of anticipatory silence, I remind myself to breathe. I cover my mouth with my fingers, unsure of which emotion might be displaying itself there. I'm not sure, myself, which emotion is tugging at the center of my chest like the string of a puppeteer, trying to pull me in the direction I'm supposed to go. My rooted feet keep me planted.

"Really?" I say, unable to believe it's actually happening. I've waited for this moment for so long, but some part of me always thought the day would never come.

"Yes. I need your application complete and on my desk in two weeks, so I can review it before you submit it."

"Of course," I say, not expecting the tight timeline, but what choice do I have? This is what I asked her for, and I won't let her down now. I'll work through the nights if I have to.

Vanessa squints her tapered eyes at me, like she can see my mind calculating the hours in a day, hours in the clinic, hours in the office, and in Labor and Delivery. She must be in her midforties but there's not a single line on her face, a result of either good genes or preserving herself inside these four walls. I glance at the curtains she always keeps drawn, blocking out the light and the world. When I started my residency here, I used to wonder how she could spend so much of her days confined in here. Now that I'm a doctor myself, I understand completely.

"Dylan," she says, "what you're trying to do is important. Don't forget that. I don't put my name on things unless I believe in them." Vanessa has spent enough time in obstetrics to have seen her fair share of pregnancy complications—many more than me. She wants the proof that we need better early pregnancy monitoring practices as much as I do. Right now, the first ultrasound doesn't take place until the eighteenth week of gestation in most cases. But so many life-threatening things can happen in those eighteen weeks, for the fetus and the mother. So many broken families. With my research, I hope to prove that the first ultrasound should be done as early as six weeks.

I take a deep breath and nod. Vanessa doesn't need to tell me how important this research is—I've seen the damage personally. "Yes, ma'am. I hope you know how seriously I take this opportunity."

Being the chief, Vanessa gets a lot of requests each year to mentor doctors with dreams of making medical breakthroughs. She can't say yes to all of them.

"I do." Vanessa almost smiles, then picks up her phone by way of dismissing me.

I close the door behind me as I leave and lean against it, close my eyes, breathe deeply.

It's time, I tell myself.

Home—a minimalist house thirty minutes outside the city with large, open windows, unobscured views of the forest, a creek that runs behind the property and my sorely underused side of the bed.

And Cooper.

I feel the day melt off me every time I turn down our street, though most nights I don't get home before it's shrouded in darkness. I don't think I'll find much refuge there tonight either with the stack of grant application paperwork on the passenger seat next to me.

When I pull into our circular driveway, I discover a familiar red truck parked diagonally across the gravel. One of the tires is elevated by a rock that lines the empty planter in the center of the drive. I shake my head, but I'm glad Stephen's here. The three of us have shared every milestone—career and otherwise—since I met him and Cooper that first week of med school almost ten years ago.

I find the guys in the backyard, sitting in the middle of the grass in chipped, lipstick-red Adirondack chairs, the legs of which are swallowed to the hilt by the overgrown lawn. All I can see of them is the back of two heads, two hands with two open beer bottles and four bare feet kicked up on a cooler between them. The trees shade them from the fading sunset but capture their laughter like fireflies in a mason jar.

"Hey," I say.

"Dylan," Stephen calls, not turning but holding up his beer in greeting.

Cooper makes the effort, flashing one blue eye, half a smile and his fallen-down hair at me. My heart flutters. He still gets to me. After all this time, he gets to me.

"Hey, babe," he says. "Come here."

I wade through the rain-damp grass in my bare feet. It's been too long since I've taken this path, through the yard and down the broken stepping-stones to the wooden bench next to the creek. The crisp air nips at my skin as night descends.

When I reach Cooper, he uses one strong hand to pull me onto his lap, and I fall into his familiar angles, the faded breath of his cologne. His warm hand resting on my hip has become less familiar, though, over these last six months as I've focused more and more on my research grant. I feel it acutely.

"Beer?" he asks. I shake my head but take a swig of his. He rests his chin on my shoulder and watches me. It catches me off guard—this act of intimacy. Like I've only just realized we'd come to an unspoken agreement that intimacy would come again later—after—but Cooper's exhibiting the weak spot in his willpower.

"Guess what," I say, my voice airy, a try at excitement. Or maybe it's the lump in my throat.

"You got it," Cooper says. Stephen raises his eyebrows.

I nod. "I got on the research clinic schedule. My spot is guaranteed as long as the grant is approved."

"Which it will be." Stephen is quick to assure me, his face lighting up. "Damn, Dylan. Congrats. I'll drink to that."

I laugh. "Thank you. But I don't know how meaningful that is. You'll drink to anything."

"And I'll drink to *that*." He winks, raises his bottle in a salute and follows through.

I turn to Cooper, my stomach tight as I wait for his response.

"I'm happy for you, Dylan," he says. His smooth fingers twist their way through my ponytail, not looking at me. "I knew you'd get it." There's tightness in his voice. Still, he presses a kiss to my forehead, pulls me closer to him.

"Thanks," I say, though I'm not reassured. Now that the possibility of getting the grant is so real, the pressure to do the right thing for my family—for Abby—is almost suffocating. I had hoped Cooper would remind me that this is the next big milestone in our shared dream for the future. This is a good thing. A great thing. I should have known I was hoping in vain.

I clear my throat. "So, what? Are you guys out here reliving the glory days?"

The hint of spring in the air reminds me of studying for finals and opening the windows in the little apartment Cooper and I used to share in the city; of when the three of us spent so much time at our favorite spot in the forest next to the Willamette River, drinking into the night by the light of a feeble campfire. We talked about what life would be like when Stephen was a sought-after neurologist, Cooper was a partner at a patient-focused pediatric practice and I had discovered the secret to diagnosing early pregnancy complications before the mother's body knows something is wrong itself. Back when the path was simple and our whole lives were ahead of us.

Now Stephen is an attending neurologist at the hospital where we completed our residencies—the same hospital where I work. Cooper is at a practice he loves and is, any day, bound to be recognized for the amazing doctor he is. And I…I have grant paperwork to fill out.

Stephen laughs and runs his hand through his shaggy hair. "I guess so. All we're missing is the fire."

"You are not starting my backyard on fire," Cooper says.

"Might do it some good," Stephen mutters behind his bottle.

Cooper kicks Stephen's feet off the cooler, making them both laugh like kids. They always have fought like brothers, even before it became official. Cooper couldn't have been happier when his best friend married his younger sister four years ago. Stephen was a force of nature—women, alcohol, adrenaline—before he fell in love with Megan. He reminded me of the way I was before I met Cooper—shallow encounters with men I hardly knew, detached, angry. Megan was exactly what he needed. The same way Cooper was what I needed.

"Behave, children. Where's Megan tonight?" I ask. Being that she's an elementary school teacher, she's better than I am at keeping the guys from getting too raucous.

Stephen shrugs. "Busy." He finishes off his beer.

"Which is what I should be."

"Can't you stay a little longer?" Cooper asks softly. "Celebrate?"

"I wish I could. I have to get my application done. Vanessa's waiting for it."

He nods, leans forward and kisses me slowly until my thighs quiver. It's been so long since he's kissed me that way.

"What's gotten into you?" I whisper. Before he can answer, my pager buzzes on my waistband and Cooper's body deflates.

"I have a—"

"Delivery," Cooper completes for me. I nod. He purses his lips, then sighs. "I'll see you when you get home."

"See ya, Doctor," Stephen says when I stand to leave. He winks as if to say it will all be okay.

I get home after midnight with every intention of sneaking into the office to work on my application for a few hours before bed. When I see the glow from Cooper's bedside lamp coming from our room, though, I know Cooper is waiting up for me.

I go to him and find him in his reading glasses, holding a copy of *Game of Thrones* open on his chest. I stop in the doorway and lean my head on the door frame. The lamplight on Cooper's face makes him look even more boyishly handsome, if possible. He hasn't aged a day since I met him. It's possible working in pediatrics keeps him young at heart, but there was so much about him that was childlike already. If opposites attract, maybe that's what drew us together. I was forced to grow up too soon.

"Is everything okay?" he asks.

The telltale line of worry is drawn across his forehead.

"Of course," I say.

He nods. He knows it's just me trying to convince myself. I cross to my side of the bed while Cooper sets his book and glasses aside. I climb in next to him.

"Listen." He shifts downward and brings his hands together in front of his lips, the way he does when we're about to have a serious conversation. I sigh inwardly. "I know you're really focused on your grant right now. And I know you go through these phases, so I try to give you your space. You don't like to feel boxed in, and I get that." He reaches down to brush his fingertips down my thigh. "You always come back to me eventually. But, I don't know... I guess I keep hoping at some point we'll get past the push and pull. I keep hoping that instead of blocking me out when things get tough, you'll open up to me and let me be there for you. It's been nine years, babe. When are you going to finally start trusting me?"

"Cooper, it's not about trust. And you are here for me. So much more than you realize. Once I get this grant—"

"Once you ace this test. Once you graduate. Once you finish your internship." He cuts me off with the list of promises I've made him, always putting my guilt over Abby first.

Because my guilt over hurting Cooper can still be forgiven. Cooper is still here. Abby isn't.

I close my eyes in an attempt to hide from his words, to go somewhere else in my mind.

For a few minutes, it's just our soft breathing, but then Cooper props his head up on his hand. I reluctantly turn onto my side to face him. The moonlight coming in from the window casts long shadows over his solemn expression.

"I know you have a hard time letting people in, Dylan. I understand that there are things I don't understand about you. Hell, the fact that you can still surprise me after nine years is one of the things I love most about you. But I worry about you. It's not healthy to keep everything locked up inside yourself. You don't have to try so hard to keep everything under control. The world isn't an operating room."

It's easy for him to say. He's lived such a charmed life. He doesn't know what it's like to have everything you know and love torn to shreds before your eyes, like my life and my family was after my sister died.

I used to tell Abby my secrets, but since her death, I've been too afraid to trust anyone else with that raw, imperfect version of myself. I've been too afraid to trust the world. But Cooper doesn't understand. He doesn't know all the details of what happened that night.

"Are you going to pull out your blood pressure cuff?" I joke.

"I'm serious, Dylan."

"I know. I'm sorry. It's not you. You know it's not you, right?" I ask him. I place my hand on his cheek. "You know how much I love you?"

My words seem to reassure him more than I would like, like he didn't know.

I tell him.

Don't I?

I *feel* it.

He takes my hand from his cheek and holds it to his chest, right over his heart.

"Maybe it's time we focus a little more on *us*," he says. I open my mouth to argue, but he goes on before I can. "I know you have the grant. But you love me. And I love you. God, Dylan, don't you get how much? I'd do anything to make you happy."

I watch my fingers run up and down the folds in the sheet instead of looking at him, instead of answering him.

"What can I do?" he urges. When I can't come up with an answer, he sighs and softens his voice. "You know once you get this grant, work is going to be busier, not slower."

"Maybe I can get fewer shifts at the hospital," I offer hopelessly.

"Can you?" he asks. "I don't mean, will they let you. I mean, will you let yourself?"

I scoot closer to him and bury my face against his chest, feel his chin against the top of my head. His body melts beneath mine, no doubt with the belief that his words have gotten through to me. But the responsibility I carry lives deep in my bones. I can't lose focus at the moment of truth.

"I just love you, Dylan. I want to see you happy, and I'm not sure you are anymore."

"I'm happy with you," I whisper.

To that, he has nothing else to say.

I close my eyes and count his heartbeats, hiding in the immediacy of him.

3

The following Tuesday morning, the rain comes down like candy from a piñata. The drops are intermittent but heavy and invasive—the kind that assault the top of your head and bleed down your scalp. I stride across the hospital parking lot, using my hand to shield my eyes from the sunrise as it rekindles its romance with seven o'clock.

Over the last week, I've hardly left these few square miles, spending all my spare time in my office preparing my application. Between patient exams and three deliveries, spare time has been hard to come by. The first couple of nights I tried to work at home, but although Cooper never said a word about me skipping dinner, I felt his disappointment permeating all the air under our roof, seeping into every word I wrote. I could no longer decipher which disappointment was his and which was mine. It was easier to stay away.

Last night, though, when I sneaked into our bedroom after working until midnight in the clinic and curled up with my back to him in the dark, he reached out for me in his sleep. That simple gesture has gotten me through many tough times—to know that even in his unconsciousness, and even when he's unsure about my choices, he's never unsure about us. Still, I didn't turn to him. I could have. He would have woken up for me. I could have let him take me in his arms, and we would have been Dylan and Cooper for a night, or just an hour. We could have been the *can't keep our hands off each other* young couple we once were, instead of Dr. Michels and Dr. Caldwell, making appointments to see each other. I know that's what he really wants from me. Putting work first was always the story of our relationship. There's never been a time when we haven't been studying, applying for grants, making it through one class at a time, one day at the hospital at a time. Except for the past two years, since Cooper finished his residency and found a nine-to-five. He's ready for me to find a comfortable routine, too—to find a comfortable ease together.

I just don't have the energy to reassure him yet again. All I can think about right now is my purpose—that which is greater than me.

As I step off the curb toward the emergency entrance, an ambulance comes barreling into the drop-off lane, the back doors flying open and EMTs pulling the patient out on a stretcher. It's a common sight, but I step back onto the curb, startled—both by its abrupt appearance, and that after all these years working in a hospital, I still associate the red-and-white lights with only one person. I close my eyes and force a deep breath into my lungs.

When I open them again, I notice a packet of flower seeds where it's been discarded in the ditch. I've seen hundreds of them in my life—scattered on the kitchen counter, hidden in drawers around the house, bound together by a rubber band in the garage, and torn open and empty on the porch. Gardening is my mom's passion. But with Abby still in the fore-front of my mind, it's her face I see, not Mom's—fragile and broken, like the seeds, with their package marred by dirt and water. It feels like a sign. I crouch down to pick up the paper envelope, wipe it with my palm and slip it into my pocket. Then I run into the hospital, out of the rain.

"Good afternoon, Erika," I say as I enter the exam room later that day.

It's Mrs. Martinez's monthly checkup. She sits straight-backed on the exam table in a flowing white blouse that's tucked into a taut pencil skirt. Her long black hair is pulled into a side ponytail, and her bright red lipstick is freshly applied. I try to imagine how much of this will change by the time she hits forty weeks, and a grin pulls at the corner of my mouth. Doctors aren't supposed to have favorite patients—I, of all people, understand why—but I've always enjoyed my visits with Erika, a strong, successful businesswoman with a sense of humor.

"Afternoon, *Dylan*," she drawls. She's always made it a point to call me by my first name, and I never felt the need to correct her, so it's become an inside joke between us. In truth, I savor the intimacy.

Her husband, Andrew, is here for the first time, and I introduce myself. He's an unassuming man behind his glasses, the reflection of a computer screen almost still visible on his lenses. This surprises me. I imagined her husband would be someone bigger with a presence large enough to rival hers, but his quiet air balances her—the yin to her yang. A good fit. That's one part of being an obstetrician I didn't expect—how much my patients would teach me about relationships.

"Erika has said a lot of good things about you," he tells me over his eager handshake.

"Likewise," I say with a smile. "You're quite the lucky guy."

"I know it," he says earnestly, casting a glance at Erika. She blushes, something I never imagined I'd see her do. There's an innocence to their love, even after six years together. In our first years together, Cooper and I were passionate, but never innocent.

"Oh, don't let him fool you," Erika says. "He calls me a pain in the ass five times a day."

"The best ones are," he says, and we all laugh.

"All right, let's take a listen to baby's heartbeat," I say, and grab the jelly. "We'll give Dad some of the good stuff. Go ahead and lie back," I tell Erika.

Andrew helps her down. "She keeps pretending she's going to take maternity leave," Andrew chatters as I help Erika pull her shirt out of the way. "But we both know that's not gonna happen. She'll probably have her assistant on the phone, barking out orders while she's pushing."

Erika narrows her eyes at him.

"Don't worry," I say. "When the baby comes, she'll have to slow down, right, Erika?" I tease. Erika turns to Andrew, the paper underneath her head crinkling.

"Actually, I'm going to stay home with the baby," Andrew says.

"Oh?"

"I can work from home," he says. "And Erika likes to be at the office. She's happy there. Stressed, but…a happy stressed, I think."

I laugh because I know exactly what he means.

"I think that's a great option," I say. "Parenting is all about working as a team."

"Teamwork makes the dream work," Erika says, and they laugh.

I picture Erika power-walking through the halls of her office in her power pumps, singing it to her colleagues as she walks by. I envy Erika, so sure of herself and how her life is going to turn out.

"You okay, *cuchura*?" she asks me.

I realize I'm frowning and refocus. Andrew gasps as the steady *swish swish* of the heartbeat fills the room, saving me from answering Erika's question. His eyes light up, and he looks over at Erika with so much adoration, I have to look away.

After the exam, as I walk down the hall, I hear footsteps approach from behind and turn to see Andrew.

"I wanted to say thank-you," he says as he stops in front of me. He pushes his glasses farther up on his nose.

"Oh, you're welcome," I say.

We both step closer to the wall as another doctor breezes by.

He lowers his voice. "It's just that…Erika doesn't trust many people. She sort of likes to be in control of everything. I'm sure you noticed."

I grin. "Not at all." We both laugh.

"She was pretty scared when she found out she was pregnant. Everything that was going to happen to her body, labor, life changing. Since she's started seeing you, she's relaxed a lot. She trusts you, and she doesn't trust easy."

My chest swells, but I keep my expression in check.

"Thank you," I say. "That means a lot to me."

And it does. It means everything that I can be worthy of my patients' trust.

Saturday night, it's our weekly dinner date with Cooper's parents, and as usual, following Cooper into his childhood home is like stepping into another world. Chatter comes from the kitchen, where I know I will find his family cooking together—a tradition, he told me, they started as a way to make the most of their visits after he and his sister moved out. After so many years with Cooper, I, too, have grown accustomed to grazing over cheeses, breads, wines and nibbles of vegetables as I help chop and throw them into simmering pots on the stove.

Cooper's relationship with his family bears a sharp contrast to mine. Cooper still sees his parents at least once a week and talks to them on the phone most days, usually to get medical advice from his mom, a nurse who has more years of experience than Cooper and I have been alive. I join their dinners when I can. Some nights their playful banter and unbridled affection for each other—and for me—is a painful reminder of what I wish for my own family. Other times, it's a refuge, a promise of a future that could still be if only I can find a way to make things right.

As Cooper closes the front door behind me, his mom, Marilyn, sweeps into the cramped space.

"There you two are. I thought I heard the door."

Marilyn plants kisses on each of our cheeks. She is a small, supple woman with a bob of box-red hair and hugs like a down comforter. I kiss her in return, and the scent of her sweet pea perfume and the Cajun spices coming from the kitchen reminds me of when I first met her, the day after Thanksgiving all those years ago. Cooper and I had been dating for three weeks. He led me into their home, small but overflowing with color and life, so different from the cool angles and empty space I'd grown up in. I was greeted by his parents and his sister like they'd already sectioned off space in their hearts and had been waiting for me to fill it.

"Your father is just about to add the wine," Marilyn says. "And you know if you don't get a glass now, it will all end up in the gumbo." She lets out her trademark high-pitched chuckle.

Cooper kisses her on the forehead and heads to the kitchen. I let Marilyn assess my face and skim her thumb over the circles under my eyes like she always does. They're darker than usual, and I can see that she notices. All week, I've either been up late working on my application or worrying about what I'll do if I actually get the grant. Or worrying about how I'll forgive myself if I don't. This research is about making amends. It's always been about making amends.

Marilyn frowns, clearly wanting to say something.

"How can I help?" I ask. She nods toward the kitchen, and I follow her.

The wine flows, and since I'm not on call I allow myself to indulge. The alcohol dulls the sharp edges of my upcoming deadline and makes the conversation flow as I listen to Cooper's dad, John, describe the latest architectural design he's sketched—his heart's work after long days spent as an electrician—as he sprinkles unmeasured and unidentified spices on the sausage I sauté on the stove. He asks about work, and I tell him about some funny moments in the delivery room, laughing along with him between sips of red wine from a juice glass. Stephen is absent, which is unusual, but Megan and Marilyn tease Cooper over a shared cutting board. His laughter pulls the strings of my heart. It's been so long since I've been the one to make him laugh like that.

During our first year of med school, Cooper and I only had one class together—genetics. Our teacher, Dr. Sands, was unbelievably enthusiastic about his subject, sometimes spending an entire period marveling at how eye color wove its way through a family. Cooper and I had taken to quoting him when we were tired of doing homework or when we needed to clear the tension after a spat.

"Isn't the human body exciting?" Cooper would mumble

against my belly button after tickling me and pinning me to his bed.

"You can't make stuff like this up," I'd intone as we shared the mirror after the shower, and in his reflection, I'd see Cooper melt a little, looking at me looking at him.

One day, Cooper and I made a bet on whether Dr. Sands said "literally" or "super" more often in class. By the time we were tied at ten, we were both laughing through our tears, and Dr. Sands had kicked us out. We went back to Cooper's car in the student parking lot and made love on the backseat, the rain our only cover. Even before I could admit it to myself, it was always Cooper and me against the world.

When the sausage is done, I follow Megan to the dining room with my glass of wine. Cooper catches my gaze over the cutting board and seems to read my mind. He gives me a tight-lipped smile, then returns to chopping.

"Do you want me to help set the table?" I ask her.

"Sure," she chirps and passes a handful of spoons. She smiles, but she looks pale.

"Where's Stephen tonight?" I ask.

"Work," she says, but the word is hollow. And though her glossy blond hair is pulled back into its usual ponytail, and her light makeup is so smooth it could easily be mistaken for the perfection of her own skin, the sparkle that lights her eyes is missing. She looks like she's lost a few pounds, too. The end of the school year must be taking its toll on her.

As I watch her from the corner of my eye, she picks up some bowls for the table but sets them back down quickly. She steadies herself on the table and places her other hand on her petite abdomen, letting out a long, slow breath.

"Are you okay?" I ask.

Her wine is untouched, and her skin is clammy.

"Sit down," I tell her and pull out a chair. "I can finish this."

She lowers herself down and shakes her head. "I'm sorry. I feel a little nauseated. One of the kids brought ice-cream cake to class for their birthday."

I pour her a glass of homemade lemonade from a pitcher on the table, then finish setting out the bowls.

"School good?" I ask her. "Or looking forward to summer?"

She laughs through her discomfort. "A little of both."

A minute later, Cooper walks through the door with a casserole dish of fresh biscuits in his bare hands, cursing.

"They make pot holders for that, you know," Megan says from behind her glass. "You wouldn't want to hurt those precious doctoring tools of yours."

Cooper sets the dish down on a mat in the center of the table and shakes out his hands. He pulls Megan close to him and musses her hair, then smooths it out again.

"Says the girl who used to beg me to pull things out of her Easy-Bake Oven when she lost that pan pusher."

"Hey, you stuck your own damn fingers in there."

"Okay, kids," John says, coming in with the pot of gumbo. "You're never too old to ground."

Marilyn follows behind him, and we all gather around the table, eating, talking and laughing the night away. It's just everyday life, but with an unwavering love that makes every moment together like snapshots in a photo album of someone else's life. Until the clock strikes midnight, I almost forget that it's been fifteen years to the day since I lost my sister.

Sometimes when the wind catches the front door of my parents' house and closes it a little too hard, a little too quickly, I'm transported back to the day Abby left our lives forever. It reminds me of the sound of the door slamming shut behind my parents when they disappeared with the ambulance siren, leaving my younger brother, Charlie, and me behind. A steady breeze blows strong on Sunday morning, so I hold the same doorknob tightly, not releasing it until it clicks shut.

Inside, I hear the voices of my dad and brother talking softly in the kitchen, glasses clinking. I smell the ever-present scent of burnt coffee in an almost empty pot. My heels echo on the tile, announcing my arrival. The chatter stops, and I see Charlie's face—eyebrows raised, the playful grin that usually curls the edges of his mouth absent—appear around the corner as he leans back on his stool. His slept-on chestnut curls are a mess on top of his head. "Hey, sis," he says.

I enter the kitchen and spot my dad standing at the island, a bottle of bourbon and highball glasses between the two of them. It's the only day of the year that the alcohol cabinet is open before noon, but it's a tradition none of us has felt the desire to look at too closely. It's a day for remembering, and a day for forgetting.

"Hey," I say to Charlie. I wrap an arm around his neck and plant a kiss on his temple.

"Hey, baby girl," my dad says.

"Hi, Daddy." My throat constricts. He looks relaxed in his Hawaiian shirt and Bermuda shorts, but his eyes are bloodshot, like he's either been crying or hasn't slept well in weeks. Maybe both. I allow him the dignity of not commenting on it and cover my own emotion with a smile. I fall into my dad's bear hug—the cure for every scraped knee, every worry, every broken heart since I was a little girl. The only thing it's never been able to do is bring my sister back.

I kiss Dad on the cheek, then slip out of his arms to walk to the window, where I know I will find the one person missing from our informal memorial. My mom's absence is as much a part of the tradition as the early cocktail hour.

The midday sun glints off the lake at the edge of the backyard, a charm on the Willamette River necklace of Oregon. When Charlie, Abby and I were kids, we used to play at the shore, throwing toy boats out as far as we could and waiting for them to wash up. Sometimes we wrote messages for each other, hidden inside on a folded piece of paper—*Can we go ride bikes now?*—scribbled our responses, then tossed them out again. It's hard to believe I could drop a message in the river outside the hospital, and, under the right circumstances, it might float here, to my mother's feet. There are so many things I haven't been able to say to her for so long, even standing right here in her kitchen.

As expected, she's kneeling on the grass at the base of the large porch. Her coffee mug is perched on the railing. Her purple gardening hat flops in the breeze, and she's digging a hole in the soil with a vigor that seems to be doing more harm than good. It's Mom's version of bourbon. Abby was always her favorite, but gardening used to be the one thing she and I did together. I'd be in charge of the hand trowel and the watering can. She'd smudge a line of dirt down my nose and call me "all knees and elbows." A lifetime ago. We stopped once Abby died, when there was no longer room there for anything less than perfection.

"Has she been out there all day?" I ask, noticing the pink of the skin on her wrists between where her gloves stop and her three-quarter sleeves end. The doctor in me winces. The daughter in me holds my tongue.

"Since the sun rose," my dad says.

I try to imagine Mom as I remember her from childhood. I try to remember her flowing skirts I used to chase around the house. How she used to lie on the couch and let me braid her hair for hours. How she used to blast Tom Petty and bake cookies with us kids after school. I can't reconcile that woman with the one I know today. The truth is, Dad, Charlie and I lost that woman long before Abby's death. But it seems that Abby's death was when Mom finally lost her, too.

I sigh and rejoin the men.

"Drink?" Charlie asks. He grabs the bottle and adds another finger-worth to his glass.

"I have to go into the clinic," I say. Working on my application is a better way to honor my sister's memory than bourbon.

"Drink?" he asks again. I roll my eyes.

"Not everyone's boss is so forgiving," I say.

"Neither is his," Dad says, "but it's not like I can fire him." After Charlie finished college, he took a job at the family finance firm because he knew it was the only place he'd be able to do as little work as possible for the most amount of pay. If he wasn't so charming, his lack of motivation would drive me crazy.

Charlie chuckles. His eyes are already glassy.

After a long silence where we put off the inevitable, Dad says, "She would have been thirty-three this year."

Thirty-three.

She was two years older than me. When we were teenagers it often seemed like a decade. Abby was a contradiction of wild and wise. She would study for a calculus exam for hours, then sneak out of her room to go to a boat party on the lake, only tiptoeing back in once the sun began to rise. She'd brush her teeth, drive her VW Bug to school, ace her test. If she'd survived, she would have been an enigma amongst teen mothers. I know she had her doubts, but I always believed in her.

"She would be...pregnant with her fourth kid," Charlie says.

"Fourth?" I sputter, then laugh.

Last year we decided that her third child had just turned two. Even though I know her first child never could have lived, even if Abby had, I like to pretend she would have been a girl—the niece I almost had, even if she only ever existed as a fetus. I think Abby would have finished high school, and then college, found a man who loved her because she was a mother, instead of abandoning her for it. Eventually, her adventurous spirit would have given way to her maternal instincts, and she would have found that motherhood was the ultimate adventure. She wasn't the nurturing type as a teenager, but I like to think she would have grown into it, given the time. That's how I like to imagine her anyway. Dad and Charlie let me lead the first time we played this game and have continued to elaborate on my initial idea. Probably because they think I need it more than they do. They're probably right.

"She's decided to have her tubes tied after this one, though," I say, giving them and my sister a break. "She recently rediscovered her passion for writing, and she'd like to go back to school once the baby stops nursing." In high school she always said she wanted to write for a magazine. She would have been good at it, too.

Dad grins, and tears form in the corners of his eyes. "I like that."

I picture her in a natural-lit room in a big white house on the other side of the lake, by a window that overlooks the water, notebook in hand. She would have stayed here in Lake Oswego. She would have married a guy who knew her in high school, but had gone unnoticed by her. In their midtwenties, they would have met at Mrs. Collins's yearly barbecue, and they would have fallen in love across the perfectly mowed grass. He would have admitted weeks later that he'd loved her since he first laid eyes on her. All the boys did.

It's a morbid game and we all know it, but it's better than hiding from it. Mom wants to remember her little girl exactly the way she was. I force myself to remember, even when I want to forget. Though truthfully, on the bad days, I wish I'd never had a sister at all.

It took many years after moving out of my parents' house to unearth who I was. I say *unearth* rather than *find* because it wasn't so much a process of adding layers as shedding the grief and confusion of my teen years. After Abby's death, I buried myself in guilt, searched for solace in the arms of the opposite sex when I couldn't find comfort at home and, at the same time, put up a wall between me and everyone I loved, or ever could love. Cooper is the only one who ever broke through, who ever made me feel worthy of being seen. I'm still working on showing him all of me. When I push through the anger that my best friend and my mother were stolen from me, I can almost see that honest version of myself—bullheaded out of love, steady enough to lean on, an unapologetic dreamer.

The layers I couldn't shed have thickened like an outer shell, covering the weaker membranes. I am fiercely defensive of the person I turned into after Abby's death, tiny and rubbed raw at first but, over the years, with the safety of Cooper's unwavering love, grown strong and powerful in my own way. I have feared the day someone in my life would crack that shell, and I'd fall to pieces again. And because I love Cooper more than I've ever loved anyone—maybe even more than I love Abby—he alone holds the power to break me. It's why I've never told him the role I played in my sister's death. If he knew, I would never be able to look at him without seeing the pity in his eyes. I would never be able to hide from that constant reminder, and I'd be robbed of my only comfort. So I let it smolder inside of me, and I foolishly allow Cooper to keep lifting me up, the friction of it eroding my shell.

Every year around the time of Abby's anniversary, I feel that urge all over again—to leave and lose myself in someone who knows nothing about me, someone with whom I can pretend to be anyone but me. And because Cooper foolishly loves me, he doesn't push, doesn't question me, knowing from the first time we met that forcing me to open up when I wasn't ready would make me run. I never hid from him how many men I'd run from before.

I find myself drawn to the window. I raise my hand to place it on the glass but think better of it. Mom hates fingerprints. She's moved to some still-dormant rosebushes farther down, pulled out her pruning shears. I fear what the poor shrubs will look like when she's done with them. I don't remember much from the days when we used to garden together, but I do remember there's such a thing as too much love. It seems that after Abby's death, she put all the love she had into that garden, and since then there hasn't been any left for us. Losing my sister broke each of us in our own way, but it was the way Mom pulled away from us afterward that broke our family as a whole.

I feel my dad's presence over my shoulder.

"You should go out there," he says.

"No," I say. "Not today."

"Dylan...you can't expect your mom to move on from it if you never do."

"I have moved on," I whisper. But we both know it isn't true.

4

After the anniversary of Abby's death, I throw myself into my grant application with more fervor. I leave before Cooper in the morning. I close myself in my office during lunch and stay at the clinic until long after Cooper is asleep. The looming deadline pushes me, but also the painful reminder of why I need this grant and why medicine needs this research.

Because my sister, at the age of eighteen, died of pregnancy.

Abby never shared the details of her sex life with me, but by the time she was sixteen, I was sure she had one. I was too embarrassed to ask. She was a good girl at heart, but she had a wild streak that pushed her further than having a drink or two at a lake party or spending eight minutes in the closet with a boy during Seven Minutes in Heaven.

When she got pregnant, I never doubted that she'd keep the baby and that she'd somehow make it look easy. She'd do it all—raise a child and continue on to college. Somehow she'd still be more successful than any of us imagined possible. More successful than I would be.

And then she died.

When it was over, the doctors told my parents it was an

ectopic pregnancy, a rare but dangerous condition when the fertilized egg embeds into the fallopian tube or the abdomen instead of in the uterus. If caught early, the pregnancy can be terminated and the mother can be saved. If it goes undiagnosed or misdiagnosed, it's a ticking time bomb. The egg that would have been my niece or nephew ruptured, and Abby died of blood loss before anyone knew what happened.

Sitting in front of my computer the night before Vanessa's deadline, my fingers on the keyboard, I think of the pain and fear Abby must have suffered that night, alone. I think of all the women who have suffered similar fates and how I can help them. I connect to that deep need inside me to fix it all. Before I leave the clinic, I put the final touches on my application, and I email it to Vanessa.

A few days later, after I've received Vanessa's response, Cooper walks into the kitchen, startling me with his "Hey."

I look up, then back to the counter, where potting soil is spilled across the granite, and I'm scooping it into ceramic seed pots with my hands. I'm home early and in the only pair of sweatpants I own—the ones I wear when I'm sick—and a glass of red wine is within reach, soil granules clinging to the stem in the shape of fingerprints.

"Hi," I bite out.

"Whatcha doing?" he asks.

"I found these seeds," I say. I thrust the dirty, rain-puckered packet at Cooper, and he takes it, stepping back to avoid my hand before it brushes against his untucked work shirt. "Do you think they'll still grow?"

Cooper shrugs. "I don't really know anything about gardening."

"I know. But just… What do you think?"

He examines them more closely. "I don't see why not. I think it would take a lot more to damage them than a little water and dirt." His mouth quirks up on one side, obviously entertained by my state, but I take his joke seriously.

"What's going on, Dylan?"

The concern in his voice drains the energy from me as quickly as a plunger into a syringe, and I stop. The kitchen is a mess. My hands are shaking.

"Vanessa called me into her office today. She isn't going to support my grant application," I say.

Cooper's head drops forward. His hair falls down around his eyes. I can't tell if he's upset for me or himself. He knows the process doesn't stop here—this is just a roadblock that makes it take even longer.

I open my mouth but nothing comes out.

Vanessa's exact words were that my goal was too ambitious. There was no way I'd be able to monitor so many women in a two-year study. I'd need more money, more research assistants, more volunteers. Or more time. I told her I didn't think the field could wait much longer. What I couldn't tell her was that I didn't think Cooper could wait much longer either.

I could ignore her—submit my application anyway—but the board won't review it without a letter from my mentor. I could try to find another mentor, but they aren't easy to come by, especially with only a couple of weeks left until the deadline. The truth is, since there are no grants listed specifically for women's health, my application will get pooled into a general category, which makes the competition stiff with or without Vanessa's support. I'm out of options right now, and it will likely be a year or more before another suitable grant becomes available. I was hesitant about whether or not I was really ready to do this research, but now that the opportunity has been ripped away from me, I don't know what to do with myself. I have no purpose.

Cooper comes over and wraps his hand around the back of

my neck, lacing his fingers into my hair. "I'm sorry, babe," he says. "That's tough."

I shrug and sniffle. "That's life, I guess." I take a sip of my wine, gathering myself.

Cooper's hand drops, and he looks out the window to the backyard, his expression vague and distant. I don't need to see his eyes to know what he's feeling. His exasperation shows in the slouch of his shoulders, the downward tilt of his head.

Finally, he opens his hands to me and says, "Come here."

"Cooper, I don't want to—"

"Come here."

"What?" I ask him, my voice bordering on hysteria.

A moment passes in silence before he drops his hands. "Dylan, you're a doctor now," he says. "You can do whatever you want. I don't understand why you have to have this grant to help people."

"It's *these* people I need to help, Cooper."

I set my glass down on the counter with too much force, and wine sloshes onto the granite like drops of blood. I escape out the back door and walk down to the creek, my breathing shallow, unwilling to defend myself again, after trying and failing with Vanessa. Doing right by the people we love should be reason enough.

No, life with Abby wasn't always easy, especially during her final months, but Abby and I had always been close growing up. Though we fought, like sisters do, I knew I could count on her when it mattered. When she became a senior in high school, though, she started to spread her wings more than my parents and I were used to—more than we were comfortable with—like she knew the freedom she'd always craved was just around the corner and she couldn't wait that long. She suddenly stopped sharing the gossip she'd heard from her friends with me when I crawled into her bed in the middle of the night. She started locking the door to her bedroom more often and disappearing with random people from school in the evenings. One Friday night, as she prepared to go to a boat party on the lake, I lay on her bed and watched her put on her makeup, hoping to get the details. An invitation would be too much to ask for.

"So who's going to be there?" I asked.

Abby finger-combed her blond hair back from her face and leaned closer to the mirror on top of her dresser. She blinked her eyes as wide as they would stretch before she pulled out the wand from her mascara tube and began to apply thick, black layers to her already long lashes.

"I don't know," she said evasively. "The usual."

I knew she didn't try to keep me at a distance on purpose. At least, I hoped she didn't. It was just one of the habits she picked up from hanging out with the popular girls. They kept everything about themselves from each other, only trading *other* people's secrets like currency.

I scooted farther forward on her floral-print comforter and tested out the question I really wanted the answer to. "Is Christian going to be there?" I asked.

Abby's cheeks flushed beneath her applied blush, and I knew the answer without her having to say it. She plunged her mascara wand back into the tube and turned to me.

"Everyone's already talking about us being prom queen and king," she said, biting her lip as if she didn't dare believe it. Up until the previous year, Abby had always flown under the radar—the kind of girl who got along with everyone, never falling into any particular clique. When her breasts filled out, though, and she started to catch the attention of the football quarterback, the popular girls had no choice but to bring the enemy closer into their fold.

"Have you kissed him yet?" I asked, pushing my luck. It was the wrong question. Abby frowned and turned back to her mirror.

"Of course we've kissed, Dylan. Don't be ridiculous. I'm eighteen, not twelve." I hated it when she talked to me like I was so much younger than her. Oftentimes, though, I felt like I was. At sixteen, I'd hardly talked to a boy I was interested in, let alone kissed one.

"Sorry," I mumbled, but Abby was already closing her makeup bag and checking her purse for the necessities. I spotted her lip gloss on her nightstand, scooted across her bed on my stomach, swiped it up and handed it to her. "You really seem to like him."

She softened. "I do," she said. "He's just so… And he makes me feel…pretty. But I don't want to be one of those forty-year-old women who married their high school sweetheart, is tied down with kids and is completely miserable because she never lived while she could, you know?"

I nodded, though I couldn't conceive of Abby ever being forty.

"You should have some fun, too," she said with a laugh and pressed her palm against the side of my head, pushing me over onto her bed. We both laughed, and long after she left, I couldn't wipe the smile from my face—not only because Abby and I both knew what a ludicrous idea it was—me going to a party, me making out with a guy behind the English building—but because I knew that she might be going through a rebellious phase, but when she came out on the other side, we'd be best friends still. I had one thing going for me that no other girl could claim, no matter how popular: I was her sister.

★ ★ ★

I come home from work on Tuesday to an unfamiliar truck parked in the driveway. It's a newer model Chevy with silver metallic paint, and though it's hidden by the shade of our trees, slivers of sunlight catch its sparkle in the places where it isn't covered in mud. Handles of miscellaneous tools stick out at all angles like Cooper's hair after a hard sleep. There's a parking sticker on the windshield for a big-time tech company in the city.

Inside, I toss my keys on the foyer table and call out Cooper's name, but he doesn't answer. I peek into the bedroom and bathroom, but it isn't until I pass through the kitchen that I hear Cooper's voice, along with that of another man, coming from the other side of the back door. When I step outside, they break from their conversation like I've caught them in the act of planning a crime. The stranger is dressed in designer jeans and a dark button-up shirt with hands covered in soil up to his elbows. He seems to have no concern of spreading it as he crosses his arms over his chest.

"There you are," Cooper says. He comes over to place a hand on my back and leads me forward a few steps. "Dylan, this is Reese. Reese, this is my…Dylan." He's always hated the word *girlfriend*. He says it makes us sound like teenagers, whose biggest concern is where to sit in the cafeteria at lunch, rather than two adults who have lived together and loved each other for the better part of a decade.

"Um…nice to meet you?" I say, more a question than a statement.

"And you," he says. He dips his head in a little bow but makes no move to shake my hand, thankfully. He looks young—midtwenties, maybe—his hair dark in purposefully unruly wisps drawn up from his head.

"Babe, Reese is a landscape architect."

"A landscape architect," I repeat in an attempt to digest this. "Like, a landscaper?"

Reese smirks.

"Well…" Cooper steps toward me and touches my fingers but doesn't take my hand. "After the thing with your application, I wanted to do something nice for you. I saw you with those seeds the other night and it reminded me of the promise I made you. I want you to have that garden you've always wanted. He's going to fit us in around other clients as a favor."

When we lived in our studio apartment, I used to tell Cooper all the time how much I wanted a garden.

But why now? Like I'll forget about my research grant? Like I'm a child he can distract with a new toy?

Cooper's eyes are bright with excitement, unaware of how I really feel, or maybe just ignoring it. He knows by now that sometimes that's all he can do. I look around our neglected yard and try to picture a garden there. I've done it dozens of times, but this time all I can see is my mom's garden and the way she was tearing into it on Abby's anniversary.

"I don't know," I say. "We don't really have time for this, Cooper."

I try to direct my words in Cooper's direction, aware of the stranger's stare. I don't want to appear ungrateful, but I'm having a hard time believing Cooper's intentions are completely selfless. I wish I knew he still believed in my research. I wish I knew he still believed in me.

Cooper takes my hand fully. "But…maybe you'll find this is what you really need."

What I really need… I wish I knew.

Tears prick the corners of my eyes, and I turn my face so neither of them can see. I let my hand fall from Cooper's.

"Fine," I spit out. "I want a moat."

Reese lets out a chuckle.

"A moat?" Cooper asks.

I sniff and stand up straighter, composing myself.

"Yep," I continue. If Cooper wants me distracted, I'll make it the biggest project either one of them has ever seen. "All the way around the house. Flowing water. And a waterfall."

"Okay," Reese says, his response smooth and amused. "What else?"

I list a few more things—flowers I like, stepping-stones, a swing.

A few minutes later, I watch through the front window as Cooper walks Reese to his truck. Cooper laughs at something Reese says, then takes his hand in a firm shake and the deal is done.

I meet Cooper at the front door when he comes in.

"What do you think?" Cooper asks, still not seeming to understand how his act of kindness is affecting me. "Happy?"

"I don't know if I'll be able to maintain it. I'm not my mom."

I clench my teeth shut to keep my chin from quivering. Cooper frowns. He knows how tenuous my relationship is with her. It's been a sore subject since he first asked me about my family—an innocent question all couples bring up at the beginning of a relationship. But without telling him the whole truth about Abby, I always had a hard time explaining our discord to him in a way that made sense.

One Christmas a few years ago, I overheard him ask my dad about it. Fumbling over his words, Dad had tried to lay it out for him—how when I was seven, his father had died and we'd moved into my grandfather's house in Lake Oswego, the most prestigious gated community in the Portland area. Everything about our lives changed—Dad taking over his father's investment company, the three of us kids going from public to private school and Mom fulfilling the implicit obligations of a woman of upper-class society. It went against everything she'd had planned for our life, and she resented it. She pulled away from all of us. All of us except Abby—her carbon copy—and I had felt most betrayed by that. With as much time as Dad spent at the office to avoid Mom's anger, I was surprised to discover he'd noticed it all those years. Cooper never brought up the subject with me again.

"Is that what all that was about?" Cooper asks. He nods toward the backyard. The moat, he means.

I release all the air in my lungs. It's all the answer Cooper needs. He takes me by the hand and pulls me over to the couch. He sits me down, then he sinks into the spot next to me. When that's not close enough, he pulls my legs onto his lap, awkwardly bumping elbows and knees. I rest my head on his shoulder.

"Do you remember when we went to Hawaii for Stephen and Megan's wedding?" he asks.

I nod against his neck, my nose brushing his loosened tie. Cooper, Stephen and I were still in the middle of our internships, but despite all three of our protests, Megan refused to put the wedding off any longer. "You're always going to be too busy," she'd said. "You just have to make the time."

"It was so beautiful there," Cooper says. "That gorgeous blue water. You waking me up in the middle of the night and making me go swimming in that cove on the beach."

That was the last time I truly lived in the moment. Being so far away from our everyday worries, it was easy to let my hair down. It was easy to forget about my mission of familial reconciliation. A long weekend of late nights on the beach, luaus and umbrella drinks, sand between our sheets and bodies. I laugh at the image in my head of Cooper naked, toeing his way into the water. "You were such a wimp."

"Hey," Cooper says. "Jellyfish near my nether regions is a very logical fear."

I laugh harder. It feels foreign, but so good. Cooper rests his head on mine.

"Do you remember," he asks, "how we told the hotel we were on our honeymoon, and that big Samoan concierge winked at us every single time we passed him on the way up to our room? Even when we were just coming back from breakfast?"

"Well, sometimes he was right."

Cooper nods. "Yes." He pauses. "Let's do that again."

"What, lie to hotel staff?"

"Let's go somewhere and pretend we're the only two people who exist. Well, the two of us and the horny bellhop." Our laughter eases the strain on my heart. He's the only one I've ever been able to count on, even when it's him I'm fighting against.

"Cooper," I say softly, afraid of shattering the moment, "neither of us has the time to go on a vacation. We can barely find time to eat a meal at the same table."

"That's exactly my point. Do you know that trip is the last time we spent any real time together without being interrupted by calls from the hospital or kids with the flu? That was four years ago."

"Coop," I say and reach out to take his hand. "I miss you, too…but I don't see how that's possible. I need to figure out what I'm doing with my career. I need to find another way to make this grant happen. Plus, you know how much my patients depend on me."

"So let's start planning now. I'm sure if you talked to your coworkers, they could spare you for a week."

"A week?" Anxiety sticks in my throat, like a pill without water. I feel like he's testing me—pushing me to see if I'm listening to him. I am. I hear him. But how do I leave when everything is up in the air? When I'm balanced at the top of a pole with nowhere to step without plummeting down?

He clasps my hands and holds them tight. "Dylan, I'm asking you, please. Please, do this for us. I know your job is important to you and you have people who need you, but I need you. I miss you. I miss the woman who used to drop everything to see a movie with me just so we could share a box of Red Vines, even though we both knew you were going to give me one and eat the rest yourself."

I smile. Those times during medical school were the best times of my life. Falling in love with Cooper, I learned to open up and trust in a way I thought I never would again. I found my first true friends in Stephen and Megan. And the responsibility I bear felt so far away. I knew I was on the right path, but I was only a student. Back then, that was the most I could do for my family and families who had suffered like ours.

But not now.

"Cooper—"

"It doesn't have to be Hawaii. You've been saying you want to go to Thailand since I first met you. Just think—*real* Thai food. I don't care where we go. I just want to be with you."

I exhale and lean back on the couch. Doesn't he know I want to be that carefree, sun-bathing, licorice-eating woman again, too?

"You know we need this."

I purse my lips. I'm failing at everything, and it's coming at me so fast, I can't keep up.

"I'll see what I can do," I say.

I spend Friday afternoon catching up on my charts, giving myself a chance to regroup on my application. Around five thirty, I run home, slip through the front door and peel off my tennis shoes. I have time to grab a bite of dinner before I head back to the hospital for a delivery. Normally I would work straight through dinner, but I'm trying to make the effort. For Cooper. He hasn't brought up the vacation again, and I'm hoping that if I can give him more time here at home, we can put it off for another year—just until I get my grant.

Cooper calls to me from the kitchen where I hear the everyday sounds of the man I love closing the refrigerator, opening a cabinet. Without the tension behind all the words we're saying and not saying lately, it's comforting. I soak in the warmth of home, add it to the collection of memories I carry with me as a reminder of why I love to bring families together and why I work so hard to keep them from falling apart. It's the simple things, like the sounds of the people you love, that end up meaning the most when they're gone. Like the way Abby used to loudly flick each page of her magazine as she turned it, and the buzz of her curling iron on the counter in our shared bathroom.

"You're home early," he says.

"Well...kind of."

I follow Cooper's voice toward the kitchen, but he appears in front of me as I round the corner, catching me off guard. He takes a strong hold of my arms before either one of us topples over.

"Hi," he says with a shy smile. He's still in the crisply pressed deep blue shirt and tie he wore to work this morning—the combination that makes the blue of his eyes ethereal. He kisses me, deeply, all of his body pressed against all of mine until I'm out of breath. I try to enjoy it, but anticipating the reason behind it sets butterflies loose in my stomach.

"Hi," I say against his lips once he's released me. "What's got you so worked up?"

"Follow me," he says.

"Okay, but I have to—"

"Follow me," he urges.

He turns toward the kitchen and drags me along. I shuffle my feet in an attempt to stay upright in my socks on the hardwood floors. He places me in front of the kitchen counter, then moves to the side, revealing a bottle of very expensive champagne—the kind my dad used to buy for special occasions, when he would let my brother, my sister and me each have half a glass—and two champagne flutes I'm sure we didn't own before. We haven't had much reason for champagne over the last few years.

"Are we celebrating something?" I ask.

"We are," he says.

I raise my eyebrows, waiting for him to elaborate.

"I did it, babe. I made partner."

I open my mouth in surprise and something that resembles excitement, but nothing comes out. I knew this was coming. I did. I just didn't expect it so soon, or that he'd reach his goal before I've even really started on mine. The air thickens around me, tense with his anticipation of my response.

I *am* happy for him. I know I am because his news stirs something in my chest. I just imagined we'd share the day, when my grant came through at least. It's illogical to think we'd reach our goals at the same time, but still, I've held a picture in my head of us celebrating together. A re-creation of the day we graduated med school. Both of us moving forward as one. Now Cooper's moving forward. I'm not.

"Dylan?" he asks, when I say nothing.

"Wow," I whisper.

His grin reveals the only evidence of his true age in the wrinkles at the corners of his eyes.

"Oh, Cooper. Wow."

I fold myself into him and he laughs.

"Can you believe it?" he asks. "Two years. They never ask doctors to become partners so soon. Didn't I say this was going to be the right place for me?"

He did, the day he started there. We'd been lying next to each other in bed that night, our legs and fingers intertwined. We said a lot of things that night, drunk on possibilities and each other, talking like reality couldn't touch us. Was that only two years ago?

I swallow hard. "I remember," I say.

"C'mon, let's have a drink," he says. I make a noncommittal noise against his warm shoulder. He places a kiss on my forehead and walks to the counter in his black-socked feet, the hem of his slacks dusting the floor. With his back turned to me, I take a deep breath to compose myself. Surely he doesn't remember everything we talked about that night. Surely he doesn't expect me to make good on those promises so soon, before I've reached my own goals.

After I make partner, he'd said, *there's nothing else I want but you…and a couple of little yous. By then, I'll finally be making enough money to give you the kind of life you're used to.*

Cooper, we could move back into that studio apartment forever, and I'd still spend the rest of my life with you.

You mean it?

I mean it.

I still do, but in the heat of the moment I didn't want to add that before I settled down with him, I needed to make some things right. Back then, I thought we had so much time to work out the details. The future stretched out like a long expanse of open road in front of us. But suddenly, it's here and I'm not there.

"You're not drinking," Cooper says. I hadn't noticed Cooper place the full glass in my hand. His brow is furrowed. I watch every emotion cross his face as realization sinks in—confusion, comprehension, frustration. Then, disappointment. "You have to go back to work, don't you?"

I look away, nod. "I'm sorry, Cooper. I didn't know this was going to happen. I have a delivery. I'm expecting the page any second."

"I thought you weren't on call tonight."

"But she's *my patient*, Cooper."

He sets his champagne on the counter. "And I'm the one who always comes last."

His words echo through the room and through my mind, tearing my heart further in half. He scrubs his hands through his hair in anger.

"It's fine," he says, but his voice is detached. "I understand."

"Cooper…" I open my mouth to apologize, but the words are meaningless.

He busies himself with trying to force the cork back into the bottle. It's useless, but it keeps him from having to look at me.

"It's okay, Dylan. Really."

I take a step toward him, but then my pager buzzes on my waistband, and that low hum, in the silence of our kitchen, is deafening.

"Go ahead," he says. He looks up at me, doing his best to reassure me, because he knows I can't leave for a delivery with my mind still here, wondering if he's okay. If we're okay.

I nod and leave the kitchen, slip my tennis shoes back on and walk out into the fading light.

Behind the wheel, I stop to look at our house. The light

from the kitchen filters through the living room to the front windows, and for a moment, I see the shadow of Cooper standing in the middle of the living room, motionless, and I don't have to wonder if we're okay because I know we're not.

Cooper is following our dreams without me.

5

I wake on Saturday morning to a note from Cooper letting me know he went on a hike with Stephen. His absence jars me—with a rare weekend off, I expected we'd make plans together—and I spend the day meandering around the house. Finally, I walk down to the creek, sit on the bench and watch the water hopscotch over the rocks to pass the time until Cooper and I are supposed to go to his parents' house for dinner. At five thirty, though, he texts me to say that since I'm on call, he went straight over. Oftentimes, when I'm on call, I like to stay home, so I don't have to bail on anyone. But I'm not on call tonight. I told him that. When I crawl into bed after ten, he still isn't home.

The next morning, Cooper is as far away from me in bed as possible, so, disheartened, I sneak out of the house with the plan to visit my dad. Other than Abby, he's the only one I've ever been able to really talk to.

When I get to my parents' house, though, his car isn't in the garage. I use my key, and I find no one in the kitchen. Dad isn't in his study, and Mom isn't in her garden. Dad often spends Sunday mornings at the office, but to be sure, I slip upstairs to his bedroom. Before I get to the door, I can already smell the scent of his aftershave, taking me back to when I was a little girl and I would curl up on his comforter and watch him get ready for work. He would make his bed with me inside it and pretend to lose me under the covers. When I peek my head inside now, though, the sheets are tucked tightly into place, and his electric shaver and comb are lined up neatly on his dresser. Dad himself is nowhere to be found.

As I pass Mom's bedroom on my way out, I hear a thump come from the other side of her door. It stops me in my tracks. A quick debate fires in my mind, the louder voice urging me to leave before she sees me, before the feelings of guilt and inadequacy overtake me. Against my better judgment, I step closer and peek in through the sliver of the open door. I see Mom sit up on her bed, having scooped something off the floor. She sets the large, purple book on her lap, pushes her lifeless gray hair behind her ears and opens the cover. I recognize it as a photo album I haven't seen in years.

I nudge the door open farther and catch sight of the storage tub we packed Abby's most prized possessions into a few months after her death. Mom had fought Dad about sorting through Abby's things to the point I thought she might actually hit him when he demanded we get rid of most of it. Left up to her, she would have turned Abby's room into a shrine, but Dad insisted it was an important step in moving forward. He thought it would give us closure. Most important, he thought it would give Mom closure. His plan backfired on him, though, because she just moved her penance to another room.

I'd be lying if I said I hadn't buried my tear-streaked face into Abby's bed many nights after her death until one Saturday it was gone without explanation. I never asked Dad about it—I was too embarrassed. It would have meant admitting that I wasn't ready to let go yet either, that I was no stronger than Mom.

Today Mom looks smaller and more fragile than ever— two words that, as a young girl, I never would have thought I'd one day use to describe my mother. Her movements are weary, lethargic. Every year it takes her weeks to recover from the anniversary of Abby's death.

The picture the photo album is open to is one I chose, selected from the dozens Abby and I had stuck to our dresser mirrors in each of our bedrooms, where there were pictures of us on family vacations at the beach, or at Disneyland, and photo booth strips showcasing her array of silly faces and my poor attempts at playfulness. With her perfect features, she could afford to be silly. She looked beautiful no matter what. The one beneath Mom's fingers is a picture she took of Abby and me before the homecoming dance the year before Abby's death. We had our hair in identical updos, curls falling down from our temples, my dark features a photo negative of her fair ones. She smiled straight at the camera, all teeth, but I was looking at her with a close-lipped grin that captured exactly how I always felt about her: awestruck.

In her last year, she had drifted further away from me as she drew closer to Christian and her cheerleader friends. Prom night, though, we got ready for the dance together, just the two of us. I let her choose my dress, one that showed off my "basketball calves," as she'd said it. Then we went to the salon, and she didn't balk when I wanted the same hairstyle as her. She'd always hated my copycatting when we were younger, but not that night. That night was ours.

Mom flips another page of the photo album, a timeline of Abby's life from birth to death. She must have every picture memorized. I don't understand what she could still need to see there, in those seventy-five four-by-sixes. But then again, maybe I do. I try to tell myself Mom's loss was no greater than the rest of ours, that her grief is overindulgent and selfish, but the truth is, we all knew there was a special connection between Mom and Abby. Everyone knew it. Everywhere we went, people commented on how much they looked alike—both of them short and petite, both with green eyes that shone like summer all year round, both with straw-blond hair. But there was more—in the way they loved to bake together, the way they could flash their smiles and talk anyone into anything, their earthiness, their impulsiveness.

I bump the bedroom door, and it creaks open another inch. Mom looks up from the photo album at me as I stand there watching her. I wait for her to get angry for invading her time with Abby's memory, to insist I leave, but her shoulders are slumped, and she looks heavy under the weight of her losses. It's been a while since I've really looked at her, and the skin around her eyes and mouth is more deeply wrinkled. She looks a decade older than her sixty years, and her eyes are vulnerable in a way I haven't seen them in a while.

"I found this in your dresser," she says. She leans over to grab another picture from the bin and holds it up. It's the one picture I'd hidden in my room—the only picture of Abby I had that was truly mine.

I move farther into the room, but not too close for fear of getting sucked back into it all.

"You didn't put it with the rest of her stuff," she said.

I shake my head. I don't apologize, though I sense she wants me to.

"Huh," she says, and tosses the picture back into the tub. She rubs at the knees of her slacks. I say nothing, afraid of being lectured, like I'm a fourteen-year-old girl all over again. With my mom, I'll always feel like a child.

She surprises me by asking, "Why that picture?"

It used to be in one of the collages Mom has hung in the living room before it got replaced by more updated pictures, posed shots of the family in matching outfits. I'd sneaked that one into my room even before Abby's death because it wasn't Abby I was looking for in that memory.

The photo was taken at our old house, in the backyard. Mom, Abby and I stood in front of the vegetable garden Mom had kept back then, before she focused all her talents into keeping up with the women in her gardening club. Abby must have been about eight years old then. I would have been six. The picture was full of color, from the vegetables themselves, to the mural of the sky Mom had allowed Abby, Charlie and I to sloppily paint on the wooden fence behind us, to Mom's flowing skirt and the delicate headband wrapped loosely around her forehead. Dad had taken the picture to capture the size of Mom's vegetables before we did our first harvest and only had us jump into the frame on a last-minute whim. But there was something about that picture that had always stirred something inside my heart when I looked at it, especially after we moved and Mom began to change into someone I didn't recognize. The picture was a reminder of who our mom used to be and who I hoped she could be again one day.

"I always thought you looked beautiful in it," I say honestly. Sure, fashion had changed since then and the picture quality wasn't great, but the look in her eyes was real. It was happy.

Mom snorts a laugh. "My hair was a disaster." She rests her elbows on her knees and runs her fingers through her hair now as if she could fix it in the past.

"It was perfect," I say, not to make her feel better but to defend my choice. I'd go back to that day in a heartbeat. "What happened, Mom?" I almost clarify that I'm not talking about Abby's death, but I think she knows that the rift in our relationship goes much deeper than that.

"Your dad's at the office," she says, avoiding the question. At her response, tears burn at the corners of my eyes, and I'm left knowing I'm not going to get an answer out of her today, and I probably never will.

"Right," I say and I back out of the room. I catch one last glance at the picture, one of my most prized memories tossed carelessly onto the heap that is all that's left of what could have been. I turn and let myself out.

I spend Sunday night in the labor and delivery unit coaxing out a little girl who isn't quite ready to leave her mother's womb. Afterward, Vanessa sends me home to catch up on some sleep. When I pull into my driveway around ten in the morning, Cooper is gone, but Reese's truck is in the driveway. I forgot he was starting on the backyard today. After my little scene the last time Reese was here, and after admitting my reluctance to get involved, Cooper took it upon himself to work out the rest of the details. But mostly, he told me, he'd given Reese free rein. I walk from the garage to the front door, watching beads of rain breach through the layer of dirt on his windshield, smudging out spots of clarity that are just as quickly blotted out by the next drop. I see no signs of Reese.

I leave my shoes in the foyer and pad to the kitchen, using the excuse of a glass of water to stand at the window and search for him. Despite my hesitation about the garden and having a stranger at the house, now that the idea has sunk in, I'm intrigued by the development of my little spot in the world. The fantasies I once harbored about a peaceful space of my own have resurfaced. I cling to that show of love more than ever with the distance Cooper has been putting between us.

From here there's nothing to see, but since I know I won't sleep, I decide to get closer.

Outside, a light rain continues to drizzle. Reese is turned away from me, so I try to make my presence known with heavier footfalls, but as I watch Reese work so attentively on the trench he's digging, I'm sure I'll startle him no matter how I approach. I stick close to the house to avoid some of the errant raindrops while he digs in a slow and steady rhythm, tossing the loose soil into a growing pile on the grass. He's knee-deep in the hole he's created, which is a few feet long, moving from the side yard toward the space beneath my bedroom windows. Despite the cool temperature, he seems unaffected by the rain on his exposed arms and the back of his neck, both a deep tan, no doubt from years of working all day in the sun. I stumble over a branch, and he looks up at me.

"Hello, Dr. Michels." I stop where I am, giving myself distance, but the way he says my name makes my mouth suddenly dry. He draws out each syllable, and somehow it sounds more intimate than calling me by my first name. Without the buffer of Cooper, or maybe because I've interrupted Reese's focus, the current that surrounds him is less contained.

"Dylan," I correct him. "How is it going?"

"Just fine," he says. He rests one foot on the lip of the shovel and leans into the handle. "You're home early."

"Actually, I'm home late. Just got done with surgery."

"Ouch. Do you work all night a lot?"

"Here and there. It's not too bad." I shrug.

"Man, I couldn't do it. I need my sleep," he says. He laughs, but I miss the joke.

After a moment of silence, his eyes narrow, gauging me— the woman who wanted the moat. I can't tell what he's looking for, or whether or not I should be threatened by it.

I cross my arms over my chest. "Well, it's not for everyone."

"Sure." After a moment, he says, "If you're not busy, I can show you what I've got so far."

"I can't. I have to get back to work," I say, which isn't true, but it comes out before I realize it isn't. He nods, smiling. The lie must be written all over my face.

I sigh. "Okay. I guess I have a minute."

He lays the shovel down on the grass and hoists himself up to my level. Like the first time I met him, I'm struck by his lightness, his agility. He seems so carefree, like someone who lives in a different world, apart from the stress and struggles of everyday life. As I look around me, at the kind of places he gets to work, I wonder if maybe he does.

"Come here," he says and waves me over. I inch forward until we're standing in front of each other, only the gap in the earth separating us.

"So here's your moat so far," he says, barely hiding a grin, teasing me. He's giving me what I asked for, clearly more for his own entertainment than thinking it's a good idea. I must have made a hell of a first impression.

"It's a pretty stupid request, isn't it?"

"Let's just say it was a first. I appreciate your bravery, though. And I admit, it is nice to have a challenge. I could use a break from the koi ponds. Want to see the rest of my ideas?" he asks. His green eyes light up against his dark hair.

"Sure," I say.

"Come with me."

He jumps across the divide in a single bound, and I let him lead me around the house to the front yard.

"Don't you have any employees?" I ask him as we traipse through the overgrown grass.

He waves the question away. "I prefer the silence."

When we reach the driveway, he opens the door of his

truck and leans far over to reach for something on the dash-board. I lower my gaze.

"Now, keep in mind, this isn't finished, it's just what I'm starting with. Most of the time, the ideas come to me as I work."

I nod and take the sketch pad he offers me. I'd expected a list or, at most, a computer-generated rendering, but inside the front cover is a hand-sketched portrait of what I recognize as my backyard from the viewpoint of the tree line. I recognize the structure of my backyard anyway. The back door and the windows of the house are clearly visible. Everything else is foreign: the water that runs around it a few feet from the exterior walls, the bridge coming out from the back door to connect to the rest of the yard, a stepping-stone path cutting through the grass into the trees. He's scribbled out vague flowers along the base of the house and patches on the outside of the moat that bleed into the grass. Vines weave it all together.

Reese's creativity and steady hand are beautiful. I always wished I had more of an eye for this type of thing, but that's my mother's forte. An unexpected yearning to ask her opinion bubbles up inside me, but I suppress it.

I clear my throat. "How did you get so good at this?" I ask.

"I don't know. Practice, I guess."

"A teenage boy practicing gardening?"

He laughs. "How old do you think I am?" he asks, and the way he says it, the way his brow furrows, does make him look older. "Never mind. Don't answer that. Yes, as a matter of fact, this previously teenaged boy practiced gardening. My mom worked—well, works—a lot. My neighbor, Abraam, used to watch me after school. He must have been in his, I don't know, seventies? But that didn't stop him from getting down in the dirt with me every day. The man had a gift.

He grew the most beautiful roses you could imagine. I always told him he should compete, but he said it wasn't about that, it was about the process." He purses his lips together to stop himself, seeming to realize he's rambling. Then he asks, "What about you? How did you become such a great doctor?"

"How do you know how good a doctor I am?"

"Well, Dr. Caldwell seems to think so. And I trust his opinion."

A tense laugh escapes my lips, but my heart warms to know Cooper's been complimenting my work, even if he's stopped sharing the compliments with me. "I wouldn't. He's biased."

"Maybe."

Reese waits for me to go on. I notice the way he's leaning slightly toward me, ready for more clues to blend into whatever picture he's painting of me. I look away.

"I'm just trying to understand what kind of person you are, the kind of things you like," he says, sensing my hesitancy. "The thing is, I can put almost anything you want in your backyard. If you don't have a preference, I can choose anything *I* want. What I'm trying to figure out is how you want the space to *feel*."

"Feel?"

"What gives gardens life is the way each individual detail adds up to something more meaningful. What will your garden mean to you? What do you want to feel when you're there?"

I ponder the question—somewhat personal coming from a stranger who was hired to dig a glorified trench in my backyard.

If I could walk into another world and feel anything, what would it be?

My mind wanders to Cooper and the look on his face when I left him alone with the champagne. It flashes to the way my mom hardly speaks to me anymore, the way I've given up on ever having a relationship with her again. I picture Abby with the oxygen mask over her face. I always picture Abby.

"Forgiveness," I say, not meeting his gaze as I utter the word. "I want to feel forgiveness."

A single raindrop hits the page, smearing a charcoal flower, and I try to brush it away.

"I'm… I… Sorry." I thrust the sketch pad at him but he doesn't take it. He stares at me for a moment, his hands in his back pockets. The way he looks at me, I'd swear he can read my mind.

He finally lifts the pad from my hand and opens the truck door to place it back inside. Before he faces me again, I walk toward the house.

"Dylan." He almost whispers my name, but I hear the very breath it rides on. I was wrong. My name on his lips is disconcerting either way. I look over my shoulder at him. "Glad you like it," he says.

On Wednesday night, I stop by the grocery store on the way home to buy the ingredients for Cooper's favorite dish— tacos—as a thank-you for the garden, and as an apology when words aren't enough. On nights like this, part of me is thankful I don't have clinical trials and paperwork to sort through and catalog. It makes me look forward to the days when this will be our life, every night, however far into the future that might be.

I drop the groceries in the kitchen, then search the house for Cooper. As I approach our bedroom door, I hear Cooper murmuring as if to a child. At first, I irrationally think he's brought a patient home from the office—those are the only children either of us knows—until I inch my way into the room where he's hunched over on the floor next to the bed, cooing and humming words I can't make out.

"What's going on?" I ask from the doorway.

He looks over his shoulder at me, a grin from ear to ear. This makes me more nervous that it should. He stands and turns to face me with a small German shepherd puppy lounging across his palms, belly up, tongue flapping lazily out of its open mouth.

"What's that?" I ask, the shock giving me no time to filter my thoughts.

"My receptionist had puppies."

"Your receptionist gave birth to puppies?"

Cooper laughs nervously, his smile shrinking down a size. "You know what I mean."

I force myself not to jump to any conclusions, calming my racing heart with one long, controlled breath. Cooper knows we don't have the time or energy to take care of a puppy. He wouldn't spring something like this on me. Except that he just sprang a landscaper on me…

No matter how bad an idea, I can't resist—I step forward and reach out to rub a finger between the puppy's ears. It nips playfully at my knuckle with its sharp little teeth. Cooper, ever naive, seems encouraged by this.

"Do you want to hold him?"

As much as I would rather crawl into bed—work clothes on and all—and pull the covers over my head, I say, "Sure."

I move to the bed and sit down on it. Cooper sets the German shepherd in my lap. The puppy yelps and begins to lick every inch of available skin on my arms. At first, I try to redirect him but soon realize it's no use. I allow him his fun until he wears himself out and rolls over onto his back again, apparently approving of me. Cooper watches the whole scenario play out without comment. I just wanted to make Cooper dinner, but it's never enough—nothing I'm able to give ever is. I place the puppy on the ground, walk past Cooper to the bathroom and shut the door.

I collapse onto the toilet and push my fingers against my temples.

A moment later, I hear a thump as Cooper leans into the door frame.

"Dylan," he says, his apologetic tone muffled. "Will you come out here and talk to me about this?"

After a few deep breaths, I stand up and place my hands flat on the counter. My bloodshot eyes, dark circles and pale skin make my reflection look washed out and scary. To escape it, I turn around and open the door. Cooper is standing there alone. I look past him and see the puppy playing with one of his old socks on the carpet.

"Did I do something wrong?" he asks. When I don't answer, he says, "I thought we talked about moving our relationship forward. And then this little guy fell into my lap. It seemed like a sign." His enthusiasm is gone. Once again, it's my fault.

"I thought we talked about going on *vacation*. How are we going to go on vacation with a puppy?"

He shrugs. "We don't have to keep him," he says, but I can see in his eyes that he's already fallen in love with it. Why wouldn't he? He fell in love with me that first night.

"This is a living thing, Cooper, not an undercooked steak you can send back to the waiter."

A silence spreads between us like an ink stain. It's broken when his phone rings on the nightstand. I look away, and he crosses the room to answer it. He says a familiar, "Hey," and then takes it out of the room, leaving me with the dog.

I heave a sigh, reluctantly cross the room and pick it—I check. *Him.*—up.

"I don't know much about dogs," I murmur to him as he licks my fingers, "but I'm guessing you'll want to go outside now."

I carry him to the back door, turn on the porch light and set him loose on the grass. I leave the door open so I can listen for him, then unpack the groceries I no longer feel like cooking. I poke at the potting soil where my daisies have yet to sprout. What the hell do I know about taking care of something?

"Babe," Cooper says, walking into the dining room. He's pulling on a T-shirt and has his phone in his hand like he's on his way out.

"What's wrong?" I ask.

He shakes his head and throws his hands in the air, as confused as I am.

"Stephen's on his way over. He and Megan are separating."

I freeze. "What? You're joking, right?" I ask.

The purse of Cooper's lips tells me he's not. I blink slowly, waiting for time to rewind or for this to be a hoax. Cooper just went hiking with Stephen last weekend and everything was fine. I saw Megan at their parents' house three weeks ago and she was…well, actually, she was a mess, now that I think about it. And I haven't seen them under the same roof for months. Funny how, after spending so many years around doctors, that didn't strike me as out of the ordinary.

"But…no." That's all I can think to say, because the more I think about it, the faster the pieces come together. Still, I shake my head, refusing to believe it. Stephen without Megan isn't possible.

Cooper says, "Megan told Mom this afternoon, and she's been at my parents' house crying all day. I just got off the phone with Stephen. Apparently he's been staying at a hotel all week. He finished his shift at the hospital fifteen minutes ago, and I told him to come over. I hope that's okay."

My fingertips go numb with shock.

"A week ago?" I breathe. "Of course it's okay. Are you okay?" *Am I okay?* The weight on my chest grows heavier in response. I can hardly see Cooper's expression in the darkness, but it's his best friend and his sister. He can't be okay.

The puppy comes racing in through the back door, his nails clicking on the floor.

"I don't know. I don't know how to feel. I guess I'll decide when he gets here," Cooper says. "C'mon."

Cooper scoops the puppy up and closes him in our bathroom, then takes me by the hand and we wait on the front porch for Stephen to arrive, both of us barefoot. He doesn't let go of me, just keeps looking over at me with sad eyes and a hopeful smile.

Of course he's hopeful. That's the kind of world Cooper grew up in, the kind of example his parents set for him during their thirty-three years of marriage. He believes in love stories and happily-ever-afters. As much as it drives me crazy that he thinks relationships should be as easy as all the good parts his parents let him see, I've always loved him for it, too.

That's not the example I was given. I used to believe in forever, but the truth about relationships revealed itself around the same time as Santa Claus's fake beard and the Grimms' version of the fairy tales, when Mom traded her flowy skirts for pressed pantsuits, and my once-affectionate parents stopped cooking together and began arguing more. Then, when Abby died, Mom shut down completely. Now my mom merely puts up with my dad's existence, and my dad tiptoes around her, like we all do. That's what I know of relationships.

It wasn't until I met Cooper's parents that I began to see

the possibility of a loving marriage again. But watching Stephen grow into a devoted husband is what really showed me I might be able to overcome my need to keep everyone at an arm's length and find happiness for myself someday, too. I thought if Stephen could overcome his self-destructive habits, I had a chance. So I don't just hope Stephen and Megan work things out; I need them to.

A few minutes later, Stephen's headlights flash through the trees, and he comes to a stop in the driveway. Cooper's hand slips from mine as he steps off the stoop to meet him at the truck and pull him into a hug. I rub my hands together for something to do with my nervous energy and allow them a minute alone. I hear Cooper ask, "Why didn't you tell me, man?"

Once they've had a chance to talk privately, I make my way toward them, taking careful steps across the gravel.

"Hey, you," I say to Stephen in a low voice. His facial hair is too long for the hospital, and the circles under his eyes are darker than when I saw him last. He and Megan have been going through this for a while. I stifle my disappointment that they didn't allow us to be there for them before it got this far, when we could have helped. Stephen frowns and pulls me into the unforgiving chest of an outdoorsman, into his earthy smell, and rests his chin on my head. I've never seen him in so much pain.

"I'm sorry," he says to me, and then to Cooper.

"You don't have anything to apologize for," I say. "What happened? Maybe you guys can talk it out." I turn my head so my voice isn't muffled against his shirt. "Cooper and I can help."

Cooper reprimands me with a single word—my name, low and insistent. It frustrates him when I try to fix things that are, according to him, "not my circus, not my monkeys," even though that's what we're all in the business of doing. Every day we fix people who are strangers to us. Why can't we fix the people we love?

"No," Stephen says, the weight of the word in the air revealing the depth of his defeat. "We can't talk it out. I've always known she was too good for me. I took her for granted, wasn't there for her when she needed me. There's no first-aid kit for this, Dylan."

"Sure there is. It's called tequila," I say, and that gets a smile out of him, but it's short-lived.

I hold Stephen tighter for a second, then let go.

"Everything's going to be okay," I say, because it has to be. "You guys will get through this."

"Okay," Stephen says, humoring me.

"You'll always be my brother. You know that, right?" Cooper says. He nudges Stephen's shoulder. "Always were."

"Damn it, dude." Stephen pushes his fingers through his hair and turns toward his truck. "I have to go." He walks away before we can invite him in for a beer, talk through it and come up with a solution, the way we used to. I guess we're too old for that now. Life has gotten too complicated for simple answers.

"I'll call you tomorrow," Cooper says. Stephen doesn't look at either of us when he nods and gets into the truck.

Cooper and I stand there until he drives away, Cooper an arm's length and a world away. I swallow hard when he sniffs and gathers himself. It's harder to watch him go through this than to feel the pain myself. I'm already jaded.

I wait for Cooper's cue, and it comes as a strong arm around my waist. He pulls me tight to him and leads me toward the house. I stumble forward beside him in our awkward embrace. Before we reach the door, Cooper leans over and kisses me hard.

"I love you," he says, clear and firm, as if trying to convince me. As if to say, *That will never happen to us.*

"I love you, too," I say, and I pray more than anything that he's right.

6

After Stephen's confession, Cooper seems more determined than ever to assert that our relationship isn't headed down a similar road. In bed one night, he wraps himself around me and whispers that he wants to spend the rest of his life with me, reminding me of the conversation I hoped he'd forgotten, at least for a little while longer. In the darkness, I keep my eyes closed and focus on deepening my breath so he'll think I'm asleep. I hate myself for it, and for my indecision but I just can't hurt him anymore. He drifts off with his heavy arm still draped over my chest, smothering me.

I sneak into the house late on Monday night. The lights are off, and Cooper and the puppy are asleep, like I hoped they would be. In the kitchen, I pour myself a glass of water and look around me, at what my life has become. There's a potted orchid on the windowsill in the kitchen that's half dead from lack of watering. The daisy seeds are hiding in their pots next to it. Pictures line the shelves in the living room, all of them a couple years old, as if Cooper and I died shortly after we moved in and someone kept the house open as a memorial. My high school and college basketball trophies sit on the shelves in the hallway without a speck of dust, thanks to the woman who comes to clean once a month. They all stand at exactly the same angle. Everything is so pristine, so organized, so untouched. I bite at the inside of my cheek when I realize it shares those qualities with my mom's house. In hers, it's because she works so avidly to keep up the appearance that she's holding everything together. In my house, it's because there's hardly anyone here to live in it in the first place.

But I love our house. We bought it after Cooper had been at the practice for three months. It was his idea. I wasn't so sure we were ready, but he insisted we could afford it, that our life was only going to get better. He had desperately wanted to get me out of the studio apartment we'd been living in, seducing me with a kitchen big enough to cook meals together, a shower that didn't make it impossible to retrieve a dropped bar of soap and a few extra bedrooms for guests, "or whatever." Even back then, we had no time to cook, and everyone we wanted to spend time with lived in the same city. I'd humored him by looking at modest homes I knew neither of us would fall in love with. I pretended I didn't hear the insinuations about what our future would entail if we chose one.

But one evening, after a double shift at the hospital, he picked me up and drove me to the outskirts of the city, past the hustle and bustle and traffic noise, to a neighborhood with more trees than sidewalk cracks. The houses were set an acre apart and strained to reach the treetops. Many of them were so hidden behind nature it seemed as if the driveways led to nowhere, but then we rounded the corner, and in front of us stood a house with sleek lines and never-ending windows. They winked the sunlight back at me.

It was this house.

Cooper had a key, and I told myself I didn't know why. He walked me from room to room, saying nothing, just letting me fill in the gaps. "This would make a great office… This could be the guest room… This would be our room…"

"So let's make it our room," he said. I laughed.

"There's no way we can afford this. It's too much. We don't need that big backyard."

Cooper took my hands in his. His expression held so much pride and hope. I already knew I wouldn't say no to him, no matter how much my conscience nagged at me.

"I know how much you've always wanted a yard of your own. This way, you can go out there whenever you want," he said. "I never want you to feel like you're sacrificing. I know life would be a lot easier if we accepted the money your dad is always trying to trick us into taking."

"He's not—"

Cooper stopped me with a raised eyebrow.

"Okay, fine. But, Cooper, I'm not sacrificing. A big, fancy house isn't important to me."

"I know. And I love that about you. But don't think of it as a house. Think of it as a daily reminder that I'll never forget how much you're worth…and that I'll always try to make you feel like you made the right choice in loving me, even if it meant living in a glorified matchbox for the first few years of our relationship."

I laughed, then pressed my lips to his until my tension and exhaustion dissipated. "I did make the right choice. I don't need the reminder."

With a wry smile, Cooper asked, "Is that a yes?"

I looked around me. I never would have picked it for myself, but Cooper always did know what I wanted better than I did. I groaned.

"We'll landscape the backyard," he added quickly. So many mornings we had stood on our second floor balcony and stared out at the city streets below, sipping our coffee, while

I imagined a waterfall, flowers, a wide plot of grass to lie in and read. I no longer had the desire to do the gardening myself, but I'd grown up used to having something beautiful to look at while I daydreamed at the back windows or outside sunbathing on the grass. Back then the dreams were a lot more fanciful.

My answer was a tired grin.

"Good," he said with finality. "Because they accepted my offer."

I rolled my eyes and nudged his shoulder, making him laugh. He wanted so much to give me everything. I let him carry me into the empty living room, where he rested me on the floor in front of the bay windows and made love to me. I felt unbelievably lucky to have a man who loved me so much, and as he pushed into me, slow and steady, I held his gaze to keep myself in the moment, hoping he wouldn't one day regret this choice, or regret loving me.

"You're home," a sleepy voice says from the hallway, pulling me from my memories.

The tinkling of the puppy's collar echoes through the quiet space. I start and busy myself with pouring the remains of my water into each of the plants as Cooper opens the back door to let the puppy out. He joins me in the kitchen.

"Did you eat?" he asks.

I set my glass in the sink and shake my head. "I'm not hungry."

I finally turn to look at him, leaning against the counter. He presses himself against me and wraps his arms around my neck, pulling my head into his chest. I breathe him in, the scent of his sleepy sweat.

"I'm sorry," he murmurs against the top of my head. ·

I pull away from him so I can see his face. His features are soft and relaxed, and even though I sense he needs to say something important, I can't stop myself from kissing him. I bury my fingers into the hair at the back of his neck and pull him to me, entwining my mouth with his. He pushes against me harder, lifting me onto the counter with one swift movement. I wrap my legs around his waist and pull him closer, drawing his energy, his love, his faith into me, losing myself in him and finding myself in him all at once. I shiver as my mind goes blissfully blank—no Abby, no Mom, no Megan and Stephen, no grant.

Our kisses turn from feverish to lazy as his stillness seeps into my pores like the effects of a good drug. I press my forehead to his, both of our eyes closed.

"I'm sorry," he repeats, determined. I wish he wouldn't. There's nothing he needs to be sorry for. "I'm sorry for not being supportive these last few months. I've always known research was what you wanted to do. It's not right for me to expect you to change your mind just because I..."

Because he changed *his* mind. Because it made sense at the time we set our lofty goals, but reality isn't quite as fulfilling as the fantasy.

I sigh and run my thumb over his cheekbone, the stubble there abrasive under my skin. My heart rate picks up, sensing this is the time to finally tell Cooper about how I could have stopped my sister's death—to help him understand and get him back on my side. As much as I like to pretend I can, I can't do this alone.

"Cooper, there's something I haven't told you."

His body stiffens, but otherwise he doesn't move, careful not to break the moment. I take a deep breath, searching for the right words. I've been close to telling Cooper a dozen times, but I've never been able to break through that final wall. And like all the other times, Abby's face flashes into my mind—the very last time I saw her without an oxygen mask, without the stretcher and the EMTs. Her face was framed by the light blue trim of her car window, pale with pain, yet lit by her smile as she tried to reassure me.

"I'm fine. Go have fun. And, Dylan…"

She'd paused, both of us aware of how long it had been since we'd had a heart-to-heart.

"Thank you for always being there for me when I need you."

I feel my eyes tear up again as her words echo through me, as clear as if she were sitting in front of me now. But for the life of me, I can never remember what I said in return. I've spent the last fifteen years trying to recall my final words to my sister. In my worst nightmares, I bring my fingers to my mouth and find that my lips are sewn shut. Did I know in that moment that mere hours later, I wouldn't be there when she needed me most?

With Cooper looking at me, his brow furrowed in concern, my throat closes. I can't speak. The fear is a physical thing, like an animal in a box it's desperate to escape from, while at the same time being terrified of what it will find outside its familiar walls. It claws at my rib cage—the fear of saying it out loud, of admitting the real reason my mother never speaks to me anymore.

"What is it, babe?" he asks. "It's okay. You can tell me."

"I…" I clear my throat.

"Dylan, there's nothing you could tell me that would change how I feel about you. Trust me. Trust what we have."

I nod. The animal scratches.

"I feel…lost again. And I'm afraid of what I might do. I'm afraid of hurting you."

It's not what I need to say most, but it's the truth. I know this feeling well, and I know what it makes me capable of. So does Cooper. It's how we got together.

Cooper's face falls blank, like he's purposefully trying to avoid letting me see his true feelings. Over our last nine years together, we've had ups and downs, backs and forths, but no matter what setbacks we faced, we always knew where we were headed. We had a Point B, a map, a compass. We could always refocus. But here, in this place, the map has been stolen from us, and we've reached a fork in the road.

I wait for his reaction. Finally, his features reanimate, and he takes my hands in his.

"You're not lost, Dylan," he says. "You're exactly where you're supposed to be. You've just been working toward the same goal for so long, you don't know what to do now that you've reached it."

"But I haven't—"

"I know," he says. "But you're so close. Another grant will pop up soon. And you know you're going to get it. No one has worked harder for it than you. So it's natural to feel the need to reassess, set new goals. Especially for you. You don't know what to do with yourself when you don't have a goal."

A laugh bubbles up from inside me and Cooper smiles. "It's like you know me better than I know myself sometimes."

I have been keeping my eye on grant listings, but nothing new has come up. Not that I expected it to.

Cooper lowers his voice and says, "You can't be a great doctor without being a great student," quoting our genetics teacher, making me laugh harder. He presses his smile to mine. In his own voice, he adds, "And you've always been my favorite subject."

He traces kisses over my jawline, on one side and then the other.

"You've always been my home," I say.

"Come to bed."

I nod. He goes to the back door to let the puppy in, then I follow him to our bed. I curl up in his arms, exactly where I'm supposed to be.

"New consult, undetermined EGA, no complications," Enrique rattles off as he comes out from behind the nurses' station. We walk through the halls of the clinic on the way to my first appointment of the day, and I latch on to the medical jargon to focus my distracted mind. An undetermined due date means I'll need an ultrasound, otherwise standard procedure.

"Got it," I say. I trade Enrique my triple shot latte for the chart as we reach the exam room door.

"I grabbed the finished charts off your desk and piled some more on there for ya. One of your patients is in L and D getting checked out. Not admitted yet."

"Perfect."

"Do you need anything else?" he asks. He takes a swallow of my latte. I shake my head.

"A nurse who's actually concerned about spreading viruses?"

"You look healthy to me," he says. "And I look healthier with caffeine in me."

"Oh, Enrique, you always look good."

He flashes me a Cheshire cat grin.

I enter the exam room and glance down at the chart in my hand for the patient's name.

"Hi, Dylan."

I hear the patient's voice at the same time I read it in all capital letters, printed across the top of the paperwork, and my heart drops. I squint at my chart to be sure and then at the woman sitting on the examination table in the hospital gown, those all-too-familiar blue eyes shining back at me.

"Megan?"

She gives a bashful laugh. "I was going to ask you to lunch today, but I thought, 'Hey, if I get pregnant, we can make it a standing date.'"

It's funny. I want to laugh. She clearly needs me to laugh. Instead I stand there, mouth agape, as my two worlds converge, and the implications settle like ash around me, suffocating.

"I'm sorry," she says. "I didn't mean to shock you. Not any more than I've shocked myself."

I should have realized at the last family dinner—the nausea, the weight loss, the fatigue.

"No… It's just… Wow. Does Stephen know? It is his, right?" I ask more quietly. I don't know how long things have been bad between them, I realize now more than ever.

"It's his. And no, he doesn't know."

I shake my head in disbelief. I still haven't accepted that they're separating, let alone the talk of divorce amongst the family. Part of me dares to hope this could bring them back together.

"I know," Megan says. "Trust me. This isn't how I expected things to go. How does the song go again? First comes love, then comes marriage, then comes divorce, then comes the baby." She forces a smile, but her hands are shaking in her lap.

"How far along are you, Megan?"

"I don't know. A few months, I guess. When I started to put two and two together, I tried to remember when my last period was, but with everything that's been going on… I thought it was just stress. And then for a while I was too

scared to tell anyone. I think half of me didn't believe it…
and the other half didn't want it to be true."

I frown and find my rolling chair, sitting in front of her.
I search for the right words in an all too familiar situation.

"Megan, I don't know what's going on with you and Stephen, but I know this isn't the ideal time for a baby." Tears
leak from the corners of her eyes, and she hides her contorted
mouth behind her hand. "I also know you will make a great
mother, and I'm not saying that just because we're…" She's
not technically my sister, though that's how I think of her. I
know she understands. "Well, I just want you to know I'm
here for you in whatever way you need me to be, okay?"

She nods emphatically and reaches her free hand out to
grasp mine. Her fingers are small and fragile-looking, such
a sharp contrast to her personality. This is the first time I've
ever seen her cry.

"No, it isn't the ideal time, but I want this baby," she says
through her tears. "Even if I have to do it alone."

"And are you sure you want me to be your doctor? Sometimes it's easier to work with someone you don't know."

She shakes her head. "You're family, Dylan. I trust you. I
wouldn't even think of anyone else. You're going to be my
doctor, whether you like it or not."

We both laugh. She wipes away her tears with a knuckle,
while I swallow down my own.

"This is going to be hard without Stephen," she says. "I'm
not too proud to admit it. But with you to guide me through
it, I feel like I can do this."

My first instinct is to tell her she does need Stephen, not
only because of the baby, but because they're meant for each
other. I bite my tongue, though. What she needs most is
nonjudgmental support, and I, of anyone, know what that
need feels like.

"I'm going to be right beside you," I say. "Every step of the way."

"Thank you," she whispers. A wrinkle forms in her brow. "Can I ask one favor?"

Still floating on her show of familial love, I say, "Of course. Anything."

"Can we keep this between us for now?"

I clear my throat, and my fingers slip from hers. I wipe my suddenly sweaty hands on the front of my slacks. It's a simple enough question, but she has no idea what she's asking of me. I think of how Cooper will feel if I keep this secret from him. I think of their parents, who have accepted me as one of their own and how I couldn't stand to disappoint them. I think of Stephen. I think of all the things that could go wrong. I've always feared losing a patient, and as doctors, it's a reality of the job—more so for some specialties than others. I've helped many patients through miscarriages, which is never easy, but I haven't lost a single patient whose eyes I've stared into. It's why I spend so much time at the hospital—to make sure it stays that way. Thankfully, in obstetrics, most of my patients are young and in good health. And for the babies, we have an incredible NICU.

But still, Megan is family. Taking her on as a patient is a whole new level of responsibility.

"Well, there's doctor-patient confidentiality, so lawfully, I can't say anything. But surely you want your family to know."

"I can't, Dylan. Not yet. You know how Mom is. She'd have a nursery fully stocked before I even got home."

I smile. It hurts my cheeks.

I know if Stephen knew about the baby, he would move his stuff back into their house, against Megan's will. He's never considered himself to be kid-friendly, but he's an honorable man, and he loves Megan. Once he got used to the idea, I know he'd be an incredible father. I wish I could tell him and bring their family back together. That's my job. It's what I do. But there was nothing in my medical training to prepare me for this.

"I won't tell anyone," I hear myself say. "Like I said, it's not my place. As long as you promise to call me anytime, day or night, if you need anything."

She thrusts her pinky toward me, herself again, and we smile at each other as I take it in my own.

In spite of my fear of ruining the moment, I can't help but ask, "Did Stephen really do something that makes it impossible for you to forgive him?"

Megan looks at her feet for a long time before she says, "He's not fighting for me, Dylan. I didn't want this. When I told him I needed more time with him, all I wanted him to do was say okay and do it. He acts like I expect him to live for nothing but me, but he knows it's not true. All I want from him is to make me feel like I'm a priority in his life. Stop acting like he's single and doing whatever the hell he wants without consequence. It isn't just his life anymore. But he said he couldn't. They need him too much at the hospital. And then when he's not at the hospital, he's out drinking with his friends. Or rock climbing. Sometimes both. I won't get into the dangers of that."

I laugh. It's so Stephen. Megan shakes her head but smiles, too.

She continues, "When I told him we'd put off having a family long enough, he said he wasn't ready yet. When I told him I was tired of spending so much time alone, he had nothing to say at all. I dragged it out as long as I could, and then I thought, maybe if he realizes he's going to lose me, he'll change. I asked him to leave, and instead of saying he would try harder, he left."

I swallow hard and wonder if that's how Cooper feels about me—that he's not a priority in my life. I've always thought of Stephen and me as being cut from the same mold, but the thought that I could make Cooper feel this way steals my breath.

There is one difference between Stephen and me: I would never walk away from Cooper willingly. He's the only thing that keeps me grounded—the only one who sees me for me.

"And now I'm waiting," Megan says, almost a whisper. "And he's still not home."

I rest my hand on her knee. "If that's all it is, let me talk to him. I know once he hears—"

"No," she says. "No. Don't you see? That wouldn't help anything. I needed to know he was ready to commit to this marriage and this family." She puts her hands on her belly. "I needed him to choose us and start living like a husband and father. I needed him to be there because he wanted to be there, not because someone gave him instructions, and he followed them. Definitely not because he feels obligated. All he was thinking about was what he needed, but relation-ships are about putting the people you love first sometimes."

I open my mouth to argue more—which point, I'm not sure—but I find I have nothing left to say.

"You're lucky," she says after a long silence. "Cooper loves you so much. He would never let you leave him. He would fight for you until his dying breath."

I avoid Megan's eyes and grab the blood pressure cuff to change the focus of the conversation. Because she's right. Cooper would fight for me. But after everything she's said today, I wonder if he should. He deserves so much better than me.

I examine Megan, then I get the Doppler wand and squeeze a dollop of jelly onto her exposed belly that is already visibly showing. I run the wand back and forth across her abdomen. It doesn't take long to find a strong heartbeat. As soon as she hears the *swish swish*, she opens her mouth to form a little O.

"Oh, wow," she whispers, and I smile. I hold the wand there, letting her enjoy the moment. Despite my concerns about what happens after this, I enjoy it, too. I've heard the first acknowledgment of a growing child inside of hundreds of new mothers, but never from someone I love.

I will take care of her. I will protect all of them.

Running forty-eight minutes late for date night with Cooper, I burst through the front door of my house, throw my keys on the foyer table and peel off my tennis shoes. I shake the rain from my hair and stumble around Cooper's Oxfords, where they're always strewn in the middle of the foyer no matter how many times I ask him to use the shoe rack. The house is alive with him—the scent of garlic and the sound of Coldplay. Cooper's flavor of romance.

"Sorry I'm late," I yell to him.

I stayed late at the hospital to attend Megan's ultrasound—she's almost in the second trimester. How she plans to keep it a secret for much longer, I don't know, but I can't think about that tonight. If I do, Cooper will see it written all over my face. Tonight is about him, about us.

"Did you put the clothes in the dryer?" I ask as I dart through the living room. "I'm going to hop in the shower, and then I'm all yours."

His swift footsteps thrum a rhythm on the hardwood behind me, then his hands grasp my elbows from behind before I reach the bedroom, stopping me with a jolt. I sigh, caught, then lean back into his firm chest.

"All that can wait," he says. His breath stirs the loose hair around my ear and sends goose bumps down my right side. "It's time to eat. The noodles are only so forgiving."

"And are you?" I tease, though the moment the words are out of my mouth, I wish I could take them back, sure I don't want to know the answer. Thankfully, he seems to be in too good a mood to pick a fight.

"You can make it up to me," he says.

Cooper turns me around and tilts my head down so he can place a kiss on my forehead. Even after all this time, my heart still flutters every time he looks at me like the world really could stop turning for us. Sometimes I wish it would.

"Date night in scrubs?" I ask.

"Date night now," he says. "You look beautiful in everything. Including mashed-pea-green scrubs."

I purse my lips and narrow my eyes at him. "You make it hard to say no."

"That's the goal." He kisses me again, on the lips. "C'mon."

I let Cooper guide me to the dining room table. He pulls my chair out for me, and I sit in it while he returns to the kitchen to serve the fettuccine. He's already showered and dressed in a pair of jeans, barefoot, a white T-shirt covered shamelessly by a blue-and-white-striped apron. He doesn't find this at all unusual, having been raised by an apron-wearing father. The apron-wearers are the good ones, I've decided.

"You're cute," I say from where I sit formally at the table, hands in my lap. He puts on a sultry half smile, never looking up as he ladles Alfredo sauce over each plate.

Cooper ducks out of his apron, lets out a deep breath and pats down his pockets, including the nonexistent one on the front of his T-shirt. He joins me at the table with the plates and a bottle of red wine.

"Are you okay?" I ask as he fills our glasses. He doesn't quite meet my gaze.

"Of course," he says. His eyes shift away almost imperceptibly when he says it, but I've loved this man for nine years. I notice.

"I really am sorry for being late," I say. If I could tell him why, I know he'd understand. But I can't.

"Don't worry about it. Seriously."

It's quiet as we take our first bites. Date night is something we started after we moved into our first apartment. The four years of med school were busy for both of us, and Cooper, having always been more knowledgeable about how relationships are supposed to work, pointed out that studying next to each other in bed wasn't exactly considered quality time. Happy to follow his lead, I agreed to monthly dates, though I wasn't sure how we'd find the time. We did. In fact, it was easier back then. It's been months since Cooper and I have blocked out work and family and other responsibilities for even an hour, and as I watch him suck a noodle into his mouth, the pain of missing him blooms in the center of my chest.

Cooper sets his fork down on his plate and rests his hand on my knee under the table. "Dylan," he says softly, just as my phone rings, a shocking buzz of vibration against the glass table. We both lean forward to look at the caller ID. It's the hospital. I glance at Cooper, then set down my own fork and pick it up. Cooper leans back in his chair, his face instantly hard.

"Cooper," I say, beseechingly.

"You promised," he says, and nothing else. He doesn't need to say another word, because we both know this is our life.

He sits up again and sighs.

"Go ahead," he says and motions toward my phone.

I excuse myself and take the call in the office, out of earshot of Cooper. After I forgive a mistaken labor and delivery nurse for not calling the on-call doctor, I breathe a sigh of relief and return to the dining room table, where Cooper's pasta sits untouched since I left. The CD must have ended because the only sound I hear is the echo of my phone ringing in my ears.

"It was nothing. I'm sorry," I mumble and hate the taste of the last word in my mouth. But I see the effort Cooper puts into smiling and into erasing the last five minutes of the night, so I try to do the same.

"There was something you wanted to talk about?" I ask as I sit and take another bite of dinner. I no longer have an appetite, but I'll be damned if I don't eat every last bite in restitution.

"Yes," he says after a moment. He touches his absent breast pocket again. "I'm really proud of you. You know that, right?"

"I know," I say. I've always known. It means a lot to hear him say it anyway. "Thank you."

"And I just keep thinking about our conversation before. About focusing more on us."

I look down. My breathing grows shallow. I wouldn't exactly call what we had a conversation. Cooper expressed his desires and I avoided responding to them. I know where he's going with this, and I can't pretend to be asleep this time.

"Yes," I whisper. When I look back up, I recognize the determined crease in his brow as he grabs my hand.

"I don't want to wait anymore," he says, then pauses to take a deep breath. I try for one of my own, but it gets caught in my throat. He slides off the dining room chair onto his knee. He looks up at me from beneath the strands of hair that stubbornly fall over his forehead. His eyes are bright and alive with anticipation—the opposite of my heart, folding in on itself and withdrawing. *No, no, no...*

"You know I've wanted to marry you since the night I met

you," he says, "but I wanted to wait until you were ready. I know this isn't the perfect time, but like my sister once told us, there's never going to be a right time. We just have to make the time. You're beautiful and smart and caring, Dylan, and you're everything I never knew I could have in a partner. If you'll have me, I'd be so proud to call you my wife."

I've stopped breathing, and I can't seem to start again.

What is wrong with me?

I love this man and he loves me.

I do want to spend the rest of my life with him—what does it matter if we get engaged right now or in five years? It all amounts to the same thing. But thinking of the weight that comes with a small ring and another big promise makes my hands shake.

How can we promise forever? It's a guarantee neither one of us can make.

I bring my hand up to cover my eyes, so I can't see Cooper and he can't see me. It's then that the real reason I won't commit to Cooper hits me: What right do I have to do what Abby will never get to do? What do I know about creating a family when mine is so broken?

The thoughts in my head are spinning so fast I can't pin down any one of them except, *He'll never forgive me for this.*

I let my hand fall to my lap and force myself to look at him. "Cooper, can we please just not do this right now? Not yet? You know I want to but…"

But I have to do something to make up for what happened to Abby. I'll never feel worthy of his love or anyone else's until I do.

"Babe," he says, his voice still gentle, knowing this is a difficult subject for me even if he doesn't know why. He's always known better than me what I want and what I need; when I need space and when I need to be pushed. But not this time.

This time it's an impossible situation—he just doesn't see it yet. "I know you're scared, but we love each other. What could be more important than that? We've already been together for nine years. We have a house together. What's really going to change besides your last name and the fact that we can start making plans for the rest of our lives together?"

"Exactly," I say, latching on to his words. "What's going to change if we wait another year...or two..."

His head falls and he clears his throat. He's losing patience with me.

"Dylan," he says with a dry laugh, "you're kind of killing my confidence here. You say you love me, but people who love each other, they get married and have kids and pick out snobby preschools together. That's what they do."

"You know I love you," I say, my voice coming back strong.

"Do you?" he asks, all signs of laughter gone. His eyes pierce straight through my heart, shattering me. "Prove it."

"Cooper, I...I'm just too focused on my career to be a good wife to you, and that's what you deserve. You deserve to have a wife who will be good to you, and I want to be her one day." Tears spring to my eyes. It's not a straight answer, but I know if I don't give him the answer he wants, it could end us. Us being over will end me.

"Prove it," he says again, softer but with an intensity that says he's not going to budge. He would never say it out loud, but the purse of his lips says it all: it's an engagement or it's over. "Dylan," he presses.

With my heartbeat thrumming in my ears, I stumble over words I don't hear myself say, I pull my hand from his grip, and suddenly I'm outside with the rain landing on my cheeks. Without a ring.

I wander the streets, wet and muddy and in a daze until the storm clears, like a sign. Finally, I find my way home, but when I call out for Cooper, he doesn't answer. I check the bedroom, the guest room, the backyard. I check the garage. Cooper's car is gone. With my hands shaking so badly I almost can't unlock my phone, I press Cooper's name on my speed dial. It rings two times and goes to voice mail. I hang up and let my phone fall to the counter.

7

Cooper doesn't come home. With each hour that passes, I don't know whether to be mad or worried. I don't know whether or not to believe the darkest thought of all: that Cooper's not staying away just to punish me. That he's really gone. But he can't be gone. Not for real. Not for good. He has our whole lives planned out. He wouldn't just walk away from that. Would he?

At dawn, I drive by Cooper's practice, but the parking lot is empty on the weekends. So I call Stephen, but he doesn't answer his phone. I go into the hospital and chart, distracting myself from the anxiety spreading and splintering beneath my rib cage. When morning turns to afternoon and the Saturday silence in the clinic becomes unbearable, I shower, change and head home to face the silence there.

I confirm before I walk into the house that Cooper still isn't here. His car isn't in the garage. The lights are off. The warmth is gone. It doesn't look like he's been home at all.

I let the puppy out in the backyard, where there's an ugly gash down the center of it, carved by Reese's shovel. He has made considerable progress on it, but for now it's torn apart for anyone to see, myself included, hidden scars revealed, imperfections exacerbated. It will get worse before it gets better.

If it gets better.

I let the puppy into the house, then walk back to the yard, searching for solitude. I extend my toes into the grass. It reaches to mid-shin, and it's wet, dampening my pant legs and squishing between my toes as I walk from one side to the other, but I don't feel it. I don't feel anything. So long ago, I placed a screen between what I think and what I feel. I can see it on the other side, but I can't touch it, and it can't touch me. I often blame Abby's death for that, but even when Abby was alive, she would urge me to open up and let people in.

"Do you even like guys?" I remember her asking me one breezy afternoon next to the lake. We'd bundled up in sweaters and blankets out on the grass in our backyard to watch a houseboat party out on the water. It was the beginning of April and after she and Christian had been dating for a couple of months. I could tell they were getting more serious but she insisted I was making more out of it than was actually there. I was tempted to answer her question with a "no" because at that moment, I didn't like what guys were doing to our relationship.

"Of course I do," I snapped. I knew what she was really asking. But I didn't like her tone, and it hurt that she had to ask at all. She knew me better than anyone.

Abby curled her loose Medusa strands behind her ear in an attempt to tame them against the wind. It didn't work.

"I'm just asking. I don't care either way. You don't have to be so snappy." She moved a little closer to me. "Why don't you ever go out with anyone?" she asked. "Why don't you make friends with people? I know you're fun to hang out with. And you're really interesting to talk to when you aren't putting up the Great Wall of China."

I pursed my lips at her. "What's the point? People are ass-holes."

She rolled her eyes. "C'mon, Dylan. You know that's not true. You're just looking for the bad in people instead of looking for the good. You don't want to have people in your life, and I don't know why."

"I'm too different, Abs. I think in…numbers, and cause and effect, and logic. People at school are more worried about who is dating who, and who said what to whom. It's all drama. I don't get other people. They don't get me."

Abby laughed. "Don't worry. Once you get out of high school, they're going to love your no-bullshit attitude. Mystery is sexy."

"I'm not mysterious," I said. I was being contrary to demonstrate my resentment toward her friends and the fact that she would be leaving for college soon, but secretly, I hoped she was right.

Abby frowned, finally seeing the seriousness on my face. She wrapped an arm around my shoulders. A group of people on the boat burst into laughter. The sound traveled across the water and was a whisper by the time it reached us.

She lifted her chin and urged me to do the same. *Us against the world.* "So prove them wrong," she said.

The sound of the back door opening pulls me from the memory. I look up, and Cooper stands in the door frame. At least, I hope he does. I pray I'm not imagining him there. From this distance, I can see he's wearing the same jeans and T-shirt from the night before, but I can't make out his expression. I can guess at a frown, though, because every muscle in his body seems too heavy for him to carry. It's the same defeat I saw in Stephen when he came over after he moved out of his house with Megan. I don't know yet if it's the rawness a man exposes because it's over or because he doesn't want it to be.

I wait, watching for the first sign of movement from him like a deer being stalked by a mountain lion. I listen, ears perked, for the words to determine our fate. Cooper leaves the stoop and wades through the grass toward me. I feel the space close between us as if it's bowing under the pressure. His eyes are locked with mine. His strides lengthen with every step closer until he's right in front of me, and his arms are around me and he lifts me off the stepping-stone to put us back on the same ground. Relief releases me into his arms. I rest my head on his shoulder, nuzzle my face into the soft skin of his neck and hold him to me like we're on the edge of a cliff, ready to fall. Maybe he can forgive me.

"I'm so sorry, Dylan," he says, but I shake my head. I won't let him take the blame for this. I was trying to protect him, or maybe myself, and instead, I turned what should have been one of the most magical nights of our lives into a night that almost drove us apart for good. He doesn't deserve to carry that on his shoulders.

"*I'm* sorry." His skin prickles at my breath on his neck, and he pulls me closer until I'm almost unable to breathe, but I let him hold me. He can hold me forever as long as he doesn't leave.

"I don't want to ruin us," he whispers. "I want to fix us."

I nod, my jaw rubbing against his. "I know. Me, too. I know."

"I don't know what's going on anymore—"

"I know," I say. "Things have gotten so out of control. But I do love you, Cooper. I'm just glad you're home."

"I know you love me. I shouldn't have given you an ulti- matum. I'm more sorry than you can know." He chokes on the words. I pull back to look at him, and his eyes are blood-shot, his skin ashen. A single night has aged him a decade.

"You don't have anything to be sorry for."

"Dylan—"

I place my fingers across his lips. Every time he apologizes, it only makes me feel worse. He's so high above me. When he lowers himself, it pushes me farther down.

I allow my fingers to slip down until the lips I've kissed thousands of times are revealed. There's a hollow space between us before he speaks, and then he says, "You're it for me, Dylan. That won't change, now or ever."

My mouth is on his almost before he finishes the sentence. His hands cup the back of my head, and he kisses me so hard there's no room for the playing of lips or teasing of tongues. It's not about lust, it's about the love we've lost the ability to convey to each other. But the connection in this moment is so strong, it's as if the energy in him and the energy in me flows together until we're humming as one. I've always tried to be strong, but with him I melt. He brings out the softness in me that, alone or with anyone else, I can't touch. Losing him would have meant losing myself.

But he's here, and he's staying.

I pull away from him, light-headed from lack of oxygen. "Come on," I breathe. I weave my fingers through his and lead the way back through the grass. We sneak inside silently as if we're in someone else's house, trailing soggy footprints on the hardwood behind us like bread crumbs.

The bedroom is orange with the sunset, and hazy—an overexposed photo. I guide Cooper to the bed, and he sits on the edge. His knees are against mine, his rapid breath palpable between us. He doesn't look up at me, but at my hands, examining them like he wonders if they are strong enough to hold us together, or maybe wondering how they'll change over the years. They're shaking with emotion and nerves. It's been so long since we've made love, and this time, it feels more important than ever. I take in a quivering breath and tell myself it's just like riding a bike. We've always been good at this part.

I reach for the hem of my shirt and pull it up over my head, the neck loosening my ponytail as it goes. I pull the band out and let it fall around my shoulders. Cooper tilts his head up to me and sucks in a breath like he's seeing me for the first time. With my heart pounding, I unclasp my bra and let it fall to the floor.

Cooper places his hands on my hips and moves me to stand between his knees. With me closer, he runs his hands up my back, then down to my buttocks. He takes big handfuls of them and hums his contentment against my belly button.

"Mmm. You smell amazing," he says. "Just you. Your skin."

I smile and lace my fingers through his hair. I lean forward until my nose is buried in the soft strands. He smells good, too.

"I love you," he whispers. In response, I tilt his head up and kiss him like the girl he first fell in love with, when I was reckless and hungry. I try to channel the assurance I had back then that Cooper saw me for who I wanted to be instead of who I was. That as long as I remained that mysterious girl, he wouldn't know the secrets buried underneath. With my secrets so close to the surface now, though, I know better than to be that naive. I take this moment for what it is: a hope, not a promise.

Cooper pulls me on top of him, and we scoot ourselves across the bed. I press my body against him. He runs his hands up and down my backside from my thighs to my hair. Any place he can reach. I slide my hands underneath his shirt and clumsily pull it up until he's forced to sit up to allow me to remove it, revealing his broad chest and shoulders. He fights off the rest of my clothes, then I pull off his. Every earned muscle of his body glistens in the dim light. His once-tight stomach has softened slightly over the years, but I love it even more for that. His kisses turn harder, almost angry. His erection is noticeably absent, but before I have a chance to decide what this means, he pulls me down on him again and into a kiss that leaves me breathless.

We wrestle like this for a long time. Kissing and caressing. Touching and moaning. At one point, I take him into my mouth. All to no avail.

"Are you okay?" I whisper in the gray light before the dark.

"Yeah." He's panting. He pulls me into another deep kiss. This one is furious, but I recognize it for the desperation it is. He bites my bottom lip too hard, but I don't allow myself to make a sound. When our teeth clank together awkwardly, his passion dissolves. He covers his eyes with his hand, and what I can see of his face has turned red.

"Coop, it's okay," I say. "It's been a long couple of days." I try to reassure him, but in truth, any hope I had flutters off my heart and lands in the pit of my stomach.

"I'm sorry. It's not you. It's not you at all, I swear. I don't know…" He tries for an explanation with a pained expression on his face. When it doesn't come, he rolls off the bed and disappears into the bathroom, closing the door to emphasize the barriers that still stand between us.

"Cooper?" I call, but my voice is so frail, I know he can't hear me. He's gone to a place where I can't reach him. I pull the blanket up to my chin to cover my nakedness and dampen the fabric with my tears.

In the days that follow, Cooper pretends the mishap never happened—pretends life has gone back to normal. He's so good at it, he almost convinces me, but there's an underlying tension I can't shake—my intuition telling me this isn't over yet. Not by a long shot.

I find an escape in the garden, just like Cooper intended. It becomes habit to wake up fifteen minutes early each morning to have an extra cup of coffee. I carry it with me as I walk barefoot around the yard to admire Reese's progress before he shows up. His appearances are sporadic, but even so, digging a moat alone appears to be a slow, strenuous job. I'm careful to sneak back to the house when I hear Reese's truck pull into the driveway.

One afternoon, I come home early to get some rest before an expected delivery, and Reese reappears. I assumed he'd left for the day since his truck wasn't in the driveway when I got home, but he surprises me while I'm sitting on the back stoop, watching the puppy prance from one side of the yard to the other.

"Are you avoiding me?" he asks before I've noticed him. I start, spilling my glass of water on the step next to my feet. I cover my heart with my hand and let out an exasperated sigh. "Sorry," he says with a laugh and that smile.

"No," I say, still trying to get my bearings.

"Did I upset you?"

"No," I say. The truth is, something about Reese makes me nervous. He looks at me too closely. I open my mouth to come up with some other excuse, but I can't think of one. He continues to look at me now with his eyes squinted from the sun.

"Can I show you something?" he asks.

I look at my watch, wondering how much time I have, but more concerned about the conclusions he'll undoubtedly make about me if I don't go…or why I even care. I set my water on the stoop and stand. Reese walks me to the side of the house.

The puppy follows us. As we walk, Reese reaches up to rub the back of his neck, making the muscles in his arm and shoulders tighten and my cheeks flush. It's then that I realize what's really bothering me about him.

I find Reese attractive.

It's been so long since I've looked at a man in that way, I didn't recognize the feeling for what it was. But it's undeniable—his light eyes in contrast to his dark features, his full lips, his lean muscles. Despite my reckless youth, since I met Cooper, I haven't assessed a man in any other way than to decide whether or not they were competition for promotions.

I see it now, though.

Understanding and labeling the feelings toward Reese makes them easier to control, and almost immediately, the wild energy surrounding him dulls.

"What do you think of these flowers?" he asks, pointing to a small assortment of plants in nursery pots. I don't know much about flowers. Mom would know the name, species and recommended amount of water and sunlight for each.

"They're pretty," I say.

He laughs. "Okay. What's your favorite flower?"

"I don't know many, but I've always loved Stargazer lilies."

When I was younger, Mom knew how much I loved them, so she always let me plant the bulbs, even though I had the habit of burying them upside down. It never ceased to baffle her that in the spring, they would break through the soil anyway and bloom more beautiful because of their longer journey. At least, that's what she told me.

"Good choice. I'm thinking of putting these ones on either side of the back door, against the house."

I shrug. "Sounds good to me. I trust your judgment."

"You do?" he asks with a laugh.

I narrow my eyes at him. "On landscaping," I say, but even I can hear the skepticism in my voice.

"I'm just about to get started. Do you want to help me?" he asks.

"You mean garden? Trying to get out of doing your job?"

"No. Trying to get you out of yours."

He stares into my eyes, and this time I don't break contact. I haven't given him enough credit for how much he sees.

"It's not your job to worry about mine."

"Just trying to help."

I scoff and turn away. There are enough people in my life who judge me for my work ethic. I don't need it from him, too. I almost make it to the back door when I hear Reese call from behind me, "Do you ever wear anything that doesn't have 'doctor' written all over it?"

I stop midstride, bite my lip. I can feel him grinning behind my back, so proud of himself. He already knows the answer, as I do. I look down at the scrubs I'm still wearing from surgery this morning, and then up at the sky. Is being a doctor really all I have the space to be?

I turn around and say, "I have twenty minutes."

He gives me a smile.

Reese turns the soil he's already fertilized and lines the plants up along the house where they will be transplanted. The puppy nips at the leaves, and I repeatedly nudge him away. Reese gives me a trowel to clear out a space for the roots and shows me how to bury them deep enough. I let him direct me. He talks with as much passion for his work as I do when talking about mine.

Once we fall into a pattern, we work in silence for a while, but it's a comfortable silence, especially for someone who makes me so uncomfortable when he speaks. I lose myself in the motion of digging, the sounds of nature and the feeling of my muscles, powerful beneath my skin. I'd forgotten how addictive it is. It slows some of the gears in my mind.

"So you never told me what made you such a good doctor," Reese says.

Our last conversation was weeks ago. I can't believe he still remembers. I laugh, shake my head. "You're one of those people who doesn't let things go, aren't you?" Just like Abby.

"Not if I think there's something interesting there." He glances at me without turning from his work.

I remind myself that once the yard is done, he'll go his own way and he'll take his opinions about me with him, and then I say, "My sister died when I was sixteen."

The words feel so foreign on my tongue. The only other person I've told the story to since it happened is Cooper, and I didn't tell him everything. I haven't told anyone the whole story. Not even my parents.

My hands stop moving, and I wait for the usual "Sorry for your loss," or "She's in a better place now," but Reese says neither of those things. He says nothing. Just nods as if to say, *I understand your pain*, and surprisingly, I believe him. So I tell Reese the same thing I told Cooper—the "official" story.

"She was eighteen, just about to graduate high school. She was pregnant, and one night she wasn't feeling well. She went to the hospital because she was having abdominal cramps. She told the ER doctor she was pregnant, but because she wasn't bleeding and a stomach virus had been going around, the doctor assumed that's what she had. Without any further tests, he told her to go home and stay hydrated. She died that night."

In clinical terms, I explain what an ectopic pregnancy is and how it took her life. That part is easier, when I can pretend it's something I read out of a book, instead of something

I lived through. As if a life can be extinguished and the rest of us can simply turn the page.

"Wow," he says when I've finished. "That must have been really hard on you and your family."

"It was." After a breath, I say, "It is."

"So now you want to help other pregnant women," Reese says.

"Yes," I say. "My patients mean everything to me."

Reese watches me with an amused expression until I realize I'm digging with unnecessary vigor, and I've shoveled more dirt into the grass than the flower bed.

"Oops," I say, and stop.

Reese laughs and comes over to help me move the dirt back to where it belongs. His face is just inches from mine, and our fingers brush once, twice as we sweep it aside with our hands. Once we're finished, I scoot away from him.

"I'm covered in dirt," I say, rubbing my hands together in a vain attempt to clean them.

"What's wrong with dirt?" He smiles and smudges the black soil across one of my forearms. Before I can react, he says, "Let's step back and see how it looks so far."

We both push off the ground and stand next to each other. I hold my hands out awkwardly at my sides so as not to smudge my pants. I can't help the smile that tugs at my lips as I take it all in. The colors and sizes and the way Reese arranged the flowers has come together beautifully.

"Those aren't evenly spaced," I say, pointing to the section I planted.

"It's fine."

"It won't take long to fix."

He puts his hand on my shoulder like he thinks I'll lunge at them before he can stop me.

"They don't have to be perfect," he says. "Life isn't about

perfection. Doesn't make it any less beautiful." He turns to me with a look in his eyes that makes my chest flush.

"Who are you? Buddha?" I ask seriously, but when he bursts into laughter, my hardened exterior crumbles and I laugh, too.

"So are you ever going to introduce me officially?"

I furrow my brow, and Reese points to the puppy.

"Oh," I say. "He doesn't have a name yet."

"You've had him for weeks."

I shrug. "He's not mine to name."

"Well, if I hear you call him 'puppy' one more time, *I'm* going to name him."

I smile. "Fine. I'll tell Cooper to name him."

"I've always liked the name Spencer for a dog."

"I'll have him take that into consideration."

The sun, getting hotter every day, beats down on the back of my neck, and a line of sweat trickles down between my shoulder blades. I'll need to shower before I head back to the hospital.

"Twenty minutes is up," I say.

"Where are we at with mom in room 1217?" I ask Enrique as I exit a delivery room and pull off my gloves. I blink as my eyes adjust to the bright lights of the hallway.

"Nine centimeters," he says. He's wearing his *how are you going to pull this off* grin, as if overseeing two deliveries at once is a challenge I'm being scored on, and there's a prize at the end.

"Shit."

Enrique and I step closer to the wall to allow a band of nurses to rush past, each one of them fighting to be heard over the other.

"Room 1215?" he asks.

"Eight. But it's not going well." The baby is still anterior, and it's getting lodged farther into her pelvis with every contraction. I think we're going to have to cut, but she's insisting we wait. "I'm going to give it twenty more minutes. That's as much as I can comfortably give her and even then… Any chance 1217 is going to shoot this thing out?"

Enrique snorts. "Crazier things have happened."

I stop to take a breath, scratch my forehead in frustration with my scrub sleeve. "Shit," I say again, shaking my head. Enrique offers me new gloves, and I let him put them on me. He follows me into the delivery room two doors down.

After performing one C-section and one assisted delivery, stitching up two women and waiting long enough to be sure neither of them showed signs of a hemorrhage, I miss Cooper again. I find him asleep in bed with his glasses on and a tattered copy of *Lord of the Rings* on the bed next to him. I pick up the book and slide his glasses off his face. My thumb brushes his cheek—the first time our skin has touched since our failed attempt at lovemaking. We've been walking on eggshells around each other, polite and cautious. Both of us waiting for the other to make the first move toward something more natural. As usual, my work schedule gets in the way, along with my guilt. I take solace, for tonight, that I'm not on call tomorrow. My phone rings in my hand— one of my dad's occasional late-night calls, when he's feeling lonely—so I slip out of the room quickly before I wake Cooper.

"Do you remember the night of the grand opening at the pizza parlor?" Dad asks without preamble, his deep voice filling my heart with warmth from his first word. I close the bedroom door behind me and muffle my laugh. Dad has brought up this memory so many times that I'm not sure I remember the day so vividly from my own experience of it or because the detailed recounting of his own memory has been so frequent that it's permanently stitched to mine.

"Of course I do," I say, but I don't stop him from reciting it again. It was one of the happiest days of my childhood, and I love going back to it as much as Dad does, even if it's only in our minds. I don't think I'm the only one who wonders if life would have been different if we'd stayed in the city, living to the beat of our own drum. It was as if, when Dad chose to accept his predetermined path as heir of the family business he'd never really wanted, we all felt we had to do the same.

"I locked up after the final customer left and turned up the stereo, and you, Abby, Charlie and your mom all danced on the tables to... What was it?" he asks. He knows, but he loves to hear me say it.

"'Dancing Queen,'" I say, a grin pulling at my lips. I open the back door and walk out into the warm night. The croaking of the frogs along the creek is so loud it almost overpowers Dad's voice, but I move farther into the yard anyway, walking along the ditch that grows longer with each passing day. The colors of the flowers Reese and I planted together are muted in the dark.

"That's it," Dad says, and I can hear his smile through the line. I imagine him in his bed, buttoned up in his striped pajamas, leaning against his headboard, looking the same as he had when we'd talked so many times during my teen years, on the nights I couldn't sleep either. I could always count on Dad to be awake, too, both of us with too many thoughts running through our heads to get a good night's sleep. He would sigh and tell me I was so much like him, as though he was proud of me and sad to have passed on the curse at the same time. "You girls looked so beautiful in those matching dresses your mom found. Your skirts swirled through the air."

"Charlie hates that story," I remind him.

"He danced to it, too!" Dad objects.

"Exactly," I say, another giggle bubbling up from my chest.

"It was your idea, you know. The dancing. We were all tired and stressed out from the long day, but you wanted to make sure we remembered what a special day it was. You've always had that way about you. You could just change the direction of things, shift the mood entirely. Abby was always the center of attention, but you…you sneaked right in there under the radar and could change the energy of the whole room without people even realizing it. You're a true leader, Dylan. I miss having that around here."

"I love you, Dad. You've always seen me as better than I actually am. But I need that sometimes," I say with a laugh.

"Uh-uh. I'm your dad. I've been watching you your whole life. No one knows you better than I do. Plus, I don't care how old you get, what I say goes."

"Ha!" I burst out. But then I say, "Yes, sir."

Dad sighs, and I stop my pacing to look up at the sky. The moon is almost full, and so bright. For a moment, I feel so far away from everyone and everything that it's like the moon and I have a divine connection. Like she's trying to remind me of what's really important, and the answer is on the tip of my tongue.

"You still have that skill," he says, as if finding the words for me. "Don't forget it."

I smile. "Yes, sir."

"So how are you?" he asks. He never dwells on anything serious for too long.

I turn my back on the moon and look through its reflection on my bedroom windows to see the outline of Cooper's sleeping form on our bed. I feel so many mixed emotions, but the most prevalent is…grateful.

"I'm good, Dad," I say. Taking his words to heart, I add, "I think things are going to be good."

The next morning, I wake without my alarm before the sun has risen, though I stayed up late talking to Dad. I look at the time: 5:17 a.m. I watch the light creep into the sky until it's rimmed with gold, and I hear the tentative chirp of the early birds outside.

For the first time in a long time, I allow myself to lie here and enjoy the comfort of my bed, the tepid air on my legs where they peek out from beneath the blanket. Soon, though, a quiet whimper comes from the other side of the room, letting me know the puppy is ready to go outside. I roll over and am shocked to see Cooper sitting on the edge of his side of the bed. I hadn't felt him move, hadn't heard him make a noise. He's facing away from me, his body hunched forward. His breathing is so shallow I can't hear it. I reach my fingers across the bed, and my arm is just long enough to allow me to brush the hem of his shirt.

"Hey," I whisper. "Do you want me to take him out?"

I wait for him to tell me he's already up, he might as well do it. Cooper may have been up many times during the night with the puppy already. So far, having a dog doesn't seem all that different from having a child.

"Coop? Are you okay?" I ask when he doesn't respond.

After a pause, he looks over at me. His face is puffy and swollen. His eyes are red.

"Cooper?"

His face crumples, and he hides his eyes again. I shoot up to a sitting position and push myself across the top of the sheets until I'm right next to him. Sweat prickles under my arms as I wait for him to tell me someone has died, or is in the hospital, or that he's sick and hasn't worked up the courage to tell me.

I run my hand across his shoulders, and my voice is firm when I say, "Cooper, tell me what's going on." I hate the speculation. My mind can run through a dozen things that are worse than the truth for every second that passes. Over Cooper's shoulder, I see the puppy stand and stretch. He wags his tail, oblivious to the tension.

Cooper turns his face to me, his eyes closed, and rests his chin on his shoulder. He opens his eyes, leans forward and presses his lips to mine. It should reassure me—if someone was hurt, he'd tell me right way—but this stall tactic, instead, makes my stomach sink lower.

"Cooper, you're scaring me," I whisper, his face still so close our breath mingles together.

"I have to tell you something, Dylan."

I stop breathing. They're the words no one wants to hear, and yet, I still have no idea what he's about to say. Is he leaving me after all? Did he finally realize he deserves more than what I can give him?

"I…" His breath catches, and I see the effort it takes him to continue in the crease between his eyes. He presses his lips together so tightly they turn white, then he opens them and says, "I slept with someone else."

My head sways. My blood runs cold. My stomach churns.

No one died, I tell myself.

No one's in the hospital.

Everyone is fine, so I wait to start breathing again, but I can't.

My lips tingle, my fingers tingle, my lungs ache from lack of oxygen, but still, I can't make myself exhale. Darkness invades the outer edges of my vision. Surely I misunderstood him.

With that small amount of hope, I breathe, "What?" The puppy whimpers again, but neither of us looks in his direction.

When several minutes pass, it becomes clear Cooper has no intention of repeating what he said, unable to force the words from his mouth again. He only stares at me, waiting for me to react, waiting to see how I feel about the fact that he lied to me—he *has* ruined us. There's no fixing this.

"You slept with someone else?" I ask. My voice is surprisingly steady. I want to make sure there's no chance of any further confusion. I want to make sure, before I walk out the door, that I heard him correctly and that I'm justified in driving away from our life together without looking back.

But this is Cooper. This is the man who promised me he would never hurt me. The man who proposed marriage to me and told me I was it for him. There must be some mistake.

Cooper bites his lip, and tears leak from the corners of his eyes. He gives a slight nod—such a small movement, but it changes everything. Absolutely everything.

"Right," I say.

I look out the window without seeing anything as my mind searches for the piece of the puzzle I somehow missed. I thought I knew everything about the man sitting so close to me that I can feel his heart beating, but with one revelation, I realize I know nothing. I know nothing about what's going through his mind, what must have been going through his mind when he made the choice to do something we'd never be able to recover from, and I know nothing about how to cope with this. So I crawl across the bed and stand.

"It was just one time," he says, reaching for me, but I shake him off. "Dylan, wait. Please. I never meant—"

But I don't want to hear it. Any of it. Who she was, when it happened, what he was thinking. None of it matters.

I lock myself in the bathroom, dress and brush my teeth. The entire time, I try to remind myself of what my dad told me the night before. I could change the direction of things. I could shift the energy. But not in this situation. In this situation, the damage has already been done. Our relationship is already broken. So when I leave the bathroom, I walk right past Cooper, out the front door, and I don't look back.

8

I drive down our street toward the city, though I don't know where I'm headed. The morning sunlight flashes between the tree trunks like a strobe in my peripheral vision, causing the pain on the top of my head to swell. My jaw is so tight my cheeks ache, and my hands grip the steering wheel with a force that originates from deep within, my knuckles bulging and angry. The hurt and indignation push against the screen in my mind. I swallow hard.

There's only one place I can think to go to clear my mind, so as I approach the city limits, I continue east and roll down the driver's-side window to allow the warm breeze to still my shaking body. I merge onto Interstate 84, through the heart of Portland and out the other side, and with every mile I put between our home and me, the easier it becomes to fight the raging river of emotions inside me. After an hour of driving, I exit Highway 26 and turn down an old dirt road, rolling up the window to keep the dust out. The car jumps and stutters over the rain-beaten path, but I don't slow down until I reach the familiar tree that marks the path Cooper, Stephen and I used to take down to the Sandy River during med school on many Friday nights.

I stumble out of the car and follow the overgrown path between the trees with memory as my only guide, leading me in a dance around every rock and every protruding root of the large Douglas firs. The humidity in the air grows heavier with every step deeper into the forest. I breathe it in, breathing out a bit of the ache that has settled beneath my sternum. I still can't think the words to myself, I just feel it—that deep emptiness inside me. It's the first time since I met Cooper that I've felt that sense of loneliness that haunted me after Abby's death, when everything I thought I knew about life was ripped away like a curtain to the truth.

Then the questions start.

Why?

What did I do?

What did I not do?

Was there some clue I missed?

Is there anything I can do to fix this?

The last question startles me so much, I stop, examine it, then shake my head until it floats away. No. I won't be that sad woman who thinks she'll be the one that's different, the woman who thinks she'll be the one to change a man.

I slog on.

I stop when I reach the break in the trees. It comes up fast, and I nearly slide down the small drop that leads to the clearing where the remnants of our fire pit still creates a mangled circle in the center, but I catch myself on a branch above my head. My heart races and my chest heaves with each heavy breath, but for the first time in years, it's because I feel alive, not because I feel like I'm slowly dying. I let go of the branch and shoot down the bank, whooping the entire way. I reach the bottom unscathed, but I can't stop my voice from releasing every emotion that will no longer fit inside my skin. What starts off as an excited howl turns to a frustrated screech to an angry roar. I imagine Cooper standing in front of me, and I scream at him for abandoning me like this. Because that's what he's done. We may not have stood in front of all our family and friends to make our vows to one another, but he betrayed all the promises we made in the dark, under the covers. He may not have moved out of our house, but he took his heart back and every other part of him I used to be able to claim as mine. Different people get different parts of him each day—his patients, his coworkers, his friends, his parents—but there was a deeper level of intimacy that was only mine to sink into. And now there isn't. Someone else has touched him the way I touch him. Someone else has whispered to him the way I whisper to him. Someone else shares his secrets. I have to swallow back the tears and bile in my throat.

If he was unsure about our future together, why didn't he tell me before he did the one thing he could never take back?

An hour later, I sit on a rock alongside the Sandy. It's hot, and sweat trickles down my back and between my breasts. My shoes are cast somewhere over my shoulder, and my feet are curved around the wet, gritty rocks beneath me. My cheeks are rough with dried, salty tears.

I shouldn't have come here. Returning to this place that sounds like Cooper, looks like Cooper, smells like Cooper, was the worst possible idea. I close my eyes and listen to the rushing water to drown out the memories of the many auspicious words he has spoken to me here—the "yes" he uttered when I asked him to take me home that first night, a thousand encouragements as we all battled our way through med school, the three little words that shifted something inside me.

I met him here nine years ago after the school's orientation BBQ. Over a hundred medical students had gathered, all dressed in three-piece suits and silk dresses, clutching long-neck bottles of beer. They talked with passion about any-thing but medicine, almost danced to the music. I located the nearest cooler, accompanied by my new roommate, who had dragged me to this party against my better judgment.

"Beer, *stat*!" she said over her shoulder, then threw her head back in laughter.

We shared the first round, before an alarming redheaded man ran up to us, said something about skinny-dipping and then took off toward the water. She followed.

Since I knew no one else, I found my way to the edge of the commotion and shuffled in a wide circle around it. I didn't mind being on my own—in fact, most of the time I preferred it—but I hated the inquisitive glances. I think it was the awkward way I stumbled in heels that gave me away, as someone who preferred shooting hoops over parties. Half an hour and two beers later, my plus-one still hadn't returned, and I was considering risking whatever I might see if I inter-rupted the group of people swimming in the river to get a ride back to my apartment. The possibilities required at least one more beer. I weaved through the ever more tipsy crowd, back to the cooler.

"Hi," someone had said too close to my ear as his fingers brushed mine, reaching the last bottle before I did. I almost snatched it from him and then felt embarrassed when he twisted off the cap and handed it to me.

"Thanks," I said and turned to leave.

"Wait."

Reluctantly, I turned back to him. I wasn't in the mood to make shallow conversation with a guy who only wanted to encourage me to drink too many beers, then try to take me home.

"I'm sorry," he said. "It's just that…I didn't come all the way over here just to open your beer."

I looked down at my dress and cursed under my breath. It was shorter and lower cut than I'd remembered it. I didn't know why I'd brought it to school with me at all. Usually I wore basketball shorts.

"Of course not," I said.

"What?"

"Nothing."

He smiled, and I knew he'd heard what I said. I would have felt bad for being rude if he wasn't so obviously good-looking and so obviously knew it.

"Stephen," he said. He reached out his hand. I kept mine to myself. "I didn't catch your name."

"That's because I didn't give it to you."

He chuckled. "Fair enough. But you see, my friend would be really disappointed if I came back without it." He pointed to another attractive…boy, really, who did his best to put on a brave face, showing off his laugh lines and the most perfect smile I'd ever seen. I was fascinated by the mole above his top lip. He lifted his bottle in greeting. I was so caught off guard by the sudden change in suitors, I smiled weakly back at him.

"He's been hoping you'd walk by all night. I told him to go talk to you, but, well…he's a pansy."

I snorted. "Is that your tactic to impress me?"

"No. My plan, if you don't agree to come over and say hi to the poor guy, is to steal your beer and go sit next to him." He winked at me. I found myself grinning.

"You're not stealing my beer," I said.

As we approached, Stephen's friend stood, and I saw that he was far from being a boy. He wore a suit that was charmingly generic and cut a little too loose, but he wore it well. His black silk bow tie hung untied around his neck, and the top buttons of his shirt were undone. He gave me a shy smile and hid his eyes behind his fallen hair.

Stephen introduced us. "Nameless woman, this is Cooper."

This time, I gave my hand willingly.

"Dylan," I said.

"Wow," Cooper said in a low voice, then he laughed. I got the impression complimenting women didn't come to him as easily as it did his friend.

Stephen bowed and strutted away, arms open to signal his job had been done. Cooper laughed and invited me to sit next to him on the log.

"I like your dress," he said, and suddenly, I was a dress person.

I didn't know it until months later, but that night, I'd found everything I didn't know I was looking for. Now I don't know how I'll make sense of a world where he isn't mine.

At ten o'clock, I park in the garage across from the hospital and trudge up to the automatic doors that lead to the emergency department. I take the elevator up, and once the nurse at the information desk buzzes me through, I slip into Labor and Delivery and melt into the endless buzz of doctors and nurses at work. I keep my head down and weave through the hallways unnoticed. I know every room, every door, every closet here. It's the only place that makes any sense today, and I find solace in its predictable rhythm.

I spend the night on a hard cot in the on-call room, staring up at the empty bunk above me. I lie under the covers, still in my clothes and shoes, my fingers laced over the center of my chest. I'm sure I won't sleep with all the questions swirling in my mind, but I must fall asleep sometime during the night because I'm awoken minutes or hours later by the opening of the door and a bright-eyed nurse intern, one of the few

I don't recognize. She must know me, though, because she says, "Dr. Michels? I didn't know you were on call tonight."

I blink a few times to soothe my dry eyes. "I'm not," I say, my voice raspy. I plaster a smile on my face so as not to alarm her.

"Oh," she whispers and puts a finger to her lips conspiratorially. She backs out of the room, and the door clicks shut behind her.

After a few minutes of lying there with the sounds of machines beeping and phones ringing and TVs playing in the rooms on all sides of me, I throw the blanket aside, straighten my clothes and walk the connecting hallway to the clinic. I walk into my office, close the door and lean back against it.

I must have walked too quickly because my skin is clammy and there's a pain in the pit of my stomach. I push my fist into it and wait for it to subside. I haven't eaten anything in more than twenty-four hours, but it doesn't feel like hunger, it feels like something else. Then an image flashes through my mind.

Cooper, sweating, heavy breathing, hands on his skin, not mine.

I take a deep breath to combat the ache between my eyes. But then...

Moaning, fingernails, blond hair. *Not mine.*

My head is in the trash can next to my desk before I know what's happening. I cough and choke on nothing, dry heaving into the bin. A single sob escapes my lips, but I choke that back, too. It won't help anything. It won't change what has already happened or what I have to do.

I spit into the trash can and drag myself off the floor to my desk chair. I fall into it, exhausted from lack of sleep and food. I look around my office, noticing how bare it is here, just like my house. Just like my mother's house. At least there's nothing at all to remind me of Cooper.

★ ★ ★

It starts to drizzle when I arrive home late the following afternoon. I sit in the garage and watch the raindrops come down through the rearview mirror. Cooper's car is here, parked next to mine. He's waiting for me to come home, the way I waited for him when he was gone all night. I wonder if that's when it happened. The thought cuts a fresh wound on my heart. And yet…

I still feel him on the other side of the walls between us.

I tilt the rearview mirror down so I can check my eyes. When I see how swollen and bloodshot they are from crying and lack of sleep, I sigh. There's nothing for it. I stare until my face no longer looks like my face, or any face at all—just shapes and colors all blurred together.

I'm not going to hurt you.

I hear Cooper's words again as if he's whispering them in my ear—what he promised me when we first started getting serious. I see the details of that day in my mind as if I'm watching a scene in a movie.

It was two weeks after Cooper and I started dating when I was already spending most nights at the apartment he shared with Stephen. Every morning, I woke up before him, both of us naked and pressed so closely together I had to peel my sweat-salted body from his to sneak into the bathroom and dress while he slept.

"Why do you get out of bed so early?" he asked me one morning.

"My first class starts before yours does," I said, applying a second coat of mascara.

"Your class doesn't start for over an hour," he said. He rolled to his side and rested his head on his hand. The sheets barely covered the parts of him that still made me blush, not because I was inexperienced with naked men, but because with Cooper, his nudity was more than just sex. It was intimacy. I wasn't used to baring so much of myself to another person, or having him bare so much to me.

I shrugged. "I like to get coffee first."

He threw back the covers and came to stand behind me. He placed his sleep-warmed hands on my hips and turned me around to face him.

"You don't have to hide from me," he said.

"What are you talking about?"

He touched his nose to mine and traced the tip playfully over my skin, teasing me.

"I've seen you naked," he said. "I've seen you without makeup."

"I know," I said and tried to turn back to the mirror, but he stopped me.

"So stop trying to hide from me. I don't expect you to be flawless."

I gasped. "Do I have *flaws*?"

Cooper laughed. "Of course not."

I'd pouted, but he kissed my frown away, soft and slow and with meaning.

"You can stop fighting, Dylan," he'd said. "I'm not going to hurt you."

Now I suck in a breath as my face re-forms in the mirror. I tilt it back into place and get out of the car.

It's darker in the house than it should be at four o'clock, but not a single light is on. The puppy is happily gnawing on a bone in the living room. I lean over to rub his head before I continue on to the bedroom.

I find Cooper sitting on the edge of our bed, in the same place as when I last saw him almost thirty-six hours ago. He could have been sitting in that spot since I left, if it weren't for the dampness of his hair and the scent of his freshly ap plied cologne in the air. He's wearing a pair of sweatpants and a sleeveless undershirt, revealing the broad lines of his shoulders and arms. I fear I'll never get to kiss those lines again, rub my hands across them when he's stressed, find solace in them when I'm lost.

"How long has it been going on?" I ask, breaking the thick silence.

"It's not going on," he says, staring at his hands, too much of a coward to look me in the eye. "I told you. It was one time, and that was it, I swear. I would never do that to you."

"You said you would never hurt me either."

What I can see of his face contorts in what looks like pain, but he keeps it in check. "I know."

"Who?" I ask next. "Who was she?"

The back of his neck blanches more, if possible. He had to have known I would ask.

"Kim," he whispers.

"Kim?"

"From the bar," he says.

"Our bar?" I ask—the place where we've often met Stephen and Megan for late-night drinks after work. I rack my brain for a Kim. "The bartender?"

Cooper nods. I remember her. A petite little brunette about the same height and build as Megan. A few years older than I am, I'd guess, and cute, but the kind of cute that can be rubbed off with a box of tissues. I imagine them on top of the bar, and my stomach churns again. Thankfully, there's nothing left inside it.

My arms hang limply at my sides. My shoulders no longer have the strength to hold them up. Cooper finally looks up to face me. He's clearly been crying, too, but I don't let myself react.

"How can I fix this?" he asks, his voice watery.

A twinge of anger pulls at the center of my chest. He had all night and all day to think about this, and the first thing he wants to know is how he can skip past the discomfort and get back to how we were?

"By making it not have happened."

"Jesus," he growls. He rubs his hands over his face and through his hair. I wish I could sit down and unburden myself of the weight of what answers he'll have next, but I decide to give the conversation space. If I've learned anything about working with people, it's that the discomfort of silence breeds truth.

Cooper stands up and comes over to me. The air around us is still, as empty as I am.

"I don't even know what to say," Cooper says. "I won't insult you by pulling out some cliché. Although they all feel true right about now." He gives a dry laugh, though we both know there's nothing funny about it. "Please, say something. I can't stand not knowing what you're thinking."

"If you didn't want to be with me anymore," I whisper, "you should have just left. You should have just stayed gone instead of making me think we had a chance."

"But I do want to be with you, Dylan."

He reaches for my hands. I step away. His voice is pleading, and I know it should affect me somehow, but when I look at him, I don't see the Cooper I love anymore. I see a stranger. I leave the bedroom, so I don't have to look at him. I feel him follow me anyway.

"No, you don't," I say over my shoulder. "You just didn't want to admit it to yourself, so you took the easy way out."

When we reach the kitchen and he still hasn't responded, I turn to face him. He shakes his head, urging me to believe that's not true, knowing I won't hear it.

"Why?" is my last question. The biggest question. What

led us to this point of no return? Could it have been pre-vented, or was it inevitable that we'd get here—at the end, one way or another?

I can tell by Cooper's reaction that it's the question he's been dreading most. He pushes his palms against his eye sock-ets and turns slightly away, but then some internal argument, no doubt, convinces him to face me.

"Please, don't make me say the words, Dylan. Please. There is absolutely no excuse for what I've done. I take full respon-sibility for... I take full responsibility for the consequences."

"No," I say, stepping forward. "There is no excuse. But there's always a reason. And if the reason is big enough for you to...*fuck* some other woman—" he winces at the words, and I find some small satisfaction in pushing the knife in fur-ther "—then I deserve to know what it is."

"You're right," he says. He opens his mouth. He's shaking his head—at himself, maybe—when he says, "I just couldn't take it anymore, Dylan. I've been waiting for you to come around for nine years, and for what? Do you know how em-barrassing it is to call you my girlfriend when all the other guys at work are married and have kids? They treat me like the bachelor of the place while they have company picnics with their families and coach Little League. Sure, they invite me, but I go hiking with Stephen instead because you're at work. You're always at work."

"Cooper, that's my job!" I yell at him, my face aflame with anger but also shame. I had no idea Cooper felt so displaced.

"I know. I know that's your job, but you take on more than you have to, and you know it. And you're always try-ing to take on more. Dylan, I love Stephen. He's my brother. But you—" His breath hitches, and he takes a step closer to me. "You're my best friend. I want to spend time with *you*. I want to make a life with *you*..." His voice trails off at the end, and my head spins. I don't know how much more of this I can take.

"I don't want our lives to pass us by, Dylan. I don't want to be a forty-year-old first-time father."

"You said you would wait," I say. "You said I was the only one for you."

"You are. I will wait."

"And you'll hate me for every second of it. I knew this would happen as soon as you made partner. It's so easy for you to expect me to set aside my own dreams, now that you've fulfilled all yours."

"Dylan," he says. "I don't want that from you. Do you think I would have asked you to marry me if I didn't love your passion?"

"Right. Well, I guess it's a good thing we didn't get married. Maybe you can go ask your new friend."

He sucks in a breath. Right now I want him to feel at least a fraction of the pain he's causing me. But the vision of another woman in a white dress walking down the aisle toward him tears me apart from the inside.

He emphasizes each word when he speaks again. "I don't want to marry anyone but you."

"But it's just one of the many things on a long list of everything I haven't given you." I pace back and forth from the stove to the counter while he stands dumbstruck, waiting for me to say something, to say that we can get past this. Finally, I stop and look at him. "Well, I hope she gave you everything you wanted."

"I hardly even remember it, Dylan. Because all I was thinking while it was happening was that it wasn't you."

The sting of my hand is what alerts me to the fact that I've slapped him, and my first instinct is to apologize, but I refuse to take it back. The sharp sound assaults my eardrums, but I stand tall.

When I can breathe again, I say, "It should have been." I walk toward the bedroom, then turn back to him. "You can stay in the guest room until you find another place." Then I close the door behind me, and the door on us.

9

Cooper doesn't move out right away. I'm not sure he even tries for the first week, maybe thinking or hoping I'll change my mind. He continues to leave dinner in the fridge for me, and I still come home on my lunch break to let the puppy out, having surprisingly light conversations with Reese on the days he's there and admiring his work on the days he's not. But when Cooper and I pass each other in the living room, all I have left for him are tight smiles. There are no words left to say, and he seems to feel the same way.

Until one night he corners me in the hallway on my way to what used to be our bed. He catches my wrist and pulls me close in the small, dark space.

"Dylan," he breathes, and the single word almost crushes me after our prolonged silence. "Is this for real?" he chokes out.

"How can I ever make love to you again," I hiss, "knowing she's touched you where I touch you? Knowing she's kissed you when I'm the only one who should be kissing you? How, Cooper? You were supposed to be mine."

It's not just about betrayal; it's about respect. How can I respect him when he disrespected us and what we had together? He shattered the bubble of intimacy that surrounded us, and there's no getting that back.

He nods and lets me go.

After that, I start to see apartment listings lying around the house and hear him taking phone calls in the guest room, asking questions about kitchens and bedrooms. I suggest Stephen's place but he says he doesn't want to get anyone else involved. He tells me he needs some time to decide how to break it to his family, and I agree to give him that much. Despite the cheating and the lies, I still feel a pang of guilt that he has to start over, not only in another home but in life. Back to being single, back to living in an apartment. He hasn't fully settled into his partnership at the practice, and he has the puppy to take care of. But then I remind myself that this wasn't my choice. He made the decision to break us all by himself.

Didn't he?

I cry myself to sleep for days, burying my face in my pillow, so Cooper won't hear me, won't think there's any opening between us that he might squeeze back into. It would have been easier if he'd left right away. I'm not the kind of person who likes to drag things out. Once I make a decision, I prefer to act on it and be done with it. It's the waiting that's killing me. It's seeing him standing in our kitchen and forgetting for just a moment that I can't walk up behind him, wrap my arms around his middle and bury my nose into the hair at the nape of his neck.

And then I get so angry at myself for missing him, especially when he's not even gone yet. But after one third of my life spent loving the man I thought I would be with forever, it's too soon to think I could surgically remove him from my heart. I don't think I'll ever get a completely clean cut— we grew up together and into each other and around each other. I just work each day to create more distance between us, mentally and physically. It's all I know to do.

Still, the changes make me restless.

Instead of sitting in my office at the clinic all afternoon, I listen to my voice mails and answer calls while I walk the hospital sidewalks just to get out of that suffocating box and breathe fresh air. Instead of eating lunch, I spend my break sitting cross-legged in the grass, silently watching Reese dig his way around the house. He seems to sense my need for silence and doesn't push me, just lets me feed off our surroundings and his peaceful energy. Many nights, I toss and turn in a sleeping bag behind my desk at the clinic. Other nights, I pace around the yard, searching for an answer inside myself, wondering if this uneasiness means more than a simple transition.

Sometimes I think I catch Cooper watching me from the kitchen window, but when I look closer, no one is there.

Finally, a few weeks later, I come home early one morning to shower and find Cooper crouched in the shade of an overhanging pine in the front yard, suitcases littered around his feet. He's petting the puppy, who's sprawled out on the ground, ears laid back on his head. Cooper's eyes are unfocused, like he's a world away.

I walk toward them, already knowing where the conversation will lead. *How did we get to this place?* I wonder. How will Cooper go create a new life that I'll know nothing about? I'm not like Stephen, who was a part of the group before he married Megan. Without Cooper, I have nothing connecting me to him, Stephen, Megan, Marilyn and John. Once Megan has her baby, I'll have no reason to see them ever again. Her child will never know who I am. This realization, now that it's real, hurts. I'm not just losing the man I love, I'm losing a family.

"Hi," I say softly, before I can fall apart. I have to keep it together in front of him, at least.

"Hi," he says. He meets my eyes for a moment, then glances away. He's dressed for work, but he's unshaven and his hair isn't styled. A soft breeze blows it across his forehead. I don't even feel the desire to run my fingers through it anymore.

I don't.

I clench my fists tightly at my sides.

"So you found a place?" I ask. I point to the bags. He's viewed several apartments already, but none he liked. College students coming and going overwhelm the market this time of year.

"No," he says. "But I don't want to overstay my welcome."

I have to fight every instinct not to uphold my mother's standard for social etiquette and tell him he can stay as long as he likes. It's better for both of us if he leaves. Maybe if the house is finally empty, I can get used to the idea of sleeping in my own bed again.

"Okay," I say.

He looks to the ground, and his jaw tightens, but after a moment, he nods to himself.

"I found a hotel where I can rent a room by the week for now," he says. "The problem is, they don't allow dogs."

"Oh," I say. I glance at the puppy. He has a stick between his paws and is working on turning it into mulch. "Well, I can keep him here until you find a place."

"Are you sure? I don't want to put you out. I'm sure my sister wouldn't mind."

"No," I say too quickly. She has enough on her plate as it is, though Cooper doesn't know. "It's fine. Really."

"Thank you."

I look over at the empty planter in the center of the circular driveway and sigh. "I guess we should tell Reese he doesn't need to finish the yard." I'm surprised by how much this pains me.

"No," Cooper says. "I want him to finish. That was a present for you."

"I may not stay," I say, though in truth, I haven't thought that far ahead. Now that I've said it, it doesn't sit well in my stomach.

"Then it will increase the value of the house."

I nod. He swallows hard. There's an awkward pause, then he meets my gaze with a struggle so obvious, it must be the hardest thing he's ever done. Tears sting my eyes, but I won't let them fall.

The sound of gravel crunching in the driveway alerts us to Reese's arrival. I keep my back to him, knowing Reese will understand what's happening if he sees my face, and soon enough, I'll have to field his questions about our separation.

Cooper picks up his suitcases. "I'll come check on the little guy as soon as I can. Let me know when he needs more food, and I'll bring some over."

"Okay," I say, still not quite able to accept that this is really it. Cooper's really leaving.

"Okay," he says and ducks out into the sun toward the garage. The puppy tries to follow him, but I scoop him into my arms.

"Cooper," I say, taking a step forward. The sunlight catches my eyelashes. He glances back at me. I want to tell him that I don't regret any of our time together, even now that it's come to this. It feels like it will muddy the waters too much, though—my feelings as much as his—so instead I ask, "Are you going to name the dog? We can't keep calling him 'puppy,' you know?"

He shrugs, pretending it doesn't matter to him—that none of this does—but I don't fall for it. He's terrible at not caring.

"I got him for you," he says. "You should pick his name."

"But you're taking him when you get a place. Right?"

He shrugs again. "It will be his going-away present."

I frown, and with no more reasons to stay, Cooper leaves.

Instead of seeking the shower for solitude, I go to the backyard where Reese is organizing his tools on the grass. He looks up at me when he hears the back door close, surprised. I approach him like I'm poised for a fight, but he doesn't wince.

"Need any help?" I ask him, when I stop a couple of feet in front of him. I plant my hands on my hips to keep them from shaking. He looks me over for a moment before leaning down to pick up a shovel. He hands it to me and motions toward the moat. I don't miss the irony. A moat was the most ridiculous request I could think to make, and now I'm the one digging it. I swipe the shovel from his hands and march toward the side of the yard where he left off.

I thrust the shovel at the dirt. From the ledge of the grass, though, I'm too high to get good leverage on it, and it jerks out of my hand and lands with a clang in the ditch below me.

"You'll have to get down in there," Reese says. I sit on the grass at the side of the trench so I can lower myself into the hole. I grab the shovel again, swing it back and heave it at the wall of dirt. The tip of the shovel hits it but bounces back. At least this time I hold on to it.

"It might be easier if you—" Reese starts, closer behind me now.

"Reese, would you just..." I feel him back off. With tears brimming my eyes, I hack at it again and again, the muscles tightening in my arms. At first, I'm taking out my frustration at Cooper, but then it becomes about my grant, and about Abby, and then my frustration with myself.

Should I have seen this coming? Or have I always been oblivious?

"Let me in," I hear my own voice shout through my memory. I was pounding on the bathroom door I shared with Abby as I had been for the last half hour. We were both going to be late for school. Abby may have been able to talk her way out of a detention for tardiness, but I couldn't. I banged the door again and heard the flush of the toilet a moment later. She took her time washing her hands and finally the door opened.

"Your Highness," she said, motioning for me to enter, a small bow curving her back. She looked sick—pale, tired eyes, a light sheen of sweat on her face. But I didn't care. I hoped she was sick. Served her right for all the late nights out of the house, leaving me to cover for her with Mom and Dad. I was tired of her dragging herself into her room in the early hours of the morning, waking up late and giving me a poor attendance record for the first time in my life.

I pushed past her and grabbed my toothbrush. "You're one to talk," I barked. "Maybe if you weren't out letting Christian worship you every night, you wouldn't look like the walking dead."

It was a low blow. Abby was gorgeous, and we both knew I resented it, though I never said it out loud. Not once did she ever do anything but try to build me up.

Abby scoffed. "Oh, Dylan. If you only knew."

I shrugged, pretending I didn't care, but as she leaned against the door frame saying nothing, my curiosity overwhelmed me. I shoved my toothbrush into my mouth and raised my eyebrows at her.

"Christian broke up with me," she said.

My hand slipped from the toothbrush, and my body sagged in regret. After a moment, I finished brushing, spit and went to her.

"You know he's an idiot, right?"

She nodded, her eyes filling with tears.

"You were going to break up with him anyway, remember? You're leaving soon."

She nodded again. "It's fine, really. He's a child. Now I can tell all the cheerleaders what a small penis he has."

I snorted a laugh, blushing at the word. Abby laughed, too, and took a deep breath.

"It's just... It's not that," she mumbled.

"Well, what it is?"

She opened her mouth to respond, but no words came out. For a second, I thought I saw genuine fear cloud her eyes, but before I could goad it out of her, Mom called from the living room and our moment of alliance was shattered.

"Girls, you're late!"

"Shit," I muttered and ran a brush through my hair a few times. "Let's go." I grabbed both our backpacks and pulled her down the stairs behind me.

By the time we met back at her car after school, her face had regained some of its color, and she was smiling again.

"I don't think he's going to be dating any more cheerleaders," she said as we got in, laughing. I took that as a sign that the sadness had passed and never asked her about it again.

Just like I didn't ask Megan that night at her parents' house.

Just like I pretended Cooper and I would be fine.

Just like I'm pretending I'm fine.

The shovel falls from my hands, and I sink down to the dirt. I press my shaking fingertips to my eyelids. Eventually, Reese hops down into the ditch and sits next to me. He says nothing, his silent presence the most comfort I've had in weeks. He doesn't ask. Maybe he knows. Maybe he doesn't care.

"Can I ask you a question?" I say. I peek out from beneath my fingers to look at him—the crazy woman who wanted a moat.

"Sure."

"How long does it take daisy seeds to sprout?"

He looks to the sky, thinking. "Depends. Two to four weeks, usually."

I frown.

"Why?" he asks.

"No reason. Can I ask you another question?"

"Sure."

"When you get the next batch of flowers, will you wait for me to help you plant them?"

He raises his eyebrows. "Will you be able to take the time off work? It may take longer to work around the flowers that are already here."

"I'll figure it out." Those few minutes of digging have been the most therapeutic thing I've done in years.

He pretends to think it over—or maybe he actually does—then says, "I think I could arrange that."

"Promise?" I ask. I've had enough of people not keeping their word to last a lifetime.

Reese purses his lips together and nods. "I promise."

"So how's your patient doing?" Reese asks me one Wednesday evening about a month after Cooper's departure. He's been working later in the day to avoid the midday heat, so even though his visits are still sporadic, when he does show up, it's right around the time I'm coming home from work. I've found comfort in that, even leaving the office early from time to time just to escape and find easy conversation with Reese. He doesn't ask about Cooper, though I'm sure the suitcases and Cooper's absence tell him everything he needs to know. Instead, we talk about work—his clients, my patients—and our passion for our respective fields bridges any gap in terminology. "The one who delivered early?" he clarifies.

"She's doing well," I tell him. I slip my tennis shoes off and sit on the edge of the trench, so I can drop my feet into it. I'm still in my scrubs after a delivery, so I don't mind so much if I get dirty. I feel especially light after today's delivery to a mother who miscarried four times before welcoming her first child early this morning. Afterward, she held me tightly and cried tears of joy into my shoulder.

The coolness of the earth on my feet lowers my body temperature, overheated from the summer sun and the busyness of the day. "I released her today. The baby is still in the NICU, but he's been stable for two days. He'll probably be in there for a few more weeks, but at least his mom can be with him all day if she wants to. I know it's been hard for her to be away from him."

"I can imagine," he says.

I can't help but laugh.

"Can you?" I ask. "What do you know about the maternal bond?"

Reese chuckles and holds up his hands, covered in dried mud. "Fair enough. But I know what love feels like. I know what it means to take care of someone."

"You do?" I ask skeptically. "Do you have a girlfriend?"

"No," he says. "But I have a dog."

I burst into laughter. Reese smiles coyly, the butt of the joke for once.

"Not exactly the same," I say.

"I respectfully disagree," he argues, pleased as ever to play devil's advocate with me. "Charlie depends on me for her health and happiness—"

"Charlie?"

"She's a fox red Lab. And I love her as much as I love any human in my life. I would be heartbroken if she was hurt or sick or if I lost her. Tell me what's different."

"I don't know," I say, pondering it. "A human's life is more valuable."

"Is it?" he asks. "Why?"

I shake my head, mouth agape, my arguments so many that I'm rendered speechless. The corner of Reese's mouth lifts in a crooked smile, and I realize it's pointless to argue with him anyway. Nothing I say will change his mind. Instead of speaking, I grab a clump of dirt and throw it at him. He dodges it and chuckles.

Spotting the puppy a few feet away, Reese nods toward him. "You'll see."

I glance at the puppy, who is chewing on a flower petal he stole from a plant he decimated a few minutes ago.

"He's not mine."

As if he senses we're talking about him, the puppy comes over and drops the flower petal in my lap proudly.

"Tell him that."

I roll my eyes. "So you live alone?"

"With Charlie." He nods. "Why do you ask?"

"I guess I'm trying to picture your life outside of digging holes and dealing with neurotic strangers."

He barks a laugh. "You're not neurotic."

I gasp and place a hand to my chest. "Who said I was talking about me?"

He kicks dirt in my direction, but it doesn't come close to me.

"Yep," he says. "In a house on the north side of town."

"A house? For some reason I always pictured you living in an apartment using pizza boxes to hold up your twelve-inch TV set."

"I'm single, not a frat boy."

"Isn't that the same thing?"

"You might be surprised," he says.

I look him over, study his face. "Maybe not. You're an artist by nature. I'm sure your house reflects that in the best way."

"What does your house say about you?" he asks.

"That I'm never in it."

He returns to digging.

"Family?" I ask.

"I have a brother. And our mom."

"No father?"

"Not in the picture. Not for a long time."

"I'm sorry." Reese shrugs it off, so I don't push him for more information. "What does your brother do?"

"He owns a tech company. They design software."

"Wow. That's impressive."

"He's a very smart man. Very creative."

"Runs in the family," I say.

"No," he says. "I just see things in my head, and I have to get them out. It's like therapy. So at best I'm on the verge of madness."

"You're the sanest person I've ever met," I say.

He laughs. "Then you need to run. Now."

I laugh until my eyes fill with tears, and I have to wipe them away. When the chirping of the birds in the trees is once again the only sound, I ask him about his mom. I realize that after all the conversations with Reese, this is the first time he's told me anything about his family. I realize just as quickly that it's the first time I've asked. Why is it that I can find out so much about my patients during their short visits, but when it comes to personal relationships, I don't know the first thing about opening up to people?

"She's an incredible woman," Reese says. "Hard-working. Smart. Beautiful. I wish I knew her better."

"What do you mean?" I dig my toes farther into the moist dirt.

"She had to raise my brother and me by herself, so it was

hard on her. When we were young, she got a job as a hotel maid and worked her way up the ladder. Now she works at the corporate office and is really successful. That didn't leave her a lot of time for us. She did what she had to, so I'll never hold a grudge against her for that. But it would be nice to see her more, now that she doesn't have to take care of us anymore."

"I'm sorry," I say, and I mean it. I know what it feels like to be alone—emotionally, if not physically—at a young age, and how it affects me even now.

"It makes her happy. I'll always be supportive of someone doing what makes them happy."

"Are you happy…doing this?"

He gives me a lopsided grin, never stopping his rhythmic dance with the shovel.

"Do you think for a second I would be here if I wasn't?"

I smile, shake my head.

"My brother has offered me a position at his company a dozen times. But I would go out of my mind sitting in an office all day. It's just not me."

I sigh. How much I wish I could make decisions based solely on what I wanted. What would my life look like? Would Cooper still be here? Would we have ever met in the first place?

"I bet you would look good in a suit," I say before I realize the way he might perceive my words. I bite my bottom lip as I wait for his response, but he just smiles at me.

"The flowers came in," he says, changing the subject. "Can you get off early tomorrow?"

I nod. "I'll be here."

The next day, I check the clock every five minutes until my last appointment. I saw the columbines in Reese's truck this morning and packed my gardening clothes before work—the first pair of jeans I've owned since I started my residency and a sleeveless T-shirt. I left them in my locker to change into as soon as the clock strikes four, prepared to leave my charting duties for another day. It's been a long time since I've felt these butterflies in my stomach, and I relish them without thinking too much about what they mean. I love the easy feeling of a breeze on my neck and someone to talk to. Nothing more.

"Dylan," Vanessa calls from down the hall after my final appointment. "Are you finished for the day?" she asks. She stops in front of me, and I focus on her face so I don't look past her toward the locker room.

"Yeah."

"Come with me," she says.

My heart sinks when she turns toward her office. I follow her. We haven't talked much since she shot down my application. I worry belatedly that her suggestion to wait until the next grant became available was a test, and I've failed it. It's not that I haven't been working on revising it, but without a benefactor to submit it to, there's been no reason to rush.

Vanessa closes the door behind me and motions for me to sit. I swallow hard. She doesn't speak until she's comfortable in her own seat and has looked me over, her eyes narrowed to slits.

"What's going on with you, Dylan?" she asks.

"G-going on?" I stammer. I take a deep breath and remind myself that I'm not a resident anymore. I've done my job very well for the last year. There's a reason Vanessa picked me to lead the research trial. "Nothing. Nothing's going on."

Except everything is going on. I can't seem to think about anything but Cooper, I barely make it through the day without tearing up in front of a patient and I've been stumbling through my work like a first year. For the first couple of weeks after Cooper left, I spent every waking minute at the hospital and many nights sleeping in my office. But after my most recent appointment with Erika and Andrew and witnessing their affectionate banter again, work seemed like another reminder that life was moving forward all around me. In the garden, time stands still, and for the last couple of weeks, I've retreated to it more than I should.

"I'm not blind, Dylan. Sure, you're spending more time here, but you aren't really here, are you? I'm starting to get complaints."

My heart stops. *Complaints?*

Vanessa leans forward and rests her chin on her hands, her fingers steepled in front of her mouth. I haven't seen this side of her since I *was* a first year, and it jars me out of my self-pity. It took me so long to build that ground with her, and now I've lost that, too.

"From…my patients?" I ask. The idea of letting any one of them down, of all people, paralyzes me.

"From the nurses," she says, softer. "They're worried about you, Dylan. Frankly, I'm more concerned about the morale here, but if whatever is going on *does* start to affect your patients, we're going to have a problem."

My body relaxes with a small amount of relief. I nod.

"I'm sorry, Dr. Lu. I've been distracted."

"Is something happening at home?" she asks, which surprises me. Vanessa is so dedicated to the hospital, she assumes everyone else is, too. Or that they should be.

"I…" My voice trails off. To admit my personal struggles would be a sign of weakness.

Vanessa sighs and leans back in her chair. "Dylan, are you still working on your grant application?"

There's no use lying to her. It doesn't help either one of us. "Not as much as I should be."

"There will be other grants, Dylan. I need you to get focused. Don't throw everything away now. Do you know how many doctors ask me to mentor them each year?"

I don't know the exact number, but I get her point.

"I get it," I say.

"Good. Don't make me wrong about you, Dylan."

When she picks up her phone, I rise and leave her office, shaken.

Afterward, I return to my office to finish my charts because I can't very well leave them undone now. I sit down at my desk with the intention of finishing the few that can't wait, but several phone calls and questions from the nurses later, and the colors in the sky have melted from light blue into a bright orange. I no longer have time to change clothes, so I run to the locker room, grab my bag and bolt out the door.

My heart sinks when I turn onto my driveway and see that Reese's truck isn't there. The clock says it's after eight. I've missed him.

I walk around the garage to the backyard, and when the scene comes into view, my chest deflates. The flowers Reese had promised to let me help with are already planted, and I find myself irrationally angry at him for doing it without me. I take off my shoes and pace across the grass, burning off my emotions. At the top of the stepping-stones, I sink to the ground, breathless. I feel nature against my skin and the longing to control one small part of this world. And as much as I hate to admit it, I understand my mom a little more in this moment.

10

By the end of June, Reese has planted flowers in the front beds and around the entry door. He's finished the back half of the moat, and is moving on to the side of the house. I've avoided seeing him for the last week, but I spend plenty of time in the backyard alone, running my fingers over the fresh blooms and the thick grass. It's only those things I can touch that feel real to me now.

Cooper flits in and out of my life unexpectedly to pick up mail or drop off more food for the puppy. He asks how I'm doing and nods when I tell him I'm fine, both of us knowing the truth—that none of this is fine. Those moments, no matter how confusing and tense, feel almost normal. But then, just as quickly, he's gone again. I thought having him out of the house would make getting on with my life easier, but the memories of him have an even stronger presence in the house than he did. Cooper could only be in one place at a time—the memories are everywhere.

On Saturday morning, I wake up facing my first weekend off alone. I roll away from the sun streaming in through the bedroom windows, wondering if today might be the first day in years my body will let me sleep in. If I could sleep the entire weekend away, it would be a welcome break. But my movement wakes up the puppy who, by some act of cunning, has worked his way into my bed. His tail thumps against the comforter, and he licks my face.

I sigh. "Okay, Spencer," I say, trying out his new name. Coming up with a name myself felt like too much pressure, but he seems to like Reese's choice. His tail wags faster, and he licks my nose with more enthusiasm. "What do you say we go for a walk this morning?" He clearly has no idea what I'm saying, but just the sound of my voice is enough to convince him to do anything. I roll myself out of bed and get dressed.

After untangling a leash and collar from the pile of things Cooper has dropped off for him during his visits and getting it on Spencer's wriggling body, I lead the puppy out into the dry heat of the morning. Spencer doesn't know what to make of his trappings and seems to have declared war on them, contorting his body into increasingly alarming shapes in an attempt to free himself from them. I watch him with amusement. I've never walked a dog before, but I have a feeling we aren't going to make it very far.

"Dude, you have got to chill out," I tell him, pulling my sunglasses down over my face. Spencer looks up at me innocently with the bottom part of his jaw wedged underneath his collar.

I hear the sound of a car approaching as I maneuver Spencer's collar around his teeth, his body pinned between my legs to keep him still. My heart flutters, expecting Cooper or Reese, but when I look up, I see Megan's car approaching. Spencer bolts toward her and, with his leash still wrapped around my legs, sweeps my feet out from underneath me. I land splayed out on the ground with a groan. I don't move for a minute, still in shock, until Spencer bolts back in my direction and covers me with his wet tongue until I'm laughing and pushing him away.

"Are you okay?" Megan calls out as she gets out of the car. Spencer disappears for a moment, and I sit up.

"Fine," I say. "That damn dog is going to be the death of me."

I stand and brush my backside off. Megan slams the car door shut, revealing her midsection, but in the loose-fitting shirt she's wearing, I see no evidence of her pregnancy. Still hiding it, then.

"Are you sure?" she asks.

"Yes," I say. "I'm surprised to see you, though. Everything okay?" I approach cautiously, unsure of how much she knows about me and Cooper. I haven't spoken to anyone in his family since it happened, avoiding Marilyn's usual calls. I'm still not ready to say goodbye to them.

"Everything's great," she says. She bends down to pet Spencer, but she hardly touches the top of his head before he's off again, zigzagging around the yard with the leash tangled between his limbs. "So that's the dog Cooper brought home, huh?"

"Suits him, right?"

Megan laughs and so do I, until I realize that Cooper isn't mine to make jokes about anymore. My laughter dies off abruptly.

"May I?" I ask Megan, reaching for her belly. She nods. I take a step closer, and when I smooth her shirt against her skin, the roundness beneath it becomes obvious. She won't be hiding it for much longer.

"I feel good," Megan says, answering my unasked question. "The morning sickness has finally stopped, and I'm getting some of my energy back. Maybe this whole pregnancy won't be as miserable as I thought."

I smile. "They say the second trimester is the best."

I drop my hand from her belly, and we stand in awkward silence for a moment. I realize then how infrequently Megan and I have spent time together just the two of us. The guys have always been our glue.

"So I take it Cooper told you—" I start, but she speaks over me.

"I've been feeling kind of—"

We both stop and laugh.

"You first," I say.

"No." She looks at me with narrowed eyes. "What didn't Cooper tell me?"

I search her face for any signs of knowledge. I see none.

"About the puppy," I say. She narrows her eyes further, but she doesn't push me. "You've been feeling…?"

Megan sighs, and her expression turns from skeptical to coy.

"I've been feeling kind of out of the loop," she admits. "I mean, I know Cooper is my brother, but I guess I don't know how to invite myself to hang out with you guys without Stephen."

I deflate. "Oh, Megan. I'm so sorry." I place my hand on her shoulder. "I'm an idiot. I should have called you. Things have just been…"

If Cooper had told his family about our breakup, she would know she wasn't being left out. I almost tell her out of spite—it's been weeks, and Cooper is still hiding in denial or shame—but I stop myself. It isn't fair to drag Megan into the middle of it, especially in her condition. And as angry as I am at Cooper, I don't want to be the one to change his family's view of him, as much for their sake as for his. I'm not the only one who has looked to Cooper as a beacon of hope in a world that's all too devoid of good anymore. Letting them down is something Cooper has to face on his own.

Besides, in truth, I haven't told my family yet either. They've never been as close to Cooper as I am with the Caldwells. I didn't realize, though, how much our separation would affect the people we love without them even knowing it.

"I know," she says. "It's not your fault. It's my own insecurity. I'm still not used to this idea of being…single." She says the word as if it's a completely foreign concept, and I turn my face away. *You and me both*, I want to say.

"I was going to take Spencer on a walk. Do you want to join me?"

Megan's face lights up. "I'd love to."

The office building my father owns is as old as the dirt it stands on, and it looks it, the brick harboring over a hundred years of soot and money dreams. I park in the garage across the street and jog through the listless one-way traffic to the glass doors only featured in government buildings anymore. The place stands six stories high and is situated near historic Portland, and though when I was younger I urged him to move to a building closer to home, he insisted he loved its history and charm. It's the same building his father rented when he first opened the doors for business. Dad always told me, "People should never forget where they come from," as if it's possible to erase it from memory. Maybe if I *could* forget my past, I'd finally get a hold on my future.

I let myself into the lobby and out of the cool, misty morning. It's Sunday, and though I've made it a habit of hiding in charts on the weekends, seeing Megan made me feel like it's time to finally start accepting the fact that I'm going to have to move on with my life and without Cooper. I can't keep living in a bubble.

The receptionist isn't here, and it feels like a ghost town without her and her constant barrage of phone calls. The sound of my heels on the ceramic floors echoes as I cross the room to the elevators. But I know Dad will be here. Sunday morning has been his favorite time to catch up at work, even when he owned the pizza parlor. He says the quiet allows him to concentrate. It's a strategy I often use myself.

Once the doors slide shut in front of me, I rest my head against the wall and close my eyes. I know talking to my dad will help. I'm his baby girl. But I'm also his only girl now, and that makes him more protective of me.

I knock lightly on his office door, then crack it open and peek my head in. My dad turns to face me from where he's standing in front of the windows overlooking downtown.

"Dylan?"

"Hi, Dad," I say. "Can I come in?"

"Of course. Of course." He lets his arms fall to his sides and motions toward the chairs in front of his desk. Instead I find a spot beside him near the window. We stand next to each other for a few minutes, watching the foot traffic below. It is relaxing, watching some people scurry by in business suits, even on the weekend, while others laugh and talk, window shop. I see a woman smiling and talking sweetly to the man who's holding her hand, and I try to imagine what her life must be like. What would be different? What has she figured out that I haven't?

"How's work?" I ask Dad.

"Same old, same old," he says.

As much as Dad has encouraged me to share my frustrations and setbacks, he's never been particularly forthcoming with his. Some parents become friends to their adult children and share the secrets that were once withheld to protect them, but mine have always just been my parents.

We stand there for another minute before I feel my dad's arm snake around my shoulders. He pulls me into the nook under his arm. I don't fit there as well as I used to.

"What's going on, baby girl? I can tell something is up."

I press a kiss to his cheek. "Let's sit down."

"Okay."

I take one of the chairs, and he takes the other. We face them toward each other, and he crosses his ankle over his knee. My stomach is alive with anxiety. I finally have to say the words aloud, and I can feel them there, lodged in my throat, fighting their way out.

"Okay." I exhale forcefully. "Cooper has moved out. He… cheated on me."

I have a hard time looking at him, as if it's my own shame. His face has gone stony. I swallow hard.

"I would never have expected this of him either but…" I go on, feeling the need to defend Cooper, or maybe my decision in choosing him. "I don't know what to do. My life is completely tied to his. The house, the cars, our finances. You know more about money and assets than anyone I know. I figured if anyone could give me some advice on how to make a clean break, it would be you." My voice gains strength as I go on, growing more sure with every word.

Dad turns away, thinking, and rubs his forefinger over his chin and the day-off stubble there.

He finally nods. "And you're sure you want to leave him?"

I furrow my brow. His question is so shocking, it takes me a moment to respond.

"He cheated on me," I say. "There's nothing else to do."

My dad stands, catching me off guard. I push myself back in my chair to give him room. He crosses the floor and resumes the position I found him in when I first walked in. He paces along the window, his lips working, not quite forming the shape of words but as if he's having a conversation with himself in his mind. I stand, but stay rooted in my spot. I prepared myself to hear him threaten to kill Cooper or to hold me in his arms. I didn't prepare for him to say nothing.

"Will you help me figure out how to get out of the mortgage and separate our bank accounts?" I finally ask, trying to pull him back in.

Dad analyzes me for a moment, then comes over to take my hands. "You know I will. I'm always here for you. But will you do me a favor? Will you think about this for a few more days? A week?"

"I…I don't know, Dad. It's been weeks already. Nothing is going to change."

The words come out shaky. Dad pulls me into his chest and holds me there, the way I wanted him to—the reason I came here. Tears leak from my eyes onto the palm trees on his Hawaiian shirt. He rubs his hand over my hair and shushes me. When I was a girl and we first moved, I often came home upset about things the girls at school said about me. I had spent the first years of my life at public schools in lower middle-class Portland, and while I was never popular, I had a few close friends. We didn't have much, but we were happy with just enough. It never occurred to me to want nicer clothes, more expensive haircuts or designer backpacks. I was thrown into a world—private school—that didn't understand me, and when people don't understand something, they shun it. The only thing that got me through those days was that my dad would hug me each night after he got home from work, and when I told him about my day, he would say, "Give your hurts to me, and I'll keep them safe until you need them." I would laugh because I could never imagine a time when I would *need* to hurt.

Now, I mumble, "Will you take my hurts?" Dad laughs his deep, throaty chuckle, and a smile tugs at the corner of my lips.

"Give 'em here," he says. He holds out his hand, but instead of pretending to place my invisible pain there, I push the real pain to the back of my mind where it will be safe, no longer roiling and swollen.

Dad holds me away from him and cups my chin in his hand. "You know Cooper loves you, baby."

I sigh, giving up hope that Dad is going to let me off the hook easily. I should have known he'd react this way. He's been trying to hold his marriage to my mom together for half my life.

"I'll think about it," I say, because I sense more is riding on the promise than just my relationship.

On the way home that night, I stop by the farmer's market to pick up some fresh produce and wine, then the grocery store for Asian noodles and spices to make my favorite stir-fry. It's one of the dishes Mom made growing up—one I adopted when I moved out—but Cooper never liked it much. I also grab the first purple comforter set I see at Bed Bath & Beyond. It's time to get used to being single again.

To my surprise, Reese's truck is in the driveway when I get home. Before I've even put my key into the front door lock, I hear Spencer whining from his crate. I announce my presence, and his whining stops, immediately replaced by the thumping of his tail on each side of the kennel.

"Yes, I'm home," I say to him and open the kennel door. As soon as I open the back door and set him down, he bolts out into the grass, right past the newest mound of earth—

next to a large hollow at the end of the trench—and a pair of muddy work boots with Reese inside them.

Reese greets the puppy first. He leans down to rub Spencer's head, and I watch from the threshold. He has smudges of dirt on his bronzed arms in places that don't make sense, like on the back of his bicep and the inside of his elbow. Spencer finds interest in his friend for only a minute before he's off to the first bush. Reese stands up again.

"You know," Reese says, "if you want, you can leave him with me in the mornings. I don't mind if he hangs out with me while I work."

"Oh, you don't have to do that. I don't want to impose."

"It wouldn't be an imposition. I like his company. Almost as much as yours," he adds. My cheeks flush with anger or embarrassment, I'm not sure. We haven't spoken since he planted the flowers without me, and some of the uneasiness between us has crept back in.

"Thanks. I'll think about it," I say. "Working on a Sunday?"

"Yeah. I tried to call Dr. Caldwell today to let him know I'll be out of town next week. I'm trying to finish up this section before I go, if that's okay."

"Oh. Sure," I say, as I back into the house. "His name is Spencer, by the way." I nod toward the puppy.

Reese beams in a way I haven't seen before. "I like it."

"Well," I say, and motion over my shoulder. "Better get dinner started." Reese tilts his head and picks up his shovel as I call Spencer. I retreat into the house.

To unwind, I turn on some music and take a shower. I dress in knit pants and a loose white blouse—comfortable but cute. It's been a while since I've dressed for myself, not for my clients or the operating room. Or, on date nights, Cooper. In the kitchen, I purposefully put everything out of my mind but chopping onion and bell peppers, and I let a lightness seep into my heart and outward into my limbs. Maybe starting over won't be the worst thing. Maybe I could even leave Oregon, try someplace new. When thoughts of Cooper's retreating figure loom in the darkness of my mind, I hum to the music, forcing all my energy into my senses, the way I do at the clinic. If my hands are busy and my mind is focused, nothing else can reach me.

By the time I start to heat the oil in a pan on the stove, an hour has passed, and the sun has almost set. Dark clouds hang heavily in the sky, but Spencer nips at my ankles anyway, whining to be let out again. With one eye on the stove, I open the door for him. Reese is in the cavity he's been digging in sight of the kitchen window, something that isn't a moat. I turn on the outside light for him.

"You're still here," I say, though I'm not as surprised as I sound. I saw him working from inside, showing no signs of stopping or slowing. "Can you even see anything?"

"The light helps," he says with a smile.

I look pointedly up at the sky. "It might rain. Are you sure you don't want to head out now? It's not a problem if you put it off until next week." My reasons aren't completely unselfish. It's hard to find my center with him on the other side of the window.

"I'd like to stay on track. I gave you a completion date, and I intend to stick to it. Again, if it's okay with you. If you need me to go, I'll go." Seeing my hesitation, he adds, "I like to be a man of my word."

"Is that why you planted the flowers without me?" I haven't been able to let it go—another disappointment by someone I was surprised to realize meant something to me. Another broken promise.

"So that's why you went missing."

Now that the words are out of my mouth, I feel silly for bringing it up. Reese doesn't owe me anything.

"I don't want to be an imposition," I repeat.

"You never are, Dylan. But life keeps moving. Every moment is another opportunity to choose how you want to spend it."

I smile ruefully. "Right."

I want for him to apologize, but, of course, he doesn't. I'm actually glad. I admire his ability to stand behind his decisions.

A light rain begins, but it's the kind of rain that alludes to worse yet to come. There's a hum of electricity in my limbs at being alone on an ominous night, but I ignore it and go inside.

Distracting myself from Reese's words, I throw all the freshly chopped ingredients into the pan, contented by the sizzle each one makes, the scent of garlic filling the house. I set a place for one at the table—place mat and a cloth napkin, a wineglass and the nice china. I go all out, proving to myself I can let go and live in the moment. I just need to do it in my own time.

While the food cooks, I make the bed with my new sheets. As I tuck them in on Cooper's side, something catches my eye. I reach down into the crevice between the wood and the bed and pull out a book Cooper must have forgotten. I turn the tattered paperback over to see the title, but of course, I already know what it is. *The Great Gatsby*. It's his favorite. I can't count how many times I've seen him reading it. He always kept it on his nightstand and always teased—like long-time couples do—that if we ever broke up, he'd fight for me until his dying breath the same way Gatsby did for Daisy. It was one of his cheesy jokes, I thought, but now I wonder if it's true. And as much as I hoped he wouldn't make it harder for both us by dredging up the pain all over again, a small part of me hoped he would. I guess Megan was wrong—Cooper gave up the fight for me after all.

But then again, he didn't pick up the book the last time he was here. No doubt he's missing it. Does that mean he still wants it here?

I don't realize I've curled up on his side of the bed, on top of my new sheets, with the book cradled against my chest, until I hear a knock at the back door. I don't get up right away, and the knock comes again, more insistent until I finally get up. When I open the door, rain is falling heavily. I hadn't noticed the pounding of it against the roof, so it's a shock to my senses. Reese stands in my doorway, drenched. His shirt is stuck to his chest. His eyes are narrowed as he stares at me with that examining gaze. They look almost black in the darkness.

"I wanted to let you know I've finished up. With the yard. I'll be back next Monday." When I don't respond, he adds, "Unless you need anything else."

"Okay." My eyes won't focus. Sadness has hollowed my chest.

Reese looks behind me. "Is everything all right in there?"

"Uh-huh."

"It smells like something is burning."

Once he mentions it, I see the thin billows of white smoke overhead. But I can't seem to react.

"He left the book on purpose," I say, as if that explains it.

Reese stares at me for a few seconds before accepting that I'm not going to move. He steps into the house and walks past me. That jolts me out of my daze.

"Your shoes," I say, but he has already kicked them off and disappeared into the kitchen. "What are you doing?"

Having another man in my house for the first time since Cooper should make me uneasy, but watching him in my kitchen gives me a surprising sense of comfort, the sense of not being alone. I close the door as he pulls the noodles off the burner. He grabs the kitchen towel and fans the smoke detector in the dining room, though it hasn't gone off yet. I watch him do all of this with an interested detachment, like watching animals at the zoo.

Once he folds the towel in half and drapes it over the sink, he says, "You're going to want to soak that before you wash it," motioning to the noodles.

I set *The Great Gatsby* on the counter, then turn my back to him in a vain attempt to pull myself together.

"Dylan, what's going on?"

"Please, don't ask me that," I whisper. "I know you know."

Reese comes around to stand in front of me. Rain drips from his hair and lands on the hardwood. The intensity of his presence and his gruff charm force me to take a step back. He glances over my shoulder at the single place setting on the table, and his face softens with understanding.

"Sit down," he says. When I don't move, he repeats himself more firmly.

I glare at him, but he doesn't back down, so I find my seat at the dining room table. He goes into the kitchen, searching for something.

"Tongs?" he asks.

"Drawer to the right of the stove."

He finds them and returns to the dining room.

"I smelled the garlic all the way outside," he says quietly. "This dinner should not go to waste."

He fills my plate with a generous helping of stir-fry, minus the noodles, then places the pan on the stove. I catch him dipping his fingers in and feeding himself a few peppers while I sit with my hands in my lap.

"You can take the rest," I say.

He returns to the dining room. "I have to go. But you enjoy."

"Thanks."

"For what? You made it."

He slips his boots on and with a half smile, closes the door behind him. I wait until I hear his truck start up and pull out of the driveway, then I eat my dinner alone.

11

Cooper told me he loved me on Thanksgiving Day, three months after we met. It was a cold, dreary day, and his family had rescheduled their celebration so Cooper could meet my family. It was the first time I'd brought someone home since my prom date, and though I worried my mom would scare him away with her dedication to holiday tradition, he assured me he'd love me if I came from a family of circus performers or even Republicans—the latter of which was true. The problem was, I didn't know if *I* would still love me, or at least the person I turned into around my mother. I didn't want Cooper to meet that girl. I worked hard to keep her hidden, especially from him.

The night started off well enough. Mom greeted Cooper with a kiss on the cheek, a sweeping once-over and a smile. He fell into conversation about golf and business with Dad and Charlie. They sipped bourbon on the back porch. Within the hour, he was in.

As soon as the boys had slipped out the back door in their hysterically festive sweaters—the Michels boys' tradition adopted to counter Mom's Martha Stewart treatment—Mom threw an apron on me and stuck me in front of a bowl of potatoes with a hand mixer. One extra guest meant three more side dishes in addition to the seven she already felt necessary for our family of four.

Family of five. Thanksgiving had been Abby's favorite holiday.

Mom had rattled off instructions for over an hour, pointing her ragged, chewed-to-the-quick fingernails at this dish, then that, before I made an excuse to escape to the laundry room, where Mom stored the overstocked pantry items she collected on sale. With the light still off, I wiped my hands on my apron and placed them on the washing machine to brace myself for the tears that would surely come. We all tried to make up for Abby's absence in different ways, and Mom's coping mechanism was pretending nothing had changed, that we were not broken. But I was not perfect. I couldn't mash the perfect potatoes or whip the perfect cream, and no amount of beautiful food would tempt Abby down from her bedroom to dip her finger into a casserole dish or pick at the corners of the corn bread. I pulled myself together in the darkness, where no one could see whether or not the turkey was the precise shade of golden brown.

The door cracked open, letting in a sliver of light. It spotlighted my face and revealed Cooper's in the space between.

"Do you have any sweet potatoes in there?" Cooper asked.

"Sweet potatoes?"

"I don't think your mom made enough food."

A grin slid across his face, and I let out a watery laugh.

"I hate you," I told him.

He laughed and said, "I know. I love you, too." He closed the door behind him, and there in the pitch-black, he pulled me into his arms and kissed me. He pushed his body against mine until my breasts were crushed against his chest, and I tingled with his touch. With one wordless gesture, there in my mother's laundry room, Cooper took over as the protector of my heart, the keeper of my hurts.

And I let him.

When I pull into the driveway at lunchtime the following Monday and see Cooper standing in the front yard talking to Reese, the sleeves of his dress shirt rolled up to mid-forearm and the sun lighting up his golden hair, I know I can no longer count on anyone else to keep them for me. I have to deal with all these new ones on my own.

I take a deep breath and step out of the car. Spencer comes bounding over and, used to our usual greeting, jumps into my arms. I groan and pull him up to my chest, letting him lick the bottom of my chin. Neither Cooper nor Reese seems at all interested in my appearance. They continue talking.

"So it will stop to the left of the door?" Cooper asks.

"Yeah. The left looking at it from here. You'll only need the one bridge." Reese's hair is freshly trimmed, and he wears a thick layer of mud around the soles of his shoes. He appears to have confined it to his boots so far today.

I approach, feeling like the third wheel.

"Good thinking," Cooper says. "Don't want to be tripping over a bridge every time we come in the front door."

I don't miss the *we*.

"Hey," I say. The guys finally look over at me. They both smile, and my heart skips a beat. Everything about this picture is wrong. "What's going on?"

"I just stopped to grab a few things." Cooper sneaks a glance at Reese. "You know, the extra pair of shoes for the office."

"Right," I say. So he is still playing that game. Against my better judgment, I follow Cooper's lead and don't ask him in front of Reese why he's checking on the landscaping while he's here.

Cooper furrows his brow. "You're getting your shirt dirty," he says, and points at the dusty Spencer in my arms. His tone is more surprised than concerned. I look down at my chest, set Spencer back down and noncommittally brush myself off. Cooper looks at me expectantly, but I plaster on a fake smile.

"The shoes?" I ask him, barely hiding my sarcasm.

"Right," he says. To Reese, "I'll catch up with you later."

"Sure." They clasp hands, then I follow Cooper into the house, Spencer trailing behind us. I cast a glance over my shoulder at Reese. His arms are crossed over his chest. He wears a grin, eyeing my shirt. I've gotten used to a little dirt, and he thinks he's climbed Mount Everest or something. I roll my eyes and hear his chuckle as I close the door.

Inside, I follow Cooper to the bedroom but stop short of entering the walk-in closet with him.

"Do you mind if I borrow this suitcase?" he asks, like we're picking up right where we left off.

I respond with the obvious question. "What the hell are you doing here, Cooper?"

"What?" Cooper asks, emerging from the closet with my carry-on luggage and a pair of tennis shoes.

"Don't 'what' me," I say. "You can't just keep showing up here. You don't live here anymore. It's been weeks. Haven't you found a place yet? A place you can take all your things to?"

The pain of discovering his discarded book has been bubbling up inside me, and after hearing him talk to Reese as if he didn't break my heart, it's boiling over.

He glances at the bed and stops. "Nice bedspread."

"Oh." My cheeks warm from being caught attempting to exorcise him from the house. "It's just…"

His eyebrows dip low over his eyes, but he quickly erases the expression. He heaves the suitcase onto the bed and places his shoes in it, returning to the closet. My embarrassment recedes as I recall his conversation with Reese.

"What was with the 'we'?" I ask him.

He comes out again with two more pairs in hand.

"What 'we'?"

"When you were talking to Reese. You said you didn't want us tripping over a bridge every time *we* came in the front door."

"Oh. Well, you know." He shrugs.

"No, I don't know." Actually, I'm sure I do, but I want to hear him say it. He's ashamed of what he did, and he doesn't want anyone to know. He's taking the coward's way out, and I want him to admit it.

Cooper busies himself arranging his shoes in the bag like a 3-D puzzle. "I don't think it's his business, okay? Besides, it's probably not safe for him to know you're here alone every night without a neighbor for half a mile in any direction."

I think about Reese coming into the house last week. If only Cooper knew how far from being a stranger Reese actually is, I'm sure he'd have a lot more to say about the subject. But to use Cooper's words, my friendship with Reese—and my safety for that matter—is not his business.

"What about your sister?" I ask. "Why didn't Megan know when I saw her last?"

"I'll tell them in my own time, okay?" he says gruffly. "Besides, Megan's been too busy to see me. That's not exactly something you tell someone over the phone."

"Wait. Do you mean your parents still don't know either?"

"Oh, c'mon, Dylan. Don't act like I'm the only one who has secrets."

"What the hell is that supposed to mean?"

He stops packing and looks at me. I purse my lips and stare him down.

"When did you see Megan?" he asks, throwing the accusing glare back at me.

"I…" My mouth goes dry as I search for an excuse.

"Look, whatever, Dylan. I'm having a shitty day, okay?" He resumes packing, throwing the shoes in haphazardly. "I had to send one of my kids to the hospital, and the only pair of shoes I took with me are giving me blisters. Will you lay off?"

I drop my hands from my hips, startled. I've never seen this side of Cooper. No matter how angry he would get at me during our relationship, he hardly ever raised his voice. He seems to realize this, too. He closes his eyes and pinches the bridge of his nose. Maybe I should feel sympathetic, but along with everything else, Cooper gave up the right to take his shitty days out on me.

"If you didn't want to hear it, you shouldn't have come here," I say.

"Goddamn it, Dylan. Do you ever think about anyone but yourself?" He throws the last pair of shoes into the bag with so much force, one of them jumps back out and lands with a thud on the floor.

"I'm selfish? *I'm* selfish?" I hiss through my teeth.

He picks up the shoe and puts it in the bag. "Never mind. Forget I said it."

I cross my arms. "No. You clearly have something to say. Say it."

"Just drop it, Dylan. For once, let it go."

"No."

The muscles in his jaw ripple, biting back his anger. I want to see him angry. I want him to be honest for once, instead of speaking in code and passive-aggressive acts.

"You want to go there?" he asks, daring me.

"Yes! Tell me what made me such a bad girlfriend that I drove you into the arms of another woman."

"This, for one," he yells back at me. "You turn everything into a fight. You are so ready to disappoint me. You've been doing it since the night we met. You can't stand the idea that you might not be perfect, so you keep me at arm's length, so I won't see your flaws. Well, guess what? We were together for nine fucking years, and I saw them all. And I still love you."

My chest heaves and my heart pounds. I want to scream at him, and his response only makes me madder.

Love? Present tense?

"You wanted to know why I did it," he goes on, before I can say anything, both of us very clear on what *it* he's talking about. "Here it is. I felt like I was living with a stranger."

I snap my mouth shut. Cooper's eyes are wide like I've never seen them before, and I know he's trying to hurt me with this…but I can also see the truth in it.

"You were never here," he goes on. "And when you were, you were asleep, or in another room, or taking phone calls from the hospital, or reading. Anything but spending time with me. And don't think I don't know you have secrets of your own. I didn't push because I knew you would tell me if it was something important, and I didn't think it would affect our relationship. Clearly I was wrong on both counts."

He raises his eyebrows, daring me to argue. I can't.

"And when we had sex… Damn it." He lowers his voice. "When we *made love*, I didn't know where you were anymore."

His eyes are locked with mine, judging my reaction to his words.

"Was she *there*?" I bite out. "Did you connect with her?"

"See," he says and throws his hands up. "I can't get anywhere with you."

He zips up his bag and stares at it for a long moment, neither of us able to speak. We've already said too much. I realize maybe I have pushed things too far. Maybe I didn't want to hear his side, because it would bring me to this moment: facing the ugly truth. I've always known I was keeping Cooper at a distance, but I hoped he didn't notice. I hoped we could somehow work around it.

But it's getting harder and harder to place the demise of our relationship solely on his shoulders. It's getting harder and harder to justify my defenses.

This isn't what Abby would have wanted for me.

"You left your book," I tell Cooper. I break free from the tension holding us in our places. I pass Cooper, and without a single movement, I can feel him wanting to reach out to touch me. I don't slow my pace for fear that he'll go through with it. I'm too confused already. I grab the book from the kitchen counter, but as I turn back, Cooper emerges from the bedroom, his head down.

"Keep it," he says, not looking at me. He crosses the living room in a few quick strides, then slams the front door behind him.

Later that week, I come home after work to catch Reese coming up the path from the creek. He comes straight up to me with a curious smile that immediately sets my nerves on edge. His green eyes are alight, apparently not holding a grudge against me for confronting him about our missed plans or for having to rescue my dinner. I, on the other hand, have not forgotten, and my cheeks burn in embarrassment, having fallen apart in front of him and because of him. He only committed to bringing a little beauty back into my busy life. He didn't commit to being my friend.

"If I asked you to do something, could you trust me and

go along with it?" he asks. Spencer circles us, snapping at air. He's been happier spending the mornings outside with space to roam.

I tuck a loose strand of hair behind my ear. "Do I have a choice?" I ask.

He purses his lips together to suppress a grin. The wind rustles his hair, styled in such a way that it never falls from its perfectly messy tousle, no matter how hot it is or how hard he works.

"I'm serious, Dylan."

"Maybe," I say. "You have to tell me what it is first."

"Can you stay away from the creek for a while? Stay up here?"

"But that's my favorite spot."

"You're going to have to trust me."

Trust is a lot to ask of someone you hardly know, is my first thought. Then I wonder if that's true anymore. Working side by side with someone on a shared mission has a way of connecting people, whether they realize it or not.

"Okay," I say.

Reese puts his hands on my arms below my sleeves so he's touching my skin, and while instinct tells me to step away, he has me in his grip.

"Thank you," he says. I never noticed how infrequently people look directly at the person they're talking to until I met Reese. It seems to be the only way he communicates—straightforward, no filters.

When he lets me go, he leaves traces of soil on my arms. I don't brush it off.

"So are you going to help me line the flower beds?" he asks. He motions toward them, and my stomach clenches at the reminder of my foolish anger. I'm surprised to hear he plans to keep working today. He should have been gone an hour ago.

"I don't think that's a good idea," I say. The line between our professional and personal relationship is blurry enough. It's probably inappropriate, but that's a hard factor to determine out here, with no one else to gauge it against.

"Really?" he asks.

"I'm really not good at this kind of thing," I admit. "It's better for both of us if I just stay out of your way."

"What kind of thing?"

"I don't know. People." What I'm thinking but don't say: Relationships are a minefield. And I'm not agile enough to navigate them.

He shakes his head. "Dylan, I don't know what you're talking about, but you don't have anything to worry about with me. We're good," he says. I turn my face away from him. He bends down to look at me. "Do you want to tell me what's really bothering you?"

I shake my head. I've made a habit of not talking to him about Cooper. It feels safer that way—a clear boundary.

He smirks. "Okay. How about you tell me anyway?"

I sigh. It's not only my fight with Cooper that's on my mind.

"I'm supposed to be working on my grant application," I say. "But I have no idea what I'm doing. I thought I knew what my boss wanted from me, but I've been wrong before."

He frowns. "I know it's important to you. I'm sure you'll figure it out."

I scoff. "I hate it when people act confident in things they have no control over."

There are doctors at the hospital like that, who expect everything to go smoothly in the delivery room each time. I don't take probability for granted, and I don't take hopes to the bank.

"Don't you believe in the Universe?" Reese asks.

"What? You mean like God?"

"I mean cause and effect. Karma. Reaping what you sow. What goes around, comes around. You've done a lot of good things in your life, Dylan. Right?"

"I don't know. I'd like to think so." With the exception of one very big mistake.

"I know your intentions are good. I know you want this for more than yourself. You'll get the grant," he says. "You've put it out there, and the Universe is going to give it back to you. It's just waiting on you."

"Waiting for what?" I ask. I genuinely want to know. I'm tired of putting everything on the line for a dream that keeps eluding me.

"You tell me," he says. I wait for him to continue with today's words of wisdom, but he doesn't. When I don't respond, he asks, "Is that why you and Dr. Caldwell broke up?"

There it is. I knew it would come up eventually.

I shrug. "We were both so busy we didn't have time for each other. Anyone would grow apart under those circumstances." It feels like too big an admission to tell him the whole truth. I don't want to know what he thinks it means in the grand scheme of things. I don't want him to ask me what role I might have played in Cooper's infidelity.

He gives me a break from the inquisition, and I pace quietly for a few minutes, but the tension is too much to take. He's playing my card—silence.

"I don't know why we broke up, Reese. I don't have everything figured out. I never said I did."

"I know." He stands there, unfazed by my irritation with him, as he is with everything. I hate the way he seems to have so few cares in the world. It's so easy for him to judge me. "Come here," he finally says and reaches a hand out to me. I stare at it for a moment before I finally take it. I fight against the messages my fingertips are telling me as he leads me over to an open patch of grass and encourages me to sit down. He sits next to me, shoulder to shoulder, and we look up at the trees, our knees bent. Spencer jumps into Reese's lap and nips at his chin, but with a few simple caresses, Reese calms him.

He finally says, "Let's refocus here. I think we both know it isn't really about Dr. Caldwell." The assumption jars me, but I don't have time to correct him before he barrels on. "Tell me why you love your job. And I'm not talking about why you started doing it or what you think you need to accomplish. On a day-to-day basis, what keeps you going back to the hospital?"

I've been so focused on my grant and Cooper lately, I have to dig deep to remember. But it is there.

"I love helping people," I say. "I love giving women a sense of strength during the most challenging hours of their lives. Reassuring them in all the uncertain moments leading up to it. It's a beautiful process to bring another living being into the world."

"What's your least favorite part of the job?"

"Letting people down."

"Who are you letting down?"

I sigh against the weight of the question. "My family, my boss, Cooper. And I always worry I'm not doing enough for my patients."

"Or maybe…maybe it's yourself you're letting down? We're always hardest on ourselves, Dylan. I don't think anyone expects you to give up your own happiness for theirs."

I pick at the grass, ignoring the possibility that he might be right. But where's the balance? How do I let go of anything without everything crumbling around me?

"Maybe," I concede.

"So how do you adjust your expectations?"

"I don't know," I say.

He smiles and leans closer to rub his shoulder against mine. "You will."

I finally get back into my regular schedule at work, not because I don't want Vanessa to be upset with me, but because she's right. And because Reese is right.

I pull out my grant application again. I've gotten so distracted with my personal life that I've let my commitment to my career and my goals slide. So on the days Reese is at the house, I leave Spencer with him and spend my lunch breaks in my office, staring at my computer screen, waiting for the right words to come to me. When Vanessa looked at it the first time, she said she thought my goals were too lofty. As I watch the blinking cursor hour after hour, day after day, I realize maybe it is time to adjust my expectations.

During one of these staring bouts, I remember my parents' wedding anniversary is coming up soon—their thirty-fourth together. Dad hasn't called since I visited him at his office, no doubt giving me time to think about Cooper without feeling pressured. I haven't called him for fear of disappointing him with the news that I haven't changed my mind, though I don't know if it would have mattered if I had. Cooper has been keeping his distance, and I have a feeling it isn't just because I asked him to.

As my parents' anniversary date grows closer, though, I wait for Dad's phone call to remind me of our usual plans. It's always been our tradition to celebrate as a family. I think it started because when I was little, my parents couldn't afford a babysitter—the reason they gave us was that the three of us kids were the ones who made their marriage special. By the time Dad received his inheritance, we wouldn't hear of being left with a stranger while they went out to do something boring like eating tiny portions at a fancy restaurant and watching a movie only one of them actually wanted to see. Together we played board games, ate popcorn and drank half a flute of champagne each. When Charlie and I reached adulthood, it became more about the champagne, but it's a tradition so strong, even Mom joins us.

When I haven't heard from Dad by the morning of their anniversary, I try calling him several times and get no answer. I try the house phone and my brother's cell phone, but no one picks up. No one calls me back.

After work, I drive over to my parents' house. Charlie's car isn't in the driveway and Dad's isn't in the garage, so I'm already anxious by the time I walk inside and see boxes stacked along the wall in the foyer.

"Mom?" I call out as I run my fingers over the cardboard so fresh I can still smell the trees it came from. In black permanent marker, the simple label: *Books*. I lift the one corner of the tiered flaps to see John Grisham's name staring back at me. *Dad's* books. I pull my hand away, as if stung. "Mom?" I call again.

"In here." Her faint voice carries from farther inside the house. I follow it through the living room and the kitchen to find her sitting at the head of the dining room table, alone. The energy around her is so stagnant, she could be a statue—not a living, breathing being at all. She's dressed in an all-white pantsuit, her hair twisted up at the nape of her neck, looking just as she would for every other anniversary dinner. But instead of us circled around her, urging her to move the game piece shaped like a gingerbread man forward two red squares, her hands are in her lap, and an open bottle of champagne sits on the table. No glass, no coaster.

"What's going on?" I ask, breaking the silence. "Are Dad and Charlie late?"

Mom shakes her head. I take another step into the room, and the tension between us tightens like a wound-up toy. Another step, another turn of the knob.

"Why are Dad's books in the foyer?"

She watches the condensation on the champagne bottle scoot down the side of the glass and pool around the bottom of it, then she lifts it out of its own mess and takes a drink.

"Mom," I push. "What's going on?"

She sets the bottle back down, never tearing her gaze from it, and says, more to the alcohol than to me, "Your dad is moving out." She looks up for my reaction. "We were going to tell you and Charlie together."

I open and close my mouth several times. When I find my voice, I say, "You think your anniversary celebration was a good time to do it?"

"Dylan—"

"No." I step back, releasing some of the pressure. This can't be true. Dad wouldn't leave. He loves Mom. In spite of everything, he loves her. "I don't believe you."

She shrugs. "It's true. He wasn't brave enough to tell you himself."

I shake my head.

"Go look in his room if you need proof." Now that she's said it, I don't need to look. She wouldn't say it if it wasn't true.

"This is your fault," I say, unthinking. Mom doesn't even flinch. She probably expected that reaction, but I take this to mean she agrees with me. "You've been closed off all these years. You've been closed off to all of us. You didn't even try. What did you expect? He'd just keep waiting for you?"

My words are harsh, even to my own ears, but they've swirled around in my head for so long, I can't keep them in anymore.

"How could you let this happen?" I go on from the doorway, quieter. "We already lost Abby. What will be left of our family now?"

Mom's mouth thins at the mention of Abby, but she still makes no move to defend herself, which makes it worse. I want her to say something, anything I can latch on to. I want her to show emotion for once. I want her to fight—fight me, fight for her life, fight for our family. She says nothing.

"Where's Dad?" I ask her, but I'm already pulling my phone out of my pocket. I find his name in my speed dial and tap it.

"He won't answer," she says as I put my phone to my ear. The first ring trills loudly, feeding my agitation. "He won't," she says again.

I cross one arm over myself—a defense mechanism—as I wait for Dad to pick up.

"Why not?"

"Because he's not ready to talk to you," she says. She smudges the condensation on the table with her thumb. "He's too ashamed."

The phone rings again. "Why should he be ashamed? He did everything he could to try to make you happy."

Ring.

Another ring.

Mom stares at the champagne bottle. "Because he slept with another woman."

My immediate reaction is to scoff. That's a hell of a lie to come up with to justify letting a marriage fall apart. Then anger burns through me. A lie like that could ruin my father's reputation. After everything he's done for our family and this community, I won't allow her to erase it all with those six words. Then the phone rings one last time and clicks over to voice mail as a sinking feeling settles into my stomach. If it's a lie, Mom seems to fully believe it. The expression on her face is all too familiar.

I've seen it in the mirror.

"You've reached Greg Michels. I'm sorry I can't take your call..."

The phone slides from my ear, and I hit the End button. Dad always takes my calls. Always.

"I don't believe you," I say again, because I don't want to believe her. Any of it. It's too much. Dad has been so patient with her over the years as he tried to understand her grief, help her through it. He's the most loving man I've ever known. One of them anyway.

My dad...and Cooper.

Mom sits back in her chair and crosses her arms over her chest. "I knew you wouldn't. That's why I've never told you. You idolize your dad. I didn't want to take that away from you."

"How generous," I say, before I realize that if she really is telling the truth, it's not her I should be angry at.

Still, her distance...her coldness. Mom's the one who pulled away. She's the one who stopped loving us. She's the one who treated us like it was our fault Abby died. Who wouldn't go looking for warmth elsewhere? That's how it started for me as a teenager—my desperate search for something to prove I was still worthy of love and, at the same time, that what happened to Abby would never happen to me. I could be with a boy without falling for him, without letting him talk me into something that would ruin my life—something that might end my life.

"What do you mean 'never'?" I ask.

"Dylan, it happened fifteen years ago."

I shake my head. "But that would mean it happened right after…" I trail off.

Could that mean she pulled away for more reasons than Abby's death?

Mom purses her lips, gives the faintest nod.

"That means you've both been lying to me all this time."

She sits up and puts her elbows on the table, leaning her body toward me. "You were still a kid, honey. You didn't need to know what was going on in your parents' personal life. You weren't ready to handle that kind of information. Especially not when you were still grieving for Abby. I'm telling you now because I thought maybe you'd understand?" Her voice goes up at the end like she's unsure, but her narrowed eyes prove she already knows.

"Dad told you about Cooper."

"I wish you would have."

A bitter laugh escapes my lips.

"Really, Mom?" I say. "Would you have made me tea and given me relationship advice?"

She recoils at my words.

"*If* it's true, why are you separating now? It's been fifteen years," I say, as evidence that she couldn't possibly be right. Sure, they sleep in separate rooms and have separate hobbies— her with her garden and cooking and self-medication, him with his business and a boat and a membership to the country club. But they've stayed. You don't get cheated on and stay.

"I know it sounds simple," she says. "We're married. We took vows. But relationships aren't simple. Sometimes you hope things will get better, and sometimes they do. But sometimes they don't. Seeing you go through the same thing, and how hurt you are…how sure you are that you can't get past it… I think we both realized that we haven't gotten past it either, and that it's time to stop pretending."

I swallow back my emotions as I try to process what she's saying—try to stitch together the two pictures of my childhood and my family. They don't line up.

"Why are you telling me all this? Do you want me to be mad at Dad?" I ask. "Because I'm not." The lie tastes metallic on my tongue. I remember my last conversation with him, and how he wanted me to forgive Cooper. And that's how I'm sure it's true. My dad cheated. He didn't just want me to forgive Cooper. He wanted me to forgive him. The floor falls out from beneath me all over again.

"I could have just said your dad was moving out because we fell out of love over the years, but I thought you had the right to know the truth."

"No," I say. "You wanted to make yourself look better. You thought you could use what Cooper did to me to get me on your side, but I'm not like you. I'll never be like you."

Even as I say the words, I fear the evidence to the contrary is stacking against me.

"Dylan, I—"

"No." I put my hand up to stop her.

"I need you to try to understand."

"I needed you to understand, too. I needed you to understand that you aren't the only one who lost Abby. I needed you to understand how important my career is to me. I needed you to understand how much I need you in my life. All I've gotten is disappointment."

Before she can say another word, I walk out.

12

The heat and humidity is nearly unbearable. Just walking from the clinic to my car forms sticky sweat under my arms and on the back of my neck. The whole city seems to be lethargic, everything moving in slow motion. It's worse for my most pregnant patients, tired and achy and ready to be done carrying the extra weight. I sympathize with their discomfort, but I also envy them. For those women, there is a definite time limit for their suffering, and on the horizon, the promise of something worth suffering for. I have no such promise. In fact, as I pull into my driveway one day after work, I fear things are about to get much worse.

I notice my dad's Land Rover first, and then Reese's truck. I maneuver between them to get my car into the garage, my pulse quickening exponentially with every passing second. Both my mom and dad have been trying to call me for the last two days, but I haven't responded to either of them. Marilyn has called several times, too, leading me to assume Cooper has finally broken the news to his parents, but I don't pick up for her either. In light of my parents' divorce, losing the Caldwells from my life is even more painful.

I don't see Dad or Reese in front of the house, and I hope I won't find them together right up until I walk around the house and do. Before I hear a word of their conversation, I already know what they're talking about as Dad watches Reese draw pictures with his hands, listening with rapt attention the same way I did when Reese first explained his vision for my garden to me.

Moving toward them, I catch Dad's eye. He's fresh from the office, still in his suit. He attempts a smile, but his eyes don't meet mine. I never would have thought the man I've always looked up to could be too ashamed to look at me.

I stop before I reach them and clear my throat. "Want to come inside?" I ask Dad.

"I'd love that," he says softly. "Nice to meet you," he says to Reese. Reese pats him on the shoulder, encouraging him like a Little League coach, and I motion Dad toward the door.

When Dad passes me, Reese mouths, "You okay?"

I nod.

In the living room, Dad methodically takes off his coat and hangs it on the rack. He slips off his shoes and leads the way to the couch. The scent of his old Italian cologne trails behind him—a musky, minty smell that I associate with him alone.

"May I sit?" he asks.

I nod. He takes one corner of the couch, and I take the other. Dad fluffs the pillow next to him, glancing everywhere but at me. Finally, he leans forward, puts his elbows on his knees, rubs his hands together.

"Your mom told me you two talked," he says.

I nod again, unable to speak.

"I take it she told you I moved out." A pause. "And why."

"Yes," I whisper.

He sits back and crosses his arms. "I know you're upset with me. And you have every reason to be. It's something

I've never forgiven myself for, and I don't expect you to forgive me either. But…you're an adult, and I feel like you might at least understand. If you're still willing to listen to your old man."

So this is real. My parents are actually divorcing. I believed it in theory, the general idea that my parents wouldn't be living in the same house anymore, but to hear it from my dad's lips, and to see the way his demeanor has already shifted, it becomes palpable. His eyes are clearer, and his face is brighter than I've seen it since I was a little girl. I thought I understood why Mom and Dad drifted apart after Abby died, but according to Mom's timeline, it was more than that. In fact, I'm starting to wonder if it had anything to do with Abby at all. All this time, I thought finding some kind of justice for Abby might bring them back together, but maybe what I've been working myself to death for never would have made a difference anyway.

"I'll listen," I say tentatively, "but Mom's already told me everything."

He nods. "I'm sure she told you her side of the story. I'm sure she painted me as the bad guy, and I don't blame her. I am. I didn't give her any excuses for what I did, and I'm not going to give you any excuses either. You're too smart for that. You always were."

I shift in my seat. I've always reveled in my dad's praise. I've lived to make him proud, to be just like him. But after discovering a secret as big as him cheating on my mom, I question everything he's ever said to me. That's the thing about secrets—they quickly become lies, and lies are a cancer, infecting every good memory, every gesture of love, every truth. He was supposed to teach me how to be strong and how a man treats the woman he loves. Maybe he did. Maybe that's why my relationship followed the same path as his.

"You remember how your mom was," he says. He shakes his head, the memory still fresh—last week instead of ages ago. "She hasn't gotten better over the years. Worse, in fact. I did try to be understanding of what she was going through, but the truth is...she broke my heart. She pushed me away. She didn't want to talk to me. She didn't want me to touch her. Sometimes I would walk into a room, and she would get up and leave. I tried everything I could to make her happy again, but she didn't see it. I was hurting, too, Dylan. But she was so caught up in her own pain, she just didn't care. So I bottled it up." He swallows hard. "And I took the pain of being rejected by her and put the lid on it."

Dad's eyes go glassy, and my own vision blurs. Some of my anger toward him dissipates. It's hard to be mad at him when I've felt the same way about Mom. I guess we all found our own ways to cope. Instead of searching for solace in each other, we found it in other things, other people.

"But how could you do it?" I ask him. "After everything we'd been through already."

"I was stupid, Dylan. I know it will be hard for you to understand, but as a man, to... This is so..." He stops and sighs. "For a man, it often has very little to do with the woman he's with. I know it doesn't make sense, but for me, I felt like less of a man because I didn't know how to make your mom happy. If I couldn't do that one thing, what kind of husband was I? So one night I had too much to drink. A woman came on to me, which made me feel a little better about myself, and I missed your mom. I regretted it while it was happening."

Did Cooper feel like less of a man because he didn't think he could make me happy? Because he thought I didn't love him enough to slow down at work? Because he didn't know the real reason behind my drive, and that it had nothing to do with putting off a life with him?

Dad sniffs and wipes his eyes with the pad of his thumb. I move to get him a tissue, but he reaches out and stops me. I stare at his hand on mine. I squeeze it back.

"I was a weak man that night," he says. "I wish I could take it back every single day. But I can't. And she won't forgive me. Sometimes the hardest thing you can do is leave. But I can't keep living like that. Maybe I don't deserve a better life, but this is the only life I get. Can you understand that?"

I don't respond, but I do understand. There's so little time in this world to make the right decision and then follow through on it. He and I have both experienced that firsthand.

Dad rubs his fingers over his face like he's trying to wash away the pain. He's held my hurts all my life, but before now, I never thought about how many of his own he's had to carry.

"I do understand, Dad. I can talk to Mom," I say. "Maybe coming from someone who can relate to what she's gone through, she'll listen."

Dad shakes his head, but I go on.

"There has to be a way to make her see," I say. "She can't want to live like that either. And she can't want you to go."

He frowns and opens his mouth to contradict me, but I cut him off, pleading.

"We can be a happy family again. I understand now. She'll understand, too."

"Dylan, I'm sorry. It's too late." He holds my hand in both of his, but it's not reassuring like it once was. "Please, do talk to her, though. You two need each other, now more than ever."

"Dad, I…"

"Listen, I know you don't particularly appreciate the woman your mom has turned into. I probably didn't appreciate her enough either. But you have to know that the choices she's made over the years were out of love. For me, and for you. For the whole family. She never wanted to move to the lake. She did it all because she knew it was what I needed, and because she knew it would mean a better life for you kids. So she gave up her own dreams and did what she felt necessary to create the lifestyle she thought we needed. Yeah, it turned her into a woman who's hard to get to know and hard to love, but I'm sure no one is more disappointed about that than her. You've got to cut her some slack, honey."

"She's never cut me any slack, Dad," I say, silent tears slipping down my cheeks. "Where's my unconditional love?"

"She loves you, Dylan."

"Did she tell you that?" I ask, embarrassed at the squeak of desperation in my voice.

"Baby girl," he says with a laugh. "She doesn't have to."

After my dad leaves, I can't sit still with this new information. I pace the house thinking about my parents, about Cooper, about how Abby would feel if she could be here to see what our family has turned into. I don't want to face any of it, so I do what I've always done. I get in my car and drive straight to the clinic. I let myself in the back way, wait for the lights to flicker on in my office and then fall into my rolling chair in front of the computer. I don't open the blinds, and I don't check my neglected email. Instead, I open my grant application and I lean back in my chair.

I close my eyes, and I remember the look on my mom's face as she slammed the door of my childhood home for the last time with Abby alive. I recall the lines of my dad's face on the anniversary of Abby's death this year, the extra finger of bourbon in his glass. I think of my brother, who is alone and may always be because he trusts love as little as I do. My parents' arguments replay in my head, my argument with Cooper and one of the last conversations I had with my sister—the one that led me here. I open my eyes and I type. And it doesn't matter that I don't know when the next grant will become available. This time I'm writing it for me.

For as much as I strive to analyze everything that happens to and around me, it was easier to accept that Cooper's infidelity was random, an aberration that had nothing to do with who he was or the road our relationship had taken. I didn't want to accept any responsibility for the end of us.

After talking to Dad, I can't ignore it anymore. It's been pulled to the forefront of my mind, and this time I want answers. I need to know the facts, whether I like them or not. I'm still not ready to hear them from Cooper, but there's another person who knows what happened that night.

I sit in my car in the back row of the Liquid Courage parking lot. The bar isn't busy yet, but my car isn't the only one here. In a few minutes, the back door will open, and a woman will come out carrying four large, overstuffed trash bags. She'll drag them out effortlessly, even in her high-heeled boots, and toss them one at a time into the Dumpster on the side of the building. I know this because I've sat in this spot for the past two days with the visor pulled down to cover my eyes, the engine off to avoid drawing attention to myself. I've sat here watching her.

On cue, the back door opens, and Kim steps out, two trash bags in each hand. She looks up at the parking lot, scanning it and the sky, like this is the first time she's left the dank sanctum all day. Then she ducks her head, lifts the bags with surprising strength for her small frame and hikes over to the Dumpster. I sit up straighter in my seat, squint and memorize the cadence of each movement, as if it will help me understand what Cooper saw in her that was worth risking our future.

Today she's wearing a pair of skintight jean shorts that cover just enough to be decent, but not enough to leave much to the imagination. She's probably in her midthirties, but a decade freer of responsibilities. It's obvious in the way she walks with her face tilted toward the sun and the way her hips sway, not because she's trying to be sultry—there's no one out here to appreciate it—but because she can't be bothered to move at a quick pace. Instead, she moves fully through each step like a feral cat.

Watching her reminds me of what I see in Reese. Time spent with Reese is time spent chasing a fantasy, a break from the real world. I owe him nothing, and he owes nothing to me. There are no disappointments between us. It's a clean slate.

Kim reaches the Dumpster, uses both hands to flip the lid back, then braces herself with a wide stance and swings each bag into the bin, using her whole body to lift each one. It only takes her a few seconds, as rehearsed as the act is, then she closes the Dumpster lid again and dusts her hands off on the back of her shorts. That's it. That's all she does before she disappears into the bar for the rest of the night.

I sink into my seat when she turns back to the building. I don't know why I come here or what I expect to find. She's not going to have an explanation of their tryst tattooed across her midriff.

I sit up and reach for my keys hanging from the ignition, but just when I've decided never to come back here, before Kim grabs for the door handle, she stops. I look around, searching for whatever caught her attention. She's still for ten swift beats of my heart, and then, before I can duck or breathe or disappear inside my own self-pity, she looks at me.

For a moment, I freeze, sure she's only looking in my general direction, not at my pale face half hidden by my visor and sunglasses. But then, even at this distance, I clearly see her lift an eyebrow and give one quick nod toward the building. She narrows her eyes at me to make sure I've gotten the message, then pulls the door open and enters the bar.

She must have seen me sitting here. Yesterday, the day before. She must know who I am.

Before I can change my mind, I open the car door and cross the blacktop. I have nothing to fear, I assure myself. There's nothing left to lose.

Once the heavy bar door falls closed behind me, it could be afternoon or midnight. The lack of windows makes the place tomb-like. I never noticed before, when the place was teeming with locals and major league sports broadcasting from every TV. Now it's only a few people setting up for a slow weeknight. Kim stands behind the bar, filling the condiment tray, like she's forgotten about me already.

I approach the bar, weaving through tables and chairs. The jukebox is off, but a hum of country music plays overhead. There are two men on the other side of the bar drinking quietly by themselves.

When I reach the bar and place my hands on the sloping carved wood, Kim says, "What can I get you?" She's served us many times before, when I've come here with Cooper, Stephen and Megan, but the deep pitch of her voice seems more noteworthy this time. Silky. Sensual. Untrustworthy.

"I didn't come here for a drink."

"C'mon. It's on the house." She finally looks up at me. Her brown eyes sweep over me without giving anything away.

"No, thanks."

She turns to grab a bottle of vodka, places a shot glass in front of me and fills it up. A few drops land on the bar top, and she swipes them away with a cocktail napkin. She sticks her hand out to offer a seat, but I refuse that, too.

"Something on your mind?" she asks and goes back to arranging maraschino cherries. She knows exactly what's on my mind, that I'm sure of. Her nonchalance about it is amusing. She thinks she holds the power here.

"You remember me?" I ask. She glances at me but says nothing. I take it as a yes. Already tired of her games, I get to the point. "Do you remember Cooper? Cooper Caldwell?"

Again, she looks at me without responding, but the answer is clear in the tic of her jaw muscle. I wait her out. After a moment of silence, she empties her hands, wipes them on the apron around her waist and faces me.

"Yes," she says. "I remember him."

Pain blooms in the center of my chest. I'm here to try to understand, but that doesn't mean it doesn't hurt to picture them together, which is made all the easier with her standing in front of me. I don't let her see it. The pain I feel doesn't belong to her. She doesn't deserve to have such an effect on me.

"Did you see him outside of the bar?"

She lifts an eyebrow—one sleek, sexy eyebrow. Stephen often commented on how attractive she was when Megan wasn't with us. I kicked him under the table every time he did.

"Yes," she says.

"Did you...?" I can't bring the words to my lips. Her eyes darken, though. She doesn't need me to finish.

"Yes." No hesitation. No sugarcoating. No apology. I write the entire scene in my head. Him sitting in the stool that now stands empty next to me. Him complaining to her about me. Having a few too many shots. Staying past closing time. Following her out the front door. Kissing against her car. Or was it his? Slipping inside. Going back to her place. Or maybe they never made it that far. Maybe it happened right there in the parking lot.

My logic wavers.

"Say it," I whisper. "Say it out loud so I... So my life hasn't been torn apart because of a misunderstanding."

She purses her lips and tilts her chin up. I understand her expression. She's impressed.

After a pause, she says, "Yes, I slept with Cooper." One of the guys across the bar looks up at us. I ignore him and give her one sharp nod.

I weigh my options. I could hit her. Drag her around the bar by her hair until someone calls the cops. I could dissolve into tears and beg her to disappear and pretend the whole thing never happened. Many women would do one or the other in my position, but I feel no desire to do any of those things. Instead, I sit down on the stool next to me, pick up the vodka and take a sip. It burns down my throat and all the way up into my nose.

Kim hasn't moved, hardly even blinked.

"You have no shame, do you?"

She shrugs. "Listen, Dylan—"

"Don't say my name. I never gave it to you. You don't know anything about me."

A grin plays at her lips. She must have expected a weaker woman to walk in here, if she expected to be confronted at all. She must have expected someone who would be intimidated by her beauty and confidence and the forceful role she played in breaking down another woman. Not me. She doesn't win unless I let her. And I won't.

"Listen," she starts again, "your relationship is with him, not me. I haven't broken any rules or lied to anybody. That's between you two." I appreciate that she didn't say his name again. I couldn't stand to hear how familiar the word would be when it rolled off her tongue.

I pick up the shot glass and choke down the rest, then stand and turn to leave. I stop.

"Thanks for being honest," I say over my shoulder. That wipes the smile from her face, and for the first time, I see some humility in her.

I break out into the fading evening light and blink away the darkness. As I walk to my car, I have no strategy or analytical assessment of the situation. I thought coming here would help me put a lid on Cooper's one-night stand, but there are no labels or categories or clean-cut understandings when it comes to love. Not even for me, no matter how much I try.

"Wait!" I hear from behind me, as well as heavy footsteps approaching quickly. "Wait."

When I turn, Kim halts a few feet in front of me. She shades her eyes with her hand, and a breeze whips her hair around her face. She really is beautiful. I'm not sure if that hurts more, or if it makes it easier to accept.

"He loves you," she says.

I snort. "Yeah, he's done a great job of proving that."

She shrugs and nods toward the bar behind her. "I spend a lot of time around men, and they don't do a whole hell of a lot that makes sense. But…he was a mess. Because of you. He loves you and…he was hurt. Drunk, too."

"So you took advantage of a man in a fragile state."

Her lips curl, and her nose wrinkles. She sniffs, and for one crazy second, I think she might cry. "I'm not proud of it," she says. "Trust me when I tell you, there aren't many good ones out there. I thought for one night…" She shakes her head and trails off, looks over her shoulder like she's waiting for someone to call her back. Then she locks eyes with me and says, "You have a good one. If I were you, I wouldn't let that go."

She holds my gaze as she takes a few steps backward, then turns away and strides back to the bar.

Saturday morning, I sit on the back step with my hands wrapped around a cup of coffee, watching Spencer attack individual blades of grass. It's early—much too early for a Saturday—but I was tired of tossing and turning, so I got out of bed and started on the caffeine. It's going to be a hot day. Already the sun has warmed my skin to almost sweating.

When a shadow crosses in front of me, it's so natural to assume it's Reese, I forget he's not supposed to be here today, not on the weekend. But I look up and it is him. The early morning sun emanates from behind him, so I can only see parts of his face; but I recognize his stance, his muddy boots, the way my head clouds when he's around. I squint up at him.

"Hi," he says.

"Hi," I breathe.

"Are you on call?" he asks.

I shake my head. He comes over to sit next to me. There's little space here, so the sides of our bodies are pressed together. It awakens me more effectively than the caffeine. I should fight these feelings, but I'm tired of fighting everything. Life could be easier if I just let go.

"Why are you here?" I ask.

"To make sure you're okay. I haven't seen you all week. I wondered how things went with your dad." He rubs his leg against mine, prodding me for an answer. "So, are you okay?"

I shake my head, being honest for once.

"What's wrong?"

"Everything," I say. "My parents are divorcing."

I tell him because I know he understands what it's like to have parents who aren't together. I tell him because I want to.

He frowns. "Why?"

"He cheated."

He sucks air in between his teeth, as if burned. "You're mad at him?" he asks like he already knows the answer.

I nod.

After a minute, he says, "Now what?"

"Hell if I know. You seem to have all the answers."

He chuckles softly. "Hardly. I just pay attention."

"And what do you see now?" I ask. I'm no longer afraid of his analyses. I might be better off if I start listening to them.

"Either you're very hungry...or you're about to have a complete emotional breakdown."

I burst into laughter, because what else can I do when things get so bad it's like life itself—or the "Universe," as Reese calls it—is plotting against me? Reese laughs, too. When I feel his fingers suddenly on the side of my face, I stop breathing. He traces my hairline with his index finger and tucks the loose strands behind my ear. Then he wipes a tear from the corner of my eye. I hadn't felt it there. His light eyes are so focused in on me, I can't look directly at them.

"What?" I breathe.

"Maybe you're closer than you think," he says.

"To what?"

"Understanding."

"Understanding what?"

"Whatever it is you need to understand."

"You're infuriating," I say and force myself to take a deep breath. His full lips spread into a smile. My heart pounds.

"You're fascinating." His fingertips on my skin are a shock to my brain, his words a shock to my heart. I reach up and wrap my fingers around his, lower them from my face.

"I can assure you I'm not."

"You don't give yourself enough credit."

I shake my head. "Don't get yourself worked up over me. I'm a mess," I say and sigh. "I just can't believe this is happening all over again."

"Again?" he asks. I realize my mistake. I never told Reese that Cooper cheated on me. Even after months to come to terms with it, I'm still carrying the shame of being the kind of woman who could be cheated on. I know I'm not perfect, but I thought I was worth more than that. I don't want Reese to see me that way, too.

Instead of explaining, I ask, "What makes a man cheat?"

"I wouldn't know," Reese says. "But…I can imagine it has a lot to do with their masculinity. Sex is power, right? If a man feels powerless in the life he's living…" He trails off, but the insinuation is there. Did my dad feel powerless to help Mom through her grief? Did Cooper feel powerless to help me through mine?

"It's not an excuse," I say, the hurt stinging my heart all over again.

"No," he says. "But it's human."

I shake my head. Sure, I did the same thing after Abby's death—searching for comfort in other people—but with one major difference. I never hurt anyone. I had no commitment to anyone, and I made no promises. Not until Cooper. And I've always been faithful to Cooper.

"It's bullshit," I say, and stand up. Startled, Reese stands, too.

"Dylan," Reese says, reaching out and stopping me with a hand on my waist. I bat it away.

"You have to stop that," I nearly shout. "What are you trying to do to me?"

He bows his head and steps back. "I'm sorry," he says, the

first time he's apologized for anything. "I guess I misunderstood."

But then, maybe he hasn't.

"I'm sorry…if I implied anything more than enjoying your company. But…"

I think of Cooper. We're not together, but it doesn't seem right to think of anyone else. He still has clothes in *our* closet, in *our* house. His dog is standing mere feet from me.

"Dr. Caldwell then?" he asks.

I loop my hair behind my ear. "You have to go."

I step into the yard, hop over the ditch, and walk around the side of the house. I don't know where I'm going or what I'm doing, but I feel like I could walk away from this house and never look back. Unfortunately, Reese is behind me every step of the way, and I think he would follow me wherever I ended up, just to hold me together or break me apart. I can't tell anymore.

"Don't leave upset." He finally gets ahead of me, but this time he keeps his hands to himself.

"I'm not upset."

He raises his eyebrows. I can't think with him so close, with those eyes digging past the walls I've worked so hard to construct. He's just a man, I remind myself. Just like the rest of them.

My breathing comes more rapidly as he lifts one hand toward me, testing me. I let him place it on my waist, and it sends shivers through my body. He places his right hand on the other side and guides me closer to him. I can't look up. I don't trust myself to. Somehow, over the last couple of months, my friendship with Reese has shifted into something more. I don't know how it started or who blurred the boundaries, but here we are. Here I am, finding comfort in another once again.

I place my hands on his and remove them from my body, pushing him away. I don't look up at him until I'm free of his touch.

"You have to go," I say. "Or I will."

13

That evening, I turn the water off and slip into the tub, inch by inch. The bubbles consume my limbs and then my middle until I am submerged up to my neck. I lean back to dip my ears underneath, searching for the thick silence. I detach myself for a little while, close my eyes and try to pretend that I'm the only person who exists, that this tub is the only thing left in the world and that if I tried really hard, I could melt right into the hot water. I slip underneath the surface, and the heat stings my face. The bubbles fill in the hole above me like I was never there.

I sit in the tub until the water is cold and my hair has dried, watching the water leak, drop by drop, from the faucet. The only indication that the rest of the world outside is still moving comes when I hear a knock on the bathroom door hours later. I start before I remember there's only one other person who has a key to the house.

"You're not supposed to drop by without asking," I say. I try to insert frustration into my voice, but I don't have it in me today. Truthfully, I find some relief in him coming back.

After our last conversation, I was sure he hated me. And I couldn't entirely blame him.

"Are you okay in there?" Cooper asks, his voice muffled.

"I'm fine," I say, fighting my contradicting emotions—hoping he'll go away quickly, so I don't have to acknowledge the confusing voice inside me begging him to stay.

I don't want to be alone. I'd let anyone stay if they'd distract me from the questions circling in my head, one of them being if Cooper would have ever loved me at all if he'd known that first night that he would never fully break through my walls. Or would I have, instead, not even been worth a memory. Just an "oh, yeah" if Stephen ever asked, "Hey, what ever happened with…"

That's why, no matter how relieved I am to hear his voice, he has to leave. I can't further muddy our relationship by making the same choice I made the night I met him—secrets and solace.

There is a long pause before Cooper asks, "Can I come in?" Through the door he sounds embarrassed by the question, as if he doesn't have the landscape of my body memorized.

As I'm about to say "no," the door clicks open, and Cooper slips in, careful not to look in my direction. My hands float to the spots over my breasts to provide a small amount of privacy, the bubbles long gone. He sits on the toilet, facing away, his shirt untucked and hanging around him.

"What is it?" I ask.

"I came by to drop off more food for Spencer," he says. "I saw your car in the garage, but you didn't answer, so I got worried."

"I'm fine," I say.

Even through the back of his head, I can see the frown he's wearing. Or maybe I'm imagining it there because I've memorized the landscape of his body, too.

"There's a bottle of wine sitting on the kitchen counter."

"It's just wine."

"It's never just wine with you, Dylan." He knows as well as I do that wine is my balm for the particularly bad days. After a pause, he asks, "Do you want to talk about it?"

I shake my head, though he can't see me. I shift against the porcelain that's growing more uncomfortable by the minute. My fingers and toes are pruned beyond recognition.

After a long silence, he says, "Can I help?"

"There's nothing to do. Besides, it's not your job to worry about me anymore."

"I never worried about you out of obligation. I do it because I love you. You can kick me out a hundred times, and that won't change."

"Cooper, please, don't." I'm trying to sound angry, but my voice is watery and breaks at the end of my plea.

He sighs. "I'm sorry. I'm not trying to upset you." I can tell it's hard for him not to turn to me, look me in the eye. It's where he finds the words on my tongue before I speak them.

My fingers ache with the need to reach out to him, to turn him to face me, to curl up in his lap, let him hold me and ease the pain away. It takes all my willpower not to. But it wouldn't be fair to him, not when half my fears are for losing a friendship with another man and the other half are for a family he can no longer be a part of. He doesn't move either. He sits there on the toilet seat, hunched over to rest his chin on his palm, like he wants to be close to me for a little longer.

"Can I make you dinner?" he finally asks.

"I'm not hungry," I say softly, my argument thinning.

"Can I pour you some wine?"

I sigh, a mournful smile below the surface. "Okay," I whisper.

When I come out of the bathroom fifteen minutes later,

though, Cooper is gone. I peek out the front window and his car is gone, too. It's probably for the best, but I can't deny my disappointment. I had no right to let him stay in the first place. I'm the one who asked him to leave. I'm the one who told him it was over and that we both needed to move on.

But as I'm staring at the soil where my daisies should have been months ago, I hear the front door open and close, and a moment later Cooper appears in the kitchen with grocery bags.

"Sorry," he says, breathing heavily. "I didn't want to bother you again. Bruschetta?"

"Sure," I say, feeling a twisted sense of relief when I know I shouldn't.

He walks up next to me and peers out the window into the backyard.

"What are you looking at?" I ask.

He shakes his head and says, "Nothing."

We make the bruschetta together. With every step Cooper makes, he stumbles, hesitates and looks to me for approval in his own house that is no longer his home. He keeps his distance, but I feel his every movement. Our connection remains unbroken like a high-pitched vibration only we can hear—a sound so strong nothing drowns it out, not even all the other noise between us.

The wine helps. I peel the tomatoes; he slices the bread. We walk around each other, careful not to touch, but the hyperawareness this requires means we don't talk. I'm okay not talking, just having him here. I know it's dangerous to pretend, for even a moment, that we could go back…that he never left. But it's such a sweet salve to my lonely heart.

"So how's the apartment hunt going?" I finally ask.

"Fine," he says with a shrug. "Actually, I haven't been looking, to be honest."

"Oh."

"I mean, it's not because I expect you to change your mind. I don't. Don't worry. It's just… I guess if I move into a place of my own, it's official. I'm not ready for that yet."

I stop chopping. I don't know how he does it—wear his heart on his sleeve. I chance a glance in his direction. His expression is grave. I knew he'd have a hard time on his own, but it hurts to see the reality on his face. He's never lived alone before. Neither have I, but being alone has never bothered me.

"Maybe you don't have to be alone, though. Couldn't you stay with your parents for a while? Or Megan?" I gauge him, watching his eyes for a flicker of hurt at being left out of her pregnancy.

"I couldn't live with my parents again. And… I don't know… Megan's been avoiding me. Maybe Mom told her about us, and she's mad at me or something." He shrugs, but I can see it bothers him. I wish I could tell him the truth to unburden him, but it's not my truth to tell.

"Stephen?" I ask. I've been avoiding him at work, not sure of where our relationship stands without Cooper or Megan in it and not ready to face another disappointment.

"Maybe," Cooper says, but I can tell he's humoring me.

"You haven't told him either," I guess. His lack of response confirms it. Maybe he's not as open with his feelings as I thought.

Cooper crosses to the sink to fill a pot with water.

"I went to visit that patient at the hospital today. The kid I told you about. His parents had brought him into the office for a cold a couple of months ago. Then again a couple of weeks later. And then a couple weeks after that. Finally, I sent him over to the hospital to get some more tests done."

"What's wrong with him?"

He stops and puts the pot down to wipe his cheek with the inside of his collar. "It's cancer," he whispers.

"Oh, Cooper."

"He wasn't getting better because his body was too busy fighting the leukemia."

"I'm so sorry."

He returns to the food and I let him. I know how staying busy eases the pain. I can't imagine what Cooper must be feeling. It's my worst fear—losing a patient. Being responsible for the loss of a life.

"I know we're doctors and this kind of thing is going to happen from time to time, but he's a kid, you know?" he says as he works. "Maybe I'm naive, but being in pediatrics, I just didn't expect it. I don't know how to handle something like this. I'm glad I'm not the one who has to tell his parents."

"They don't know yet?"

"They're going to the hospital tonight after his dad gets off work. I keep imagining the look on their faces when they hear the news. Over and over it plays in my head." Cooper pauses. "I'm sorry. I didn't mean to make tonight about me."

"Don't apologize."

I want to go to him and wrap my arms around him, but I stop myself. Instead, I swirl my wine around the glass, pick up a piece of tomato with my fingers and suck it into my mouth. The juice drips down my hand. I wipe it off on my pants. As I chew, I notice Cooper is watching me.

"Something has changed," Cooper says.

"What?" I ask. He doesn't answer right away. He studies me further.

"I don't know," he says. "Something about you is different."

"About me?" I laugh, because if anything has changed, it's that more of my sanity and strength have been chipped away, and at an alarming rate. I feel vulnerable in a way I never have before, no longer able to hold myself together, no longer able to put on a facade. "I don't think so."

"I think so," he says.

He sweeps his gaze over me again, then locks eyes with me until I can't move. My heart beats faster, and I'm breathless under the power of his longing, the way he grips the counter as if physically stopping himself from coming to me. His hands must lose the battle because after a long, wordless moment, he steps forward and pushes me against the sink. Either the alcohol or the need for some semblance of normalcy in my life keeps me from stopping him. He presses his forehead against mine and, gently, he kisses my cheeks, whisper soft. He brushes his lips over my forehead and nose, and my own lips tingle in anticipation of what will come next. Instead, he bites his bottom lip and closes his eyes. I close mine, too. My chest rises, further closing the space between us, then falls.

"I should go," Cooper says.

We're emotional and treading in dangerous waters, and we both know it. Without opening my eyes, I nod. I feel his hands slip from my body, and my skin is icy where they once were.

"Good night," he says.

"Good night."

He hovers there for another moment, then takes one last sip of his wine and leaves.

I finish making my bruschetta alone, and all the fears creep back in, along with one more: that I will never get over Cooper.

My phone rings later that night as I'm lying in bed, still imagining Cooper's touch in the privacy of the dark. I expect it to be the hospital, but when I place the phone against my ear, an unexpected voice says my name. Cooper's voice.

"Oh," I say, sitting up. "Hi, Coop—" I stop myself and clear my throat. I'm not sure if it's appropriate to call him by that nickname anymore. "Hi, Cooper."

There's an uncertain pause, a question. It's late. I worry that something is wrong. I worry that it's Megan, but I can't ask.

"Is everything okay?"

"Oh, yeah. Everything's fine," he says.

"Oh," I say. Then, "Good."

I wait for more, anticipation buzzing through my veins.

"It was good to see you tonight," he finally says.

I hesitate, then melt back into bed. I shouldn't be letting him say these things to me. I shouldn't feel so happy that he is.

"It was," I say.

"I...I miss you."

I open my mouth to return the words, my heart thrumming a beat against my chest. "I...know," I say. I scrunch my eyes shut.

We're silent for a while, and then he says, "Dylan?"

His voice still makes my heart speed up. And then I hear the faintest sound of someone calling, "Coop," on the other end of the line. A woman's voice.

I hang up the phone before I hear any more and bring my fingers to my lips. They're cool with shock. I shouldn't be surprised. What Cooper does with his life no longer involves me. I know that. I shouldn't have let myself get caught up in the moment. And yet, I sit there staring at my phone in my hand for minutes, hours, days, wondering why the stars stopped lining up for us.

The labor and delivery unit doors open seven minutes after a page from Enrique, and I nearly run headlong into him where he waits for me with a surgical gown.

"You told me there was coffee," I say.

"I'm making it just the way you like it," he says. "That fresh pot will be an hour stale by the time you finish up here."

"You know me too well."

I let him slip the gown over my arms as he updates me on Erika's progress. I've been monitoring her labor via phone for the better part of the day.

"She reached ten centimeters five minutes ago and has already done some practice pushes," he tells me. "You're good to go."

I follow him to the delivery room door, and he opens it for me. Before I walk through, I stop to take a steadying breath. No matter how many times I cross this threshold into these rooms that are my second home, I still have to tame the butterflies in my stomach. I do it because, regardless of the patient's condition, there is no more important part of my job than bringing an air of confidence to the situation.

"How are you, Erika?" I ask as I enter the room. Several nurses shuffle silently from one side of the room to another, grabbing supplies and preparing them on sterilized tray tables. I greet them all with a nod and a smile while I scrub in, then I take a seat in front of Erika as a nurse rolls a chair underneath me.

The room is dim aside from the delivery lights overhead. Andrew holds Erika's hand and wears an expression of panic and awe. The mom-to-be is already on her back with her legs pulled up to her chest, strands of thick black hair stuck to her forehead with sweat. Her face is red, and her eyes are glazed over with pain. I adopt the soft voice I reserve for the delivery room.

"How is she doing?" I ask Andrew.

"Amazing." He sounds composed, though he nods his head vigorously.

Erika gives a low, guttural moan, and I can tell without checking that she's ready to go. I can always hear that subtle shift in a woman's voice from being overwhelmed by the pain of labor to being in control of it. I glance at the monitor over her right shoulder to ensure a normal fetal heart rate. When the contraction graph indicates the current one has waned, I speak to her again.

"You're doing fantastic. I know it's tough, but it's almost over. Are you ready to meet your baby?" I ask her.

She gives a pained smile, and a tear streaks down her cheek into her hair as she nods. "Yes. *Dios mío, por favor,*" she moans.

The next contraction begins to rise. Erika has a nurse next to her who holds one foot and encourages Andrew to hold the other. The warm delivery lights hum above me. As I run two gloved fingers over the crown of the baby's head and a tuft of thick, black hair, I hear Andrew whisper to his wife, "You can do this. You're almost there."

I focus my attention on Erika's eyes, while my hands fall into position instinctively.

"It's time," I say to Erika. "If you feel ready, I want you to push." She whimpers uncertainly, but I know she's strong. "Your baby is right here. I can feel his head. Let's introduce him to the world."

She chokes back a sob and nods. "Okay."

Erika takes a deep breath, and when the contraction peaks, she braces herself and noiselessly thrusts the baby downward. Andrew's knuckles whiten as Erika clamps down on his hand, and her lips purse together until they're white, too.

"Again," I say and watch the baby breach the threshold. Erika takes another deep breath and then grunts as she bears down. Other than the nurse counting beside her, the room is silent with anticipation. Every number reverberates in my ears. "Can you give me one more?"

She does, and the baby crowns, emerging from her womb.

"Keep pushing. Keep pushing," I urge.

With one more count of ten, the baby's head slips out, and I cradle it in my hands like blown glass. Erika gasps for air and drops her head back on the pillow. The baby's swollen face is tinged with purple, and my heart skips a beat, but my training kicks in before the panic.

"Hold it for one second," I say and run my fingers around the baby's neck. The umbilical cord is wrapped around once, so I work my fingers gently underneath it and loosen it until I can loop it over its head. I check the baby's heartbeat on the monitor—too low—then take the bulb sucker from the nurse at my shoulder and sweep the baby's mouth and nose.

I peer up at Erika between the frame of her legs, all business.

"This is it," I say. "One more big push. Give it everything you've got. Here we go."

I take a big, synchronized breath with her and watch as the baby bulges out, and then, in a split second, a tiny body slides into my palms. In every way, I feel the weight of a life in my hands, and as blood pumps loudly in my ears, the movement around me fades into the background like static on an old radio.

He's a boy. So perfect, with little hands and little feet. A precious head with sticky black hair. The sweetest combination of his mother and father in a tiny bundle that will bond them together forever. When he fears monsters in the closet, he'll lie between them in their bed, and they'll sing him to sleep. In ten years, his weekly soccer games will bring them side by side in the stands, even if only for an hour when taking time off work for a vacation is impossible. In twenty years, when they look at each other like strangers and wonder why they stayed, he will always be the answer.

And he's limp.

"Dr. Michels." Enrique's sharp voice snaps me back to the hospital room, and he snatches the baby from my hands. Another nurse cuts through the umbilical cord, and he's whisked away.

"What's happening?" Erika shrieks, but no one answers

her as everyone but me crowds around the warming table, frantically buzzing above the child, pulling equipment closer, grabbing more blankets. "Is he okay?"

My mouth goes dry, and I feel beads of sweat form across my forehead and prickle under my arms.

What did I do wrong?

Erika stirs in the bed like she might try to escape it, but I pull myself back to the moment and reach out to steady her. I swallow hard and palpate her abdomen, clinging to procedure to keep the situation under control.

"Tell me what's going on," Erika shrieks.

This isn't the first time a baby has come out with the umbilical cord wrapped around its neck, and this isn't the first time a baby has needed resuscitation after birth, but this is the first time I've ever felt a baby so lifeless.

This isn't happening. I chose this profession to make sure this didn't happen. I live my whole life at this hospital to make sure this doesn't happen.

My breathing is shallow, but I face Erika with a facade of reassurance.

"Erika, you have an experienced team of people over there taking care of your baby, I promise you that. I know it's hard, but they need to focus on doing their job right now, and I need to focus on doing mine. Let me take care of you, so that when your baby is ready for you, you will be ready for him, okay?"

"Him?" she asks.

I nod.

Her body jolts with each escaped sob, and Andrew looks back and forth between me and the huddle of nurses in the corner, clearly unsure of whether he should stay with his wife or go to the baby.

"Give them their space," I say to him quietly. Half of my

attention is on gently tugging the umbilical cord, while the other half is listening to every zing of sterilized tools being released from the packaging, every hushed prayer exchanged by the nurses. I pick up the suturing needle, but my hand is shaking so badly, I don't trust it to do its job. I take a few steadying breaths.

"Give me just a minute," I say so softly I'm not sure if anyone hears me, and place the needle back on the tray.

I assess the situation.

Erika's bleeding is normal. Andrew is there to take care of her. He won't be losing a wife today.

But the baby behind me still isn't crying. I won't allow this sweet, young couple to suffer the loss of their child. Not them.

I rise from my chair and break through the nurses in the corner to find the boy as pale and ashen as death. The warming lamps beat down on my hair as I wedge myself into the group and lean over the plastic barrier of the baby warmer to touch his icy paper skin. I know the nurses' procedure as well as my own. I know they've suctioned his lungs and stomach. I know they've cleared all airways. I know they've called the neonatal nurse practitioner. All that's left to do is to perform CPR, and so I do, because I can't sit over there and do nothing while the threat of losing a child hangs over my head. I place my fingers over the center of his rib cage and thrust them down with so much force, I'm afraid I'll do more harm than good. After a moment of stillness and confusion amongst the nurses, I recognize Enrique's hands as they return to stimulating whatever circulation there might be in the baby's arms and legs. Another nurse places the oxygen mask to the baby's nose and mouth, and he's so small, it covers most of his face.

"C'mon. C'mon," I say. The baby looks helpless with his little features staring up at me, pleading for a chance at life. I swat a loose hair away from my eyes with the sleeve of my gown.

Nothing.

Nothing.

It's too late.

It's too late.

It can't be too late.

"I've got it," a voice says at my side, and two hands reach in around the baby. I step away and allow the space to be filled by the neonatal nurse. I stumble over my feet, my hands still outstretched until the tiny body is blocked from view. I turn to Enrique, staring at him without seeing him. My heavily beating heart tracks the passage of time as it thrums in my ears. After the longest minute of my life, Enrique reaches out to me, but I step back. I'm not the one who needs to be consoled.

"Do you want me to page Dr. Galloway to finish up with Mrs. Martinez?" he asks. I can barely hear him over the quiet roar of the nurses working behind me.

I've never lost a patient before.

Not this couple.

"No," I say immediately and look away from the pity on his face. "No," I say again, more to myself than to him.

I snap off my gloves and dispose of them without another glance behind me. I return to Erika's side where she cries uncontrollably, craning her head for any glimpse of her lost child. I glance back and forth between mother and father, seeing their anguished cries but not hearing them. For now, I do the only thing that's left to do. I take Erika's hand and hold it in mine while the baby is wheeled away.

14

Promise you won't tell anyone.

The familiar rapid rhythm of my heart transports me back to my sister's bedroom in my parents' house, and for a minute the delivery room fades away and all I see is the fear in my sister's eyes as she tells me she's pregnant at eighteen...a statistic. After catching her with her head in the toilet one Saturday morning and calling to Mom for help, she'd shushed me, wiped her mouth and dragged me into her room with the promise of a secret written in her fearful eyes. I never expected what she'd tell me next or the impossible position she would put me in.

"Dylan, say it out loud," she told me. "You have to promise you won't tell Mom and Dad. Not yet. Mom's going to kill me." Her green eyes had pooled with water. I was in too much shock to cry. I'd looked down at our hands, clasped together on her baby-pink bedspread. Ironic, I remember thinking.

"Abby, I don't want to. I don't think it's a good idea. You know I can't lie to Dad."

"I'm not asking you to lie. I'm just asking you not to say anything. If Dad specifically asks you if I'm pregnant, I give you full permission to tell him." A nervous laugh escaped her lips. She tucked her silky blond hair behind her ear. "Sis, please. You're the only one I can trust. I need you."

And that was the clincher—she hadn't told her friends, she'd told me. I bit my lip, and going against my better judgment, I nodded. When she swept me up into her arms and told me I was the best sister a girl could ask for, I thought I'd made the right decision. What kind of sister threw her best friend under the bus in her time of greatest need?

But three days later, she pulled me into the bathroom and locked the door. She'd been holed up in her bedroom since after lunch. Under the harsh lighting in the bathroom, she looked like a ghost. "Something's wrong," she whispered frantically. "I'm cramping. I don't know what to do."

"Why are you telling me?" I asked her, my voice rising with panic. I was only sixteen. What did I know about pregnancy? I'd hardly kissed a boy. "You need to tell Mom and Dad now."

"No, Dylan. No," she urged. She pulled me farther into the bathroom, holding on to me like she expected me to burst out of the bathroom or take flight. But she was my older sister, and she trusted me. I would never risk that. "I just need to go to the doctor. Will you take me?"

It was eight o'clock. I didn't know how I'd get her to a doctor at that hour, but I knew I wasn't going to let her down.

"Wait here," I told her. I stepped toward the door, and my hands slipped from hers. I'll never forget her wide eyes, her reddened cheeks.

By the time I made it to the bottom of the stairs, I had a plan. I told Mom I was going to spend the night at my friend's house around the corner and that Abby was going to drop me off. I told her Abby would probably hang out for a while before coming back home. Mom was so happy to hear

I had a friend that she agreed to the lies without any further questions.

While Mom was cooking and Charlie was in his room playing video games, I packed a bag and sneaked Abby down the stairs. She had her arms wrapped around her middle and walked hunched over. Every once in a while, a low moan escaped her lips, but she kept quiet. We tiptoed past Dad's study, where he was reading the newspaper. We slipped out into the night, and I helped her into the passenger side of the car, then drove her to the nearest hospital.

We sat in the waiting room for an hour before someone finally called us into the back. By that time, Abby had broken out in a sweat, her cheeks were more flushed than before and her moaning had grown uncontrollable. I had to wrap her arm over my shoulders to get her back to the tiny room with little more than a shower curtain for privacy.

"What seems to be the problem?" the gruff doctor asked, looking down at the paperwork I'd filled out for her when we arrived. He must have been in his late fifties, his jowls hanging from his jaw like his cheeks were melting and his shaggy silver hair as tired as he was.

"She's cramping and nauseous," I answered for Abby, rubbing her back as I spoke. In a thinner voice, I said, "And she's pregnant."

"Have you been to an OB/GYN yet?" he asked.

Abby focused on her lap and shook her head.

The doctor looked over her paperwork a moment longer, unconcerned. He saw bleeding head wounds and gunshot victims and people with exploding appendixes on a regular basis. What were a few stomach cramps?

"All right," he said. "Go ahead and lie back, and I'll take a look."

I helped Abby onto her back, though she was reluctant to

uncurl herself. The paper crinkled beneath her, and I stood behind her head, using my fingers to pull her hair away from her face and blowing on her forehead to cool her.

"How far along are you?" the doctor asked.

"Just a few weeks," Abby said through gritted teeth. "Five, I think."

"And how long have you been feeling the symptoms?" The doctor pushed his fingers into her abdomen, and she winced.

"Since after lunch," she said.

He asked her a few more questions and gave her a quick examination. Finally, he said, "Miscarriages can happen this early on, but if you're not bleeding, I'm not concerned. It's probably just that stomach flu that's going around. We've seen a lot of cases in the last few weeks, and it's all the same symptoms. I can't do anything for it. All you can do is stay hydrated. If you start to bleed, come back right away."

"That's it?" Abby asked.

"That's it. And get an appointment with your OB/GYN scheduled."

He tipped his head toward us, then disappeared.

The drive over to my friend's house was silent aside from Abby's occasional moans.

"Do you want some Gatorade? Crackers?" I asked her, trying to convince myself the doctor was right.

"No. I just want to sleep." She had her eyes closed, and her head leaned back on the headrest.

"I don't want to leave you when you're not feeling well. Especially if no one else knows. Someone should be there in case you need to go back to the hospital."

"I'll be fine," she said. "You go to Lauren's. Her parents won't care if you just show up. Their house has a revolving door for the neighborhood."

I wanted to argue with her, but that had never worked in

all our sixteen years of being sisters. "Let me at least drive you home. I can walk to Lauren's."

"Dylan, if we don't stick to the plan, Mom will be suspicious."

"We should tell—"

"Don't," she said, cutting me off. "You know if Mom and Dad know, they will want to involve Christian's family, and I never want to lay eyes on that asshole again."

So we stuck with the plan. She dropped me off at Lauren's and drove herself home. I made her call me when she got there. I tried to focus on the scary movies we watched that night, boy talk, be a normal teenager who wasn't worried about pregnancy and babies. But my mind was on Abby. As soon as the sun rose the next morning, I sneaked out of Lauren's house and walked home. I saw the flashing lights of the ambulance down the street, and my heart went wild. I ran the rest of the way home, getting there just in time to see the paramedics bringing Abby down the stairs on a stretcher. Mom had her hands covering her mouth as she followed them, sobbing. Dad gripped Abby's lifeless hand with one of his own and reached out for mine with the other. I didn't take it, too stunned to grasp the simple gesture. Charlie clung to me from behind, and we watched them disappear out the front door, slamming it behind them.

Three days later, as we stood over Abby's grave, and the minister droned on about the loss of a young life, Mom leaned toward Dad, and I heard her whisper, "Why didn't she tell us? If we'd known, we could have gotten her to a doctor a month ago. We could have stopped this." She'd dissolved into tears, and as a single tear slid down my own cheek, I vowed to keep Abby's secret—now my secret—forever. When Abby was admitted the morning of her death, the hospital visit from the night before was on her records, but there was one detail that never made it on paper: I was there. I could have stopped this. My parents assumed she went after she dropped me off at Lauren's. If they knew, they would never forgive me for not telling them…for letting her die.

The delivery room door opens, jarring me from the memory of Abby that has been replaying in my mind on repeat. I vaguely remember stitching up Erika and leaving her in recovery. I even more vaguely remember grabbing a stack of charts and visiting other patients in various stages of labor.

Did I perform a C-section?

Everyone around me shuffles to allow Enrique to reach me. The nurses in the room are all looking at me with uncertainty and pity in their expressions. I'm shocked and terrified to realize I don't recognize the woman on the delivery table, and I'm not sure how I got here. How many hours have passed since I left Erika's delivery room? How many days? My hair feels greasy against my scalp, and my forehead and underarms are sweaty. My vision is blurred from lack of sleep, and I'm jittery from too many cups of coffee.

What am I doing?

"Dr. Lu said you were taking the rest of the week off," Enrique says. The laboring mother moans, another contraction taking hold. The woman who must be her mother is holding her hand and is as white as the hospital walls behind her, clearly afraid for her daughter and her grandchild. Afraid of me. Enrique takes hold of my arm, but I shake him off.

Despite my panic, I say, "I don't need the rest of the week off. I need to get back to work." I reach for the forceps, but he pulls them out of my reach.

"There are other doctors who can handle this," he says. In a lower voice, he adds, "Did you sleep at all last night?" Last night? I've been working for over twenty-four hours, and I don't remember any of it? My heart pounds faster.

"Where are we at?" I hear Dr. Galloway's voice say from the sink, where he's scrubbing up with the clear intention of taking over.

"What's going on?" the soon-to-be mother in front of me asks. I try to respond, but I realize I don't have the answer. I look at the nurses, one by one, each of them silently encouraging me to go with Enrique. After working so hard to earn their trust, I've lost it in a single night. My vision blurs around the edges.

"How did I get here?" I whisper.

"Dylan, come on," Enrique says in my ear. He grabs me by the elbows and lifts me off my chair. "*Vamanos, muñeca.* Dr. Galloway can handle it from here."

I allow myself to be pulled away from the scene in a daze. The patient never even looks up, doesn't notice the transition, or that I'm no longer there. She doesn't need *me*, she just needs someone.

"That's it," Enrique says when I finally put my weight on my own two feet. The door seals off behind us. In the hallway, he says, "Dylan, go home," in a firm whisper. He holds my chin between his thumb and forefinger, bringing his dark features into focus. "You didn't do anything wrong yesterday. Shit happens. There's no shame in taking a couple of days to deal with it. But don't come in here like this and make an actual mistake. You don't have to prove anything to anyone."

"I'm sorry," I mutter, hot tears stinging my eyes. "What did I do, Enrique?"

"It's okay, Dr. Michels. Just get home safely, okay? She'll be fine. We'll see you next week." Enrique squeezes my arm one last time, then goes back into the delivery room. I nod and stumble to the elevator.

I don't know how I make it home. I don't remember getting to my car or driving across the city or pulling into the garage. I'm just suddenly bursting through my front door and fumbling in the dark to find the light switch. I yank my shoes off and walk to the kitchen for some water. I've never been so thirsty in my life. I fumble with the glass, almost dropping it, then fill it up under the tap. I gulp down the first glass, then refill it. As I'm swallowing the last of it, I see the empty flowerpots lining the windowsill. I've been watering them every few days for months, making sure they get the right amount of sunlight, even talking to them. I followed the instructions on the package precisely and yet, nothing. Why do they bother giving instructions at all if you can do everything right and still get it wrong? Why do I try so hard when in the end, everything comes down to chance? No matter what I did, I couldn't save Erika's baby, I couldn't save my sister and I couldn't save the goddamn daisies.

I set my glass on the counter, pick up the pots and stare at them for a long moment before I hurl them across the kitchen. They hit the refrigerator and explode into a thousand pieces of shattered dreams and shattered lives.

I wake up at 5:00 a.m. the next morning in a cold sweat, to a cold, empty house, not sure what's left for me. I stare up at the ceiling, my limbs filled with cotton, my mind filled with white noise. I can't think of a single reason to get out of this bed. I gave up everything for my patients, and in the end, I couldn't save them all anyway.

Eventually, I drag myself to the kitchen for my first cup of coffee, ignoring the broken shards of ceramic and soil strewn across the floor, settling my attention on Cooper's book still on the counter. I stare at it as I sip my coffee, focus in on it for a long time, those haunting eyes staring back at me, accusing. I dump my coffee in the sink, throw on my jeans and a T-shirt and snatch the book off the counter on my way out the door.

Rain starts to sprinkle as I pull into the parking lot of Cooper's office, and I bring my car to a stop in the space reserved for me, rarely used. I reach for the book on the passenger seat. Before I get out of the car, I clutch it close to my heart. Before I rid myself of it, I latch on to the reminder that there are no happy endings.

I jump out of the car and duck my head from the rain, taking long strides to the front door.

"Dylan?" A man's voice says my name, but it isn't Cooper's. It sounds familiar, yet out of context here. I look up from beneath the shield of my hand to see Reese standing there at the edge of the sidewalk, between me and the entrance. He smiles and my heart stops.

It takes me a moment to put the pieces together—Reese, here to see Cooper. I never thought about them speaking to each other away from the house, without me. A nagging discomfort digs at the pit of my stomach, feeling oddly like betrayal.

"What are you doing here?" I breathe.

"I'm..." He motions toward the door but trails off.

"Is Cooper trying to change the plans for the yard?"

"No. Of course not," he's quick to say.

"Oh. Are...are you here to tell him about us?"

He narrows his eyes at me. "Tell him what about us?"

I take a few deep breaths to steady myself, and once my frazzled mind clears, I realize I'm overreacting. Nothing has happened with Reese. Not really. And even if it had, what would it matter to Cooper?

Cool rain lands on Reese's dark skin, and his eyes soften in a new way. I drop my gaze, suddenly feeling exposed.

"Why *are* you here?" I ask in the direction of my feet.

Reese hesitates for another moment. "I'm here to pick up paperwork for my brother." He lifts the stack of papers as evidence. "Dr. Caldwell is my nephew's doctor. I take Patrick to some of his appointments."

"*Some* of his appointments?"

"He was recently diagnosed with leukemia." Before I can react, he barrels on. "My brother is busy at work. He's working a lot these days, so he doesn't have to think about it. And so he can afford the best treatments for Patrick. I try to help where I can."

"Oh, Reese," I sigh. "I'm so…"

Forgetting where I am, I reach up to place a hand on his cheek. He closes his eyes and turns into it. His lips brush my palm, and it sends a shock through me.

My hand falls to my side as I remember the boy Cooper told me about the other night. I remember the way Cooper was searching for something out the kitchen window. He was searching for Reese—the uncle of the patient who was breaking his heart.

"Is that how you two met?" I mumble. "You and Cooper." Of course, I'd never thought about that before, too caught up in my own concerns.

Reese nods, his mouth a grim line.

"I'm so sorry." Tears fill my eyes, still burning from yesterday's tears. It's too much. It's all too much.

"Are you okay, Dylan?" he asks.

I nod, unable to speak. I turn back toward my car.

"Dylan." He stops me with a hand on my waist. "Where are you going?" he asks.

"I don't know," I say.

"Go somewhere with me."

I shake my head in disbelief.

"Reese, I—"

"Don't say 'can't.' You can do anything you want, Dylan. You either will or you won't."

I search his face for an indication of what he wants from

me. The crease between his eyebrows. His eyes, smoky with longing. His lips drawn together in anticipation.

I feel it, too. It's been there all along between us. I was oblivious to it at first, then in denial.

But I'm so tired of fighting.

"I know a place," I say. "Follow me."

I get in my car, and Reese in his truck. As we pull out of the parking lot, Reese close behind me, I start when I catch Cooper's reflection in the rearview mirror. He stands in the doorway of the office, his keys in his hand as he heads out for lunch. His eyebrows are furrowed. Behind the screen in my mind, the disappointment of him seeing me this way stings. I tear my gaze away from the mirror to my hands that are surprisingly steady on the steering wheel. Because this is who I really am, the woman I should have accepted all along.

I look up and pull out into the street.

As I stand at the edge of the forest along the Sandy River, I look down at my cell phone vibrating in my hand and see Cooper's name on the caller ID. I silence it and set it on my hood. The door of Reese's truck slams behind me, and with a few steps, he crosses the old dirt road and stands behind me. He touches the back of my neck, but I move forward into the trees without looking back.

He follows close behind me on the thin trail. I step over the rocks, duck below branches, feel his hands on my hips, guiding me. When we break through the brush and into the clearing, I stop, and he comes to stand beside me. I feel his presence there with every cell in my body.

"What do you think?" I ask. I try to look at the clearing with new eyes—the way Reese would see it with his artistic mind. The treetops are dense enough to create a canopy to protect us from the drizzling rain and the melancholy sky and the rest of humanity. It's like a world all its own—a fairy tale—green, with fern and moss climbing the length of each trunk, and hidden below, the Sandy River rushes through. There's not another living soul here to tell us what's wrong or right.

"Beautiful," he murmurs.

"There's more," I say. I tentatively reach out my hand for his. I worry he won't take it. Maybe his feelings for me have all been in my head. But he does. He laces his fingers between mine, rough with calluses, and warm.

I smile from deep within and then bound forward down the slope. We run free like children, laughing and calling out to the heavens. I hear the water ahead, smell it, taste its pureness in the otherwise dry air. Across the clearing, through the fire pit, I pull back a few overgrown branches and reveal the clear, inviting water. He gives me a half smile that makes me weak in the knees, then steps through.

"This is incredible," he says, raising his voice slightly over the sound of the water.

This part of the river is deep, but a hundred feet down, it narrows and hopscotches down a bed of stones. Reese walks forward and dips his hand into the water. I watch him with eyes from a different time, a previous life.

"Feels good," he says.

"Want to stick your feet in?"

He shakes his head, steps toward me and reaches out his hands. I take them and let him lead me forward, closer to the water, closer to him.

"Do you trust me?" he says softly. I nod. He releases my hands, takes the bottom of his shirt, and pulls it up over his head. Instinctively, I look away, but I can't help my eyes as they wander back to him. He looks at me, waiting for my reaction. His body is more than I imagined.

I open my mouth to ask him a question. Anything to slow this down. But now is not the time for words; it's the time for action.

I'm letting go.

I step out of my shoes and close the space between us. I stop before I touch his bare skin and look up at him, then I let my eyelids flutter shut and surrender. There's a long moment when nothing happens, as if he's waiting for me to change my mind, but I stand there until I feel the tips of his fingers reach beneath my shirt. I shudder as they trace lines over my hips and up my body as he lifts the hem higher and higher. I raise my arms, and he pulls it over my head, dropping it to the dirt below.

My breath is heavy and his chest swells, too. Our bare skin is so close it leaves little room for restraint. He never looks away from my face, but I know he sees all of me, and I feel his physical response. To solicit such a reaction from him fulfills a need I've ignored for so long. My skin tingles with the desire to be touched by his knowing hands.

He unbuttons his jeans next, and I'm acutely aware of the sound of his zipper moving downward. His face reveals no abashment as he leans forward to pull them off. He lost his shoes at some point, but I was too distracted to notice when. Wearing nothing more than boxer briefs, he awaits my next signal, but unable to wait any longer, I unbutton my own slacks and let them pool around my feet. I smile, step out of my pants and dash toward the water. The last thing I hear is his laughter and then I'm under.

Goose bumps and air bubbles ripple over my skin, awakening every nerve in my body. The water explodes with bubbles again when Reese jumps in next to me. I come up for air and open my arms wide to the steady rain that showers down on me. The beauty of the moment is surreal.

Reese surfaces and shakes out his hair with a laugh. The expression on his face as he wades toward me proves I've surprised even him.

"Who knew you had it in you, Dr. Michels?"

"Not me," I say.

We swim for a while, up and down the river, splashing each other. It reminds me of being at the beach with Cooper in Hawaii, but I push that thought from my mind. The sun turns orange in the sky as it starts its descent behind the trees. Once we're tired, we find a place where our feet touch the ground and steady ourselves like stones in the stream, listening to the sounds of nature that surrounds us. But I'm more aware of the fluttering in my chest and the way the sunset lights up Reese's bronze skin.

"Thank you," he says softly, like he doesn't want to disrupt this faraway world either. "Thank you for sharing this place with me."

"I've never done this before, you know. Skinny-dipping."

The gravity of the situation finally hits me. When he sees the seriousness on my face, his expression turns from playful to lusting, one degree at a time.

"Come here," he says.

We're only a couple of feet from each other, but my body is an anchor against the strength of the current and my uncertainty. Beneath the water, my hand grazes his chest, so smooth and flawless. His eyes close for a moment. He takes my offered hand and reaches around blindly until he finds the other one. Then, finally, he pulls me against him. My bare stomach is pressed against his, his chest against mine with only the thin fabric of my bra to separate us. Raindrops land on his face, and I watch them bead on his eyelashes or streak down his cheek and rejoin the water between us.

The part of me that isn't comfortable with the truth in silence wants to speak, but I can't. Instead, I open myself up to the honesty on his face, to what he's been trying to tell me from the beginning: that I am a woman worth being fought for—not only by him, or by Cooper, but by myself.

The stillness presses in on us until Reese lifts a hand and runs his thumb across my bottom lip. I close my eyes, feel him move closer. His lips—those full lips I have so longed for—touch the skin of my neck. I sigh. He breathes a path across my collarbone as his hands move down my back, trying to pull me closer even though it's impossible. His lips move farther down, and I know where he will go next.

Up until now everything I have done with Reese has been borderline. But if I let him continue, that will be it. I will be carried away, unable to stop myself. I will return to being the girl I left behind nine years ago—the one who refused to love, who took the easy way out. If we give in to our desires, the line will be crossed forever, and even if no one ever knows but the two of us, I will face the consequences every time I look in the mirror.

He moans against my skin and traces the tip of his nose upward until it finds mine. His breath is warm and moist. His lips brush lightly against my lips—an almost kiss—and hover there, his eyes closed, ready. His hands cup the back of my head, his fingers laced into my hair, pulling a little too hard.

It's animalistic.

It's sex.

It's not making love.

"Reese," I breathe.

"I know," he says, his disappointment apparent, but I exhale my relief. As much as I want this—as much as I want him—I can't do it. Because even when I'm wrapped in the arms of everything I've been needing, the only man I can think of is Cooper.

"I'm sorry," I say.

"Don't be." He rests his forehead on mine and lets his hands fall to my shoulders. He squeezes me tightly like it's taking all his strength to stop, then he lets me go.

15

There's something my dad said when he visited me last that has stuck in my head ever since. He said, "Sometimes the hardest thing you can do is leave." I think for him that's true. He tried to leave his old life behind once, to open his pizza parlor and start a different kind of home with Mom. He left behind his childhood, the family business and the approval of his parents. Yet he returned without a second thought. He sold his business and resigned himself to living the life his dad had laid out for him. To him, it was easier to follow in those familiar footsteps than to create a new world without his father in it.

For me, the hardest thing I could do is stay. Leaving is easy. Wiping away all the past mistakes and severing all connections to people who have seen me at my worst would mean a fresh start. Maybe I'd have a chance at forgetting my mistakes, too, if I wasn't reminded of them every day, every time I walk into the hospital or into the house that has encapsulated every argument I've shared with Cooper and everything that could have been.

Leaving with Reese would have been easy.

But it wouldn't have been honest. Like with Cooper, he would have only known part of who I am. And whether I like it or not, Abby's death is, and will always be, a big part of what has shaped me into this person I've become. I thought keeping that from Cooper would give me a blank slate with him, away from my family, but all it did was put a wall between us that we were never able to overcome. Because keeping a secret doesn't mean it never happened. My past *is* me, for better or worse.

So when I get home that night, my hair still damp with river water, I make the hardest choice for me. I decide to stay.

I get back to the clinic, easing my way in with my patients and keeping Enrique close during deliveries. He's forgiving of my skittishness, and I try to be forgiving of it, too.

I keep my appointments with Megan, even when she makes it easy for me to check out by calling to reschedule. For her August appointment, I offer to stop by her house instead.

Stephen and Megan's house is a warm country-style home outside the city, mere miles from mine and Cooper's. Stephen rented an apartment near the hospital when he left, but I refuse to think of this place as anything other than theirs. The hum of wildlife in the leaves above is the only sound that greets me when I get out of my car. It's one of the things I love most about living on the outskirts—room to breathe. I pull my bag out of the trunk.

Something feels different as soon as Megan opens her front door, but I try to write it off as my own uneasiness. When she fumbles as she pushes the screen toward me, though, and nearly hits me with it, I realize it's hers.

"Come on in," she says, her hair mussed and her lips pale with the lack of her usual red lipstick.

"Look at you," I say. Her face is aglow with pregnancy hormones and happiness. In fact, despite her restlessness, she's never looked better. Her shirt is taut against the ball of her stomach, no longer a secret to anyone. "How are you feeling?"

"Good," she says. "Really good."

I reach out to rub her belly.

"Hi, Dylan," a man's voice says behind me, and I jump, clutching at my heart. When I turn, Stephen emerges from the kitchen, looking proud and shrunken in uncertainty at the same time.

"Hi," I say breathlessly, then look back to Megan, worried I might have said something I shouldn't have.

"He knows everything," she says.

Stephen walks over and places one arm around her, a hand on her belly. It's been a while since I've seen him. He looks thinner, the scruff on his face the longest I've known him to wear it, but the glow emanating from within him tells me he's going to be okay.

I stammer, "So...are you..." I waggle a finger back and forth between them.

"We're...considering our options," Megan says.

Stephen smirks but says nothing.

"Tea?" Megan asks, bouncing on the balls of her feet. She goes to the kitchen before I respond. Stephen laughs softly.

"She's nervous about what her family is going to think," he says by way of explanation.

I nod. "They're going to be thrilled," I say, sadness creeping into my voice as I picture them all back together as a family. Without me.

"Come here," he says, holding open his arms. I set my bag on the coffee table and allow him to fold me up against his chest. "How are you holding up, kiddo?" he asks.

"You heard about the baby, didn't you?"

"Uh-huh."

"Is everyone at the hospital talking about it?"

"No," he says and runs a hand over my hair soothingly. "Aaron interned a couple of years behind us, remember? He knows we're close, so he wanted to make sure you had someone to talk to." Aaron is the neonatal nurse who looked at the baby after he was wheeled out, and who pronounced him dead not long after.

"I'm getting through," I say. "So you came home." I step back so I can look at him.

"I did," he says. "I missed my wife. And I missed being a husband. Who would have thought?"

We both smile. "Me. I'd hold on this time."

"I intend to. Don't you worry about that. And what about you?"

"What do you mean?"

"Do you miss Cooper?" he asks.

I huff out a dry laugh. "So he finally told you, huh?"

"I can't exactly be mad at the guy for taking so long. It's hard to admit it to yourself when things don't turn out the way you hope, let alone to other people. But you were right about me and Megan."

"That you're meant to be?"

"Something like that," he says with a laugh. "So are you and Cooper, you know?"

Megan comes out of the kitchen, holding two mugs of tea, and hands one over to me, saving me from responding.

"You ready?" she asks.

I nod.

Once we're alone in her room, I palpate her belly and she stares at me.

"You seem different," she says.

"What do you mean by different?" I ask.

"I don't know," she says. "I can't put my finger on it. Something just seems different. Calmer, maybe?"

I shrug. "I don't know. I guess you could say that."

"Have you found a new grant to apply to?" she asks. I focus on the Doppler as I find the baby's heartbeat. It's there, strong and steady.

I shake my head. "Can I tell you something?" I ask as I wipe the jelly off the Doppler.

"Of course."

"I'm afraid of getting approved for one." I'm almost ashamed to admit it, but my focus has been elsewhere, and I wonder if that's the way it needed to be. She's right—something is different inside me, and I don't know what it means yet.

"Really? Why?"

"I don't know," I say, thoughtfully. "I guess I'm questioning whether it's still the right path for me."

I remember one of my conversations with Reese, about how the Universe is waiting on me to be ready for the grant. I feel like committing to sticking out this tough transition in my life is a step in the right direction, but there are still so many decisions to make, like what part my parents are going to play in my future, as well as to what extent Abby's memory is going to guide my present.

I stand up and cross the room to my bag to replace my equipment. I hesitate there for a moment.

"You know how you can have a goal and be so focused on getting to it that you don't bother to look around you? Just straight ahead?"

"Sure. That's why I stubbed my toe yesterday on the way to get a bag of cookies from the kitchen."

I laugh and lean against the hard wooden dresser. "The thing is, I feel like I've finally stopped to look around and realize I wasn't running toward something, I was running away from something. But I don't think there's anything chasing me anymore."

I thought by trying to save everyone, I could forgive myself for not doing the right thing for Abby. I thought if I could redeem myself by establishing the need for earlier pregnancy testing, I could finally admit to my parents what really happened the night before Abby's death, and we could work through it. But after losing Erika's baby, I realize saving everyone is impossible. I'm just going to have to find a way to forgive myself anyway.

Megan narrows her eyes. "I'm not sure I follow."

I sigh and push myself off the dresser. "I don't know if I do either. I just haven't always made the best decisions. It's hard to trust them anymore."

"Like with Cooper?" she asks. I raise my eyebrows in question. "Yes, I know. He told me."

"So he knows you're pregnant, too? Are you okay?"

"You're worried about me?" She laughs. "I'm worried about you."

"Well, it's been months."

"That doesn't mean anything," she says. "Stephen was gone half a year, and not a single day went by that I didn't pray he'd come back. When you love someone, when they're *the one*, you don't forget. Those feelings don't go away."

"No," I say, sitting back down on the bed. "They don't. I guess I wasn't the one for him, though. He's already moved on."

Megan furrows her brow. "Dylan? Honey? What the hell are you talking about?"

I try to smile. "I heard her in the background on the phone when I talked to him a few weeks ago. She called him 'Coop.'" I spit the word. "You and I are the only ones who call him that."

"When?" she asks, still skeptical.

"I don't know. The night his patient was diagnosed with cancer, I think."

Megan shakes her head. "You two. It *was* me. He came over after he left your house. He was so torn up about his patient and about you. He was afraid he did the wrong thing by almost kissing you, but more afraid he'd always regret it if he wasn't honest with you about how he's feeling."

This news sends an avalanche of emotions shooting through my bloodstream. I take a shaky breath. Megan reaches out and takes my hands in hers.

"Don't give up on Cooper, Dylan. I know he made the worst mistake a man can make, but he loves you. That deep, walk-to-the-ends-of-the-earth kind of love. The kind of love that only comes once in a lifetime, if you're lucky. The only woman he wants—the only woman he's ever wanted—is you."

My eyes tear up, and I nod. I know this. I've always known this. That's what scares me.

"So why does it have to be so hard?"

Megan reaches out to touch the tips of my hair, loose around my shoulders for once, and says, "Because that's the only way to discover how strong you are."

I smile. "Where did you learn that?"

"In my birthing class," she says and we burst into laughter.

I stand up and grab my bag, ready to head home for the day. Before I leave the room, she stops me.

"If it means anything," she says, "I support you. With your grant and with Cooper. No matter what you choose, I know you're going to do great things. You can't help it."

I turn her hand over and kiss it, lean over to kiss her belly. "It means everything," I say.

★ ★ ★

"What are you doing here today?" I ask Enrique in the clinic one morning later that week.

He keeps his head down as he sorts through charts. "Jenna needed the day off, so I covered her shift."

"Weren't you scheduled to work in Labor and Delivery?"

Enrique shrugs and hands me a stack of charts—my appointments for the day. There are a few missed call slips on top. "They'll survive without me."

"I doubt that's true," I say over my shoulder as I walk to my office. He winks.

I sort through my missed calls and nearly drop the charts when I see the second to last one. A patient called yesterday to schedule an early morning meeting with me today, which is exactly why Enrique is here. Erika is already in my office waiting for me.

I turn to see him watching me with a frown.

"Thank you," I mouth. He bows his head in a subtle nod, then returns to his work.

I take a deep breath and open my office door slowly, prepared for anything. There she is, sitting upright in one of my chairs, the picture of grace in a skirt suit, her legs crossed, hands in her lap.

"Hi, Dr. Michels," she says with a weak smile.

"Hi, Mrs. Martinez." I close the door and unload the charts onto my desk. I need another minute—or year—to prepare for this moment. In truth, I'll never be ready. Still, I'm not running.

"How are you?" I ask, my gaze still on the charts. I walk around my desk and sit down. There's a long pause that sends a chill down my spine.

"I'm okay," she says. Her voice is soft, but I hear the

strength there that I've always seen in her. "It's hard to be here again."

Her honesty prompts my own. "Yes, it is."

I finally look at her. Her eyes are distant, and she's still carrying much of the baby weight. This bothers me more than anything else. Her body went through all the changes a mother goes through to develop a fetus, but she has no child to show for it. And yet she looks every bit the mother she still somehow is.

I sit in silence as she tells me about the therapy she and Andrew have been going to together. She says they're both taking some time off work to focus on their relationship, so the loss doesn't come between them. She tells me how they're coping at home and that they've decided to wait a year to try for another child. They want to love their next baby in a new way, not as a way to grieve the one they are without.

The hardest part about the conversation is that she and Andrew have always reminded me of the way Cooper and I could have been if I'd been courageous enough to let him in, if I'd asked for help with my pain instead of keeping it bottled up inside me. Erika and Andrew have gone through one of the worst experiences a couple could ever face, and somehow, they are making it through.

I nod in all the right places, but I can't find the words to respond. How can I tell her she amazes me and that she'll make the best mother when the time comes? That time should already be here, and there's nothing I can say to make it better.

"Dr. Michels," she finally says, her voice lowering an octave or two. She fidgets with the hem of her skirt, pulling it farther down. "I've been wanting to say something to you since that day."

I put on a brave face and sit up more attentively, but I feel the blood drain from my cheeks.

"I just wanted to thank you," she says. Her eyes swim with water. Mine do, too. "That day was the best and the worst day of my life."

A gasp escapes my lips, and I press my fist to my mouth to keep myself from dissolving.

"Losing Andrew Junior is the hardest thing I've ever had to face. The hardest thing I hope I'll ever have to face. But I want you to know, I never blamed you. I saw what you did for him, and I know you did everything you could. And you were there for me in a way you didn't have to be. For that, I can never thank you enough."

I was prepared to carry her heartache and anger for the rest of my life, right next to my grief over Abby, but I never could have prepared for her gratitude or the heavy load of guilt that falls from my shoulders with her words. My throat aches with unshed tears. My arms ache to hug her.

"I can't tell you…" I take a deep breath. "I can't even begin to tell you what that means to me."

"You're an amazing doctor, and because of that, I figured this has probably been hard on you, too. I wanted to make sure you knew you have nothing to be sorry for. I hope when the day comes, you'll deliver my next baby. And all the ones after that." It's too good. This isn't real. "Yes, it's been unbearable to lose my sweet angel, but Andrew and I…we've never been stronger. If there's one thing I've learned from all this, it's that you can't blame yourself for the things life throws at you. So don't let this or anything else hold you back, Dylan, okay?"

I nod, and through my tears, I smile.

Since the night of my parents' anniversary—the night I discovered my father's infidelity—my mom has called every couple of days, without fail. At first I didn't answer because

I was too angry to hear any more about her side. When Dad came to my house to ask for forgiveness, he explained some of the deeper issues in their relationship that I couldn't understand as a teenager, but old habits die hard, and I still didn't know how to speak to my mother.

Eventually, as she continued to call, the anger melted into shock. It had been more than a decade since Mom had tried to reestablish our relationship, and I didn't know how to take it. My anger for my mom has become as much a part of my identity as Abby's death, as sad as that is. I didn't know what it would mean to let go of that. Would it mean letting go of Abby, too?

Once the shock wore off, I ignored her calls because I felt ashamed of my behavior. Time with my mom was all I had ever wanted—here was my opportunity, and I was letting it slip by. I was cruel to her in our last conversation, and it was just another thing I owed her an apology for. I may have had a right to be angry, but that hurtful, combative Dylan isn't the Dylan I want to be. Erika's forgiveness reminded me of that.

On Saturday morning, I drive to my parents' house. I let myself in, and my tennis shoes squelch against the tile floor in the foyer. I don't know what I expected to see or how I expected to feel when I came here for the first time without Dad in the house, but as I look around, it doesn't seem all that different. The decor, the photos, the furniture—they were all Mom's choosing. Dad would have no use for them anyway in a downtown apartment by himself. When I peek into his study, it's empty.

I don't bother looking for Mom in the kitchen because I know where I will find her.

Outside, the weather has started to cool, and a breeze flows off the lake. Mom kneels next to a flower bed, her petite frame curled up like a snail in a shell. Her hair is flat and hangs in clumps around her face, uncombed, and she's wearing a pair of jeans and an old T-shirt.

In her lethargic and weary state, she doesn't notice me watching her from the top of the porch steps as she picks dead leaves off her rosebushes. She picks healthy leaves, too. That's what people do sometimes—in order to remove the bad from life, we remove some of the good.

"I owe you an apology," I say, my voice carrying to her on the breeze.

Mom starts and looks up at me where I'm standing on the porch, my hands balled into fists, anxiously awaiting the conversation we should have had years ago. For the first time in a long time, her eyes are alert, and I feel like she's really seeing me.

"No, you don't," she says. She shakes her head and carefully pulls her gardening gloves off one at a time. She stands and brushes herself off.

"I do," I say. "Those things I said to you when I saw you last…they were harsh. And not true. I, of all people, know that it takes two to make a relationship work. Or not work."

Mom nods but doesn't make a move to come closer. "I appreciate that."

"That's not all," I go on, before I can change my mind. "It's about Abby."

She sucks in a breath at the mention of Abby's name. It's been so long since we've said it in each other's presence. I realize now that I've feared it, worried my shame would be written all over my face.

Mom doesn't speak. I can see by her expression that she's afraid, too.

"I knew," I say. "I knew she was pregnant."

She blinks hard, trying to comprehend. Before she can say anything, I get it all out, purging the guilt from my body.

"She made me promise not tell anyone. And I knew she was sick. The night before, she was in pain. You know that she went to the hospital that night, but what I never told you is that I was with her. Since she was eighteen, she could check herself in, so…I drove her. I sat there with her for two hours, knowing the whole time I should have called you. I listened to that doctor say she had the stomach flu. And I believed him. And then I lied for her, so she could hide up in her room, and then…she died." My breath hitches on the last word. I've never spoken any of this out loud, not to anyone. "If I'd been braver, or stronger, or smarter, I would have made the right decision. Abby would still be here. And I'm just so, so sorry."

"Oh, Dylan," Mom breathes. She brings her fingers to her mouth, a gesture I realize I've gotten from her. I didn't want to turn into my mom—thought it would be the worst possible insult—but I see I already have. Finally, though, I understand that she hasn't wanted to create this gap between her and the people she loves—it was the only thing she knew how to do to survive the pain. The same way I made sure there was always a safe distance between Cooper and my heart.

Minutes pass as Mom watches the grass turn from summer to fall. I can see the wheels turning behind her eyes—processing, digesting—as I listen to my heartbeat pounding in my ears. I've avoided telling her the truth for fifteen years, but these few minutes feel like an eternity.

Finally, she looks at me with tears in her eyes and says, "Why didn't you tell me?"

My heart breaks. Tears fill my eyes. It's a question I've asked myself a thousand times.

"I don't know. I don't know. I didn't want Abby to be mad at me. I didn't want you and Dad to be mad at me for not telling you sooner. I was so scared."

She puts up a hand to stop me, unsatisfied with my answer.

"No," she says, her voice softer than I expect. "I mean, why didn't you tell me all this a long time ago?"

I shake my head, unable to answer. Silent tears pour down my cheeks and drip off my chin. I hide my face behind my hands. It's too hard to face her. Teenagers make mistakes all the time, but I never thought I would have to live with the consequences of my mistake for the rest of my life.

For a long minute, all I hear is my own sniffling, then the sound of Mom's footsteps as she walks away from me. I thought I'd prepared myself for the reality that this conversation would never bring us back together, but now that it's happening, I realize I've never heard a more painful sound in my life.

But then, inexplicably, I feel hands on my hair and Mom's soft cheek against mine. I peek out from beneath my hands to see her red, tear-stained face looking back at me. She pulls me closer, and I bury my face in the fabric of her shirt and cry like I never allowed myself to—not when I was sixteen, not ever. Back then, I didn't feel I had the right to ask for comfort. And in the years since, I blamed our distance on Mom because it was easier than admitting to myself that I pulled away first, too afraid to face my inquisition. But now, Mom squeezes me to her so tightly it hurts, and I revel in it because it's the ferocity of a mother's love, something I thought I'd never feel again.

She whispers my name over and over again, and her body shakes with her own sobs.

When neither one of us can cry anymore, we wipe our eyes, and Mom leads me to the patio table. She pulls two chairs out so we can sit facing each other. Once we're settled, she says, "Dylan, I need you to listen to me, okay? For once in your life, hear me."

I let out a strangled laugh. "Okay."

She takes a deep breath. "I am so sorry you ever felt like Abby's death was your fault. I know it must have been incredibly scary for you to have to deal with something like that when you were so young. But, sweetie...you did the right thing."

I shake my head, but she cuts me off, placing her hand on mine.

"You did. You were loyal to your sister, and you helped her the best you could at the time. That's what your dad and I have always wanted for you kids. We knew we couldn't be involved in every part of your lives, but we hoped when you couldn't come to us, you would lean on each other, and that's exactly what you did. I couldn't have asked anything more of you."

"But if you'd known, maybe she would have had a chance," I say.

"Maybe," she says with a shrug. "But maybe that's not true either. Maybe even with the doctor's help, it wouldn't have been diagnosed in time."

I know she's right. That's the reason I want my grant—because early testing for complications isn't standard, even if the patient sees her doctor in the first weeks of pregnancy.

"We'll never know," Mom goes on. "But you can't plague yourself with maybes. Trust me. I know. I've been doing it, too, and I didn't realize how much it was hurting all of us. I've pushed everyone away, and I have to face the consequences of that." She looks at her dirty, cracked fingernails. I flip my hand over and cover them with mine.

"I don't want us to keep pushing each other away," I say.

"Dylan, honey, I never meant to make you feel like I was pushing you away," she chokes. She can barely get the words out. "I thought I was doing the right thing. After Abby died, you were so angry and withdrawn. I felt like I had already done everything wrong with Abby, and I didn't want to do the same thing with you. So I gave you space, thinking that if I pushed you, you'd only push back harder. You got your stubbornness from me, you know," she says with a wry laugh. "But I was wrong again. I should have made sure you knew without a doubt that I was there whenever you needed me. I wish Abby had known that, too. Maybe if she had, she wouldn't have kept her pregnancy a secret from me. Maybe, maybe, maybe."

We're both crying again, and my understanding of her self-condemnation is so deep that I'm rendered speechless.

Mom takes a deep breath and exhales slowly.

"The last time you were here," she says softly, "you said you would never be like me."

"Mom, I'm—"

She cuts me off. "You were right. I gave up—on my dreams, on my marriage, on finding new ways to be happy. But, Dylan, after everything you've been through, and all the adversity you've faced, you've never given up. I couldn't be more proud to have you not be like me."

I shake my head, fat tears rolling down my cheeks, wanting more than anything to close the gap between who we are as women.

Mom pulls me into another tight hug, and I feel like it's the first step.

16

"You're thinking about it," Reese says from behind me, making the hair on the back of my neck stand up. Before I've even looked at him, the memories of the last time we were together flash through my mind. Electricity shoots through me. Still.

"No, I'm not," I say, but my smile gives me away. I stand in my backyard at the tree line, looking down at the staircase that leads to the creek—the place he made me promise to stay away from. I haven't been tempted until now—now that the rest of the yard is complete. When I came home from work this afternoon, the moat had water running through it for the first time, starting to the left of the front door, wrapping around the house, traveling downward across our sideways-sloped backyard, and ending in a pool in a quiet corner surrounded by stone and grass. The bridge and the swing are both in place, and colorful flowers billow from beds along the house, almost like the flowers were there first, and the house had been carefully placed between them.

"Are you ready?" Reese asks me. An afternoon breeze blows and lifts my hair off my shoulders. I look back at him and smile.

"Yes."

"Close your eyes then," he says. He doesn't seem the least bit dampened by me leaving him at the river, and I'm glad for that. He has other heartaches to sadden his spirit, and the world needs his smile.

I laugh but close my eyes. He doesn't have to ask if I trust him. Trust is coming a lot easier these days.

Reese's hand slips into mine, and he navigates me forward. "Steps," he says.

I guide my foot down the first one and then the second. With every step, the scent in the humid air begins to change—water, and a certain unmistakable pollen. A scent I know very well. I open my mouth to identify it, but he stops me.

"Just pretend to be surprised, okay?"

I feel the ground soften when I step off the last stair and then Reese's hands as he places them over my eyes. His chest is against my back, and his arms are around me. I smell his earthy fragrance mixed with that of my favorite flowers, stronger than I've ever smelled them before.

He puts his lips close to my ear and counts down, "Three... two...one..." Then he removes his hands, revealing his surprise. I bring my hand to my mouth, unable to breathe, unable to speak. Stargazer lilies. Everywhere. All around the bench I love to sit on while I watch fallen leaves ride the water downstream, and clumped together in corners. There are small flowering vines woven into the creases of the staircase where one step meets the next, so they look like they've been growing there for decades. Stepping-stones lead from the staircase down to the creek. Added up, it's a Monet. It's the most beautiful thing I've ever seen, and I can't believe it's mine.

I turn to Reese, another beautiful thing that could have

been mine in another time or place. I breathe in his smile, taking it inside me to sustain me for whatever lies ahead, to remind me of the woman I have become and the woman I still hope to be.

He says nothing, just reads me the way he does. I'll miss that, too.

"Thank you for this," I say. "It's perfect. And so unexpected."

"Well," he says, "I wish I could take all the credit, but to tell you the truth…it was Dr. Caldwell's idea."

I look around. It's everything I didn't know I wanted. I should have known.

"Oh, Cooper," I say. No matter where I go or what I do, he's there.

Reese turns his back to me, walks over to one of the flowers and runs a petal through his fingertips. The creek bubbles over the rocks beside us, punctuating the silence.

"These are from me, though," he says, cupping the bulb of a white flower in his hand. I crouch down and put my nose to the petals. "Tulips. They represent serenity…and forgiveness."

Forgiveness.

"You remembered," I say, smiling.

"I'll always remember you, Dylan."

He wears a pensive grin and looks more like the man I first met months ago—the mysterious stranger. He's pulling away. Or I am.

"I figured out what the Universe was waiting for," I tell him.

He nods, mulls it over. "And?"

"I needed to find the courage to be honest," I say. "And to come to the realization that I can't change the past."

"No," he says, agreeing with me. "You can't. But you can choose the future."

"You helped me see that. So I have a lot more to thank you for than this."

I reach for his hand, turn it over and trace my fingers along the calluses on his palm. There is so much evidence of life there. I wish I had more time to learn.

He turns my hand over in his and brings it up to his lips, places a kiss on my wrist.

"Dylan, I'm going to tell you something you don't want to hear."

I grin. "I would expect nothing different."

"You love Cooper. You never stopped."

I look away. I wanted to stop. I tried to.

I release his hand, but it isn't disappointment that crosses his face. Instead, a quiet satisfaction.

"I guess you finally figured me out," I say.

"No, you finally figured you out."

I smile and give him a peck on the cheek, his facial hair tickling my jaw. I'll always remember him, too. There's so much of him here to remind me. I don't want to forget. He will move on to another place, another yard, another woman, but his wisdom will stay here to guide me back to what's important whenever I feel lost.

"Thank you. Truly," I say.

"For what?"

"The yard. Listening. Understanding."

"All part of the job," he says with a wink.

He steps forward to smooth a hand over my hair and places a kiss on my forehead.

Colder weather is around the corner, and everything Reese built here will soon wither and die. I know it will all come back next year, but I mourn for it anyway—this sweet perfection that has been so short-lived. Right now, it just feels like goodbye.

★ ★ ★

Dad's apartment is two blocks from his office. It's surreal to walk into the new building, trying to take in the unfamiliar surroundings and attach them to the image of my father I've spent a lifetime cultivating. The lobby is contemporary, decorated in classy beiges and cool blues. The feel is exactly the opposite of Dad's antiquated office building and the classic elegance of the house he spent his entire life in. The security guard at the entrance bows his head at me as I pass. I take the elevator to the eighth floor.

Dad answers the door before I've finished knocking. I didn't warn him I'd be stopping by, but I'm guessing he doesn't get many visitors here yet. The open door reveals a smile and his longer gray curls just touching his forehead. His cheeks are rosy, and his face has a subtle fullness to it. He looks happy.

"Dylan!"

My name bursts out of Dad's mouth, and he pulls me into a hug. I allow the small amount of moisture in my eyes to soak into Dad's shirt. I recognize that my emotions aren't sadness, per se, but more a reminiscence for a chapter of our lives that is forever closed. Crossing the threshold into Dad's one-bedroom apartment makes that more evident than anything else has.

"Make yourself at home," Dad says as he closes the door and bustles into the kitchen. "Do you want something to drink?"

I don't. "Water would be great," I say.

I cross the living room to the large windows that allow the sunlight to fill every corner of the small space. There's a thin strip of balcony on the other side of the glass and a view that's even better than the one outside Dad's office. Below is a lush canopy of trees and, beyond that, a café with cute two-top outdoor tables. I can picture Dad down there, sipping his black coffee and reading his newspaper on Saturday mornings. I can picture him having a life without Mom, without family holidays, without all of us under the same roof at the same time. It's like a punch to the stomach.

"Here you go, baby girl," Dad says.

I turn back to Dad and take the water, setting it on the coffee table. All of the furniture is new, giving it a model-home feel. I wonder if he hired someone to furnish it for him—he never had a knack for that type of thing. But across from the couch, instead of a TV, is a row of bookshelves, proving that Dad is finding ways to make this place his own.

"Why did you decide you should be the one to move out?" I ask him. "The house has been in your family for generations."

"That's exactly why," he says with a lopsided grin. "It was time for something new. Besides, I wouldn't do that to your mother. That's been her home for almost thirty years. And that's where all our memories of Abby are. She needs those reminders more than I do."

I nod, not sure what to say.

"Sit down," Dad encourages. I take a place on the couch, and he takes the reading chair next to me. "How are you?" he asks. "How are things with Cooper?"

I laugh. "No beating around the bush, huh?"

"You never called me about separating your assets. I'd hoped maybe you worked things out."

"Always the optimist," I muse. "But, no. He's finally told his friends and family. I think it's finally real now."

Dad looks down at the glass of water in his hands with a frown. "I'm sorry to hear that."

"Yeah," I say. "Me, too. But I'll be okay. I'm in a good place, actually."

"I can see that," Dad says. "You look lighter."

I smile. "I didn't call you for a different reason." Dad raises his eyebrows in question. "I was mad at you," I say bluntly.

Dad nods, not surprised. His shoulders fall a little.

I clear my throat, working up the courage to say the words I scripted on the way over here. As hard as it was to talk to my mom, it's easier to be straightforward with her. With Dad, I live in perpetual fear of letting him down.

"I don't know what I was mad about most," I start. "That you did it in the first place? That you and Mom kept it a secret for so long? That I think it interfered with my relationship with Mom more than it had to *because* it was a secret? Or that you used my situation with Cooper to try to get me to forgive you?"

Dad swallows hard, and I hate this reversal in our relationship. It was always demoralizing to be on the receiving end of one of Dad's lectures, but it's even more painful to be the one giving it. That's the thing about parents, though: you grow up and find out that they're people, no more or less than you are. They make mistakes. They're still learning. They will let you down, and you will let them down, and somehow, you will all find a way to keep loving each other anyway.

"The thing is," I go on, "I don't forgive you."

Dad's jaw tightens and I can see that he is hurt, so I continue quickly.

"I don't forgive you, because it's not my place to forgive you. You didn't betray *me*, Dad. Whatever happens between you and Mom, you've always been there for me. You've been an amazing teacher, a gentle leader, a kind role model. You've been everything a girl could hope for in a father, and one mistake you made a long time ago doesn't erase all that."

Dad has always been the more affectionate one of my parents, but my words shock him so much, he doesn't move. He sits there, nodding his head, tears threatening to jump from his eyelids with every jarring movement.

"I'll always love your mom," he finally says. "I always have. I want you to know that. And maybe one day, she and I can find a way to be friends, for you and Charlie, if nothing else."

"That would be nice," I say. "But I don't want you to worry about me. I don't want you to feel like you have to hold on to the past to the detriment of your future."

"No," Dad agrees. "But we can't pretend it didn't happen either. We hold on to the good times, learn from the tough times, and let go of things we can't change. You and Charlie and Abby and your mom will always be my family."

I nod, wondering if it will still feel that way when Dad finds someone else. If Mom finds someone else. If I do. I can't picture it, but I mean it when I say, "We'll just have to take it one day at a time."

"Right," Dad says with a smile. Then, "I'm proud of you, Dylan. If I screw up everything else in my life, I'll die happy knowing I must have done one thing right."

I laugh and take a sip of my water to wash away the tears building in the back of my throat. "I don't know that I would give you *all* the credit."

Dad laughs, too, and says, "No. You've always been stubborn about making your own way in life." He pauses, like he's debating whether or not he should say the next part. "There's one other person who's been a big support to you."

Cooper. But unlike with my dad, in this situation, the forgiveness is mine to give. With him, though, it isn't so easy.

"I know. I'll always be grateful for that."

"But you still can't forgive him."

I sigh. "You know that forgiveness in a relationship is a two-way street."

Dad purses his lips and nods. "That I do."

★ ★ ★

Later that week, Vanessa comes into my office while I'm finishing up my charts for the night. Even though hardly anyone is still in the clinic, she closes the door before she points at my computer.

"Check your email," she says, barely containing a grin.

"Okay," I say. I rotate my chair away from the charts and open the window. At the top is an unopened message from Vanessa, and in the subject line: Women's Reproductive Health Grant. My heart skips a beat. I click to open it and scan the contents. It's a private grant specifically for research in my field, rather than a pool of general applicants. The parameters are exactly what I've hoped for—more money and more time than any other grant I've seen so far. It's like someone designed it specifically for me.

I turn to Vanessa, mouth agape.

"It's perfect," I say.

Vanessa nods. "I've been talking to people about your application, and one of my colleagues came across the listing. She forwarded it to me."

"My application…" I mumble to myself. I've made progress on it the last few weeks, but it's been slow going. I've decided it's time to share Abby's story, to allow it to be the reason people trust my passion for my work instead of the painful secret that keeps me disconnected from everyone…even the people I want to help. But it turns out, pouring your heart out on paper isn't so easy. Reliving those final moments with Abby has been almost as painful as they were the first time, but I'm older and wiser now, and I can look at them with an objective perspective. I can look at them with self-compassion.

"I want you to submit it," Vanessa says. "I want you to send it to them."

I frown. "It's not ready," I woefully admit. It pains me to

let her down after all the time and trust she's invested in me, but I want my application to be a reflection of who I am now, not who I was the first time I gave it to Vanessa. I want it to convey the confidence I feel that I am more ready than ever to dedicate myself to this research.

"That's fine," Vanessa says, waving my concern away. "The deadline is next week."

I laugh, though Vanessa doesn't get the joke. She never has.

I stand and walk around my desk. I lean against it and clasp my hands in front of me.

"It's not just that," I say.

"Oh?" Dr. Lu shifts her weight. I can tell she feels off balance. She's used to being the one relaying information, passing off orders. She doesn't like not being the one in control.

"Dr. Lu, I can't tell you how much I appreciate you for being an incredible teacher over the years. You inspire me. You really do. And I want to do this research more than I've wanted almost anything in my life." *Almost* anything.

Vanessa crosses her arms, sensing where this conversation is going. "But?"

"But when you pulled me aside a couple of months ago, I apologized for being distracted with my personal life. The thing is…I realize now that having a personal life isn't a distraction. I think relationships are what make the work worthwhile. And I don't want to keep putting my relationships second."

She raises her eyebrows. The sharpness of her features has never been so apparent. I don't mean to offend her, but I also don't want to become her. I want to live my life with the windows open.

"What are you saying, Dylan?"

"I'm saying it's time to cut back on my patient load." The

words come out unsteady. I never thought they'd pass through my lips. But I'm certain it's the right thing. It's what I want. Maybe I won't have Cooper or Megan or Stephen to spend time with anymore, but I'll start with my mom and my dad and my brother, and see where things go from there. Or maybe I'll just start with my relationship with myself.

Vanessa shakes her head, taken aback. "Well, if you get the grant, of course you'd cut back on your patient load."

"I want to do it either way," I'm quick to say. "Starting immediately."

She scoffs. I've never been so forward with her. I'm not sure if anyone has.

She lets her arms fall to her sides and takes a step back. "I don't understand. You're the one who's always asking for more patients. Your initiative is why I chose you to mentor this year."

"I know," I say. "And I hope it doesn't change your mind. I don't know how to explain it, but I just… I need more than this. I want to do my life's work, and I want to live while I'm doing it. Maybe that seems like a disastrous career move to you, but I have to believe that there's some way to have both."

Her laugh is humorless. "You're living in a fantasy, Dylan."

I shrug, but I don't back down. I can't expect everyone to see things my way, but I've been through too much these last few months to second guess my instincts anymore. I have to trust them.

"I guess we'll see," I say.

She opens her mouth to respond, but for the first time ever, she's speechless. For a minute she's frozen in time, but finally, she taps her knuckle on my desk with finality and turns toward the door. Over her shoulder, she says, "Don't miss that deadline, Dr. Michels."

I smile. "Yes, ma'am."

★ ★ ★

Later that night, an unusually heavy rain for autumn pours down as I climb into bed. When I close my eyes, thunder claps overhead and lightning flashes through the room on the other side of my eyelids. Before, on nights like this, I would curl into Cooper, and he'd make me feel safe. We'd watch the lightning brighten the room, then together we'd count the seconds until we heard the accompanying thunder. It would bring me peace, like counting contractions in the delivery room. I miss Cooper tonight more than I have in a long time, but I'm getting used to being strong on my own.

My phone rings, startling me. It's nearly midnight. The caller ID shows it's Megan.

"Hey, you," I say when I pick up.

"Dylan, I'm so sorry," she says, her voice panicked.

I bolt upright in bed. "Sorry for what?" I ask her.

I hear whimpers coming from her end. "I think I'm in labor. I'm scared."

I throw the covers back. She can't be in labor. It's too early. Much too early.

"Okay. It's going to be okay," I say, already climbing out of bed and pulling on some clothes. "I'll meet you at the hospital."

"I can't," she says. "Stephen is still at work, and I don't think I can drive. I'm afraid I won't make it."

I close my eyes and pinch the bridge of my nose. Thunder rolls outside, as if I need the reminder of the raging storm. "Okay, I'll come get you," I say. "I'll be there in ten minutes."

17

The night is black, the moon suffocated by thick, dark clouds. I pull out of my driveway onto the stormy streets, my blood pumping in my ears. I can't remember the last time Oregon has seen weather like this. The trees are so dense on my secluded road that they block much of the rain coming down, but when I come to a halt at the first stop sign, water pooled at the corner of the intersection sprays up over the windshield, and I can't see anything. I curse, set my wipers at a higher speed and make a left turn.

I can't do this again, a voice in the back of my mind tells me. *I can't do this by myself.* Then I realize, as the lightning strikes and I begin to count, that I don't have to. I blindly fish around for my phone on the passenger seat, then I tap the number that's still at the top of my speed dial.

"Hey," Cooper says when he answers. His voice is soft but not like he's been sleeping. It's also surprised and hopeful.

"I need your help," I say without preamble.

"What's wrong?" He goes into doctor mode in an instant.

"Your sister is in labor."

"In labor? Now?"

"I'm in the car. I can't talk. Can you meet me at her house? And call Stephen and an ambulance, too?" After a pause: "I really need you."

"I'm on my way."

The drive to Megan's house on a good day is ten minutes, but with the excess water on the roads after a long, dry summer, two-lane streets are narrowed down to one. I drive carefully. At least the roads are mostly clear of other drivers. We Oregonians may be used to the constant cloud cover and drizzle, but storms sequester us like birds in a hurricane, same as any other part of the world.

The closer I get to Megan's, the more frequently I have to dip into the pool of water on the right side of the street to allow oncoming traffic to pass. The rain shows no signs of stopping.

When I finally turn into Megan's driveway, all the lights in the house appear to be off. I slam the car into Park, almost forget to yank the keys from the ignition and then run up the front porch steps, sloshing through the puddles in my jeans. I hardly notice how wet my hair is or how muddy my tennis shoes are.

"Megan?" I call as I burst into the house. It's so dark, I can't see my hand in front of my face.

"In here," she moans. I don't even try to find a light switch, I just reach my hands out in front of me and follow the sound of her frail voice to her bedroom. Coming from the end of the hallway is the faint flicker of candlelight, and I find Megan kneeling beside her bed, hunched over it with her fingers digging into the comforter. Her hair is pulled back into a ponytail, but stray strands are stuck to her temples with sweat, her face red.

"I'm here," I say. "I'm here. Have you heard from Stephen?"

She gives me a strained nod. "He's trying to get out of the hospital, but I guess it's crazy there."

"I bet it is," I mumble. I take a deep breath and look around to find an anchor in an unfamiliar situation. Here, there's no pre-delivery ritual, no Enrique at my side. A clap of thunder makes me jump. I reach for the light switch, but after a few flicks, it's clear the power is out. "How close are the contractions?" I ask.

"I don't know exactly. Every few minutes, I think. It feels like they're right on top of each other. I think something's wrong, Dylan."

"No, there isn't. Nothing's wrong," I reassure her, though they're false words. Any of a dozen things could have caused Megan to go into labor early, some of those things life-threatening to her and her baby. "You're probably just progressing quickly."

She releases a guttural moan, and her face contorts with the pain of another contraction. I bend down next to her, and, careful not to disturb her too much, I place two fingers on the inside of her wrist to find her pulse. Blessedly, it's within a normal range.

"It's too soon," Megan says, once the contraction passes. "Why is this happening?"

Cooper appears outside the bedroom door and relief washes over me. His reaction is the opposite when he sees Megan on the floor in tears. I rush over to him before he can start asking questions and speak quietly so Megan won't hear me.

"If we don't get her to the hospital soon," I say, "she's going to have this baby right here on the floor."

Cooper runs his fingers through his hair to steady himself. "I called the ambulance, but I don't know how long it's going to take them to get here with the weather. The woman I spoke to said there have been a lot of accidents in the city."

The light coming from the candle on the dresser makes the lines of worry carved into his forehead more apparent. I fight to keep a certain little blue face from haunting my thoughts.

I open and close my fists as I debate my options. There aren't any. It would be too dangerous to drive Megan to the hospital myself in her condition. I would have even less to work with if she delivered her baby in the back of a moving vehicle.

"All we can do is hope the ambulance arrives in time and make her as comfortable as possible," I tell Cooper, and he nods in agreement.

I go back into the room and lean down to run a reassuring hand over Megan's back. "I'm going to check you, okay?"

She moans into another contraction, shaking her head.

"I know, sweetie, but I have to. I'll do it quickly. Cooper, I think I have some gloves in my bag in the trunk."

"I'll get them," he says and disappears.

"Is there anything I can do for you?" I ask Megan while we wait. "What would make the pain easier to cope with?"

"Stephen," she cries.

"I know. He's going to get here as soon as he possibly can. Can we get your pants off for a minute?"

She nods, and I help her to her feet. Cooper returns and looks away when he sees me pulling her sweatpants off. He holds the bag out, and I grab it.

"Just get into any position that's comfortable," I tell her as I open the bag and find a single pair of gloves. During med school, I was taught how to deliver with the help of machines and sometimes with the slice of a scalpel, and throughout my career, I have come to rely on these things. Tonight, when it matters most, I have little more than a pair of gloves. I pull one on.

Megan gets back onto her knees so I duck down and maneuver my way underneath her. Immediately, I feel her bag of waters bulging out but not broken. In fact, I can feel it a little too easily.

"Shit," I say, and immediately regret it.

"What?" she asks. "What's wrong?"

"Nothing," I say softly. "Everything is fine…except you're eight centimeters."

"Does that mean what I think it means?" She knows exactly what it means. She's probably read every book about birthing a baby ever written by now. Since her water hasn't broken yet, we may be able to prolong her labor until the ambulance gets here. Even if we don't make it to the hospital, they would have more tools than what I carry around in my bag. If her water breaks, though, this baby will be making its debut within the hour, ready or not.

I sigh and push my hair behind my ear. While Megan is still turned away from me, I take a moment to gather myself. I remind myself that when I accepted Megan as a patient, I vowed I would get her through this, whatever it took. I plan to keep that promise. I refuse to buckle under the pressure, so I'll have to learn to improvise quickly.

Megan looks over her shoulder at me, fear written all over her face. With my gloveless hand, I take hers.

"Feel like taking a relaxing bath?" I ask her. I've never overseen a home birth, let alone a water birth, but the nurse-midwives at the hospital have performed them for more than a decade. Since I have nothing else to offer Megan by way of pain relief, it's the best I can do.

Her smile looks more like a grimace when she says, "Relaxing, huh?"

"Candlelit, even."

I remove my glove and help her off the floor. With one hand, I carry our single source of light, and with the other,

I get her into the master bathroom, complete with a deep, round tub. I start the water running and help her in. Her oversize flowy white shirt floats around her, making her look like either a ghost or an angel. I can't decide.

"Are you okay in here for a minute?" I ask.

She curls down over her belly and goes red in the face as she moans through another contraction. I hold her hand. When she lets up again, she nods me away.

I find Cooper pacing in the living room. Rain pounds angrily at the roof, and with the glow of a streak of lightning, I catch a glimpse of Cooper with his hand wrapped around the back of his neck. I hope his stress is only because of Megan's predicament and not because he's upset with me. The last time he saw me was when I left his office with Reese.

"Have you heard from Stephen?"

"Yeah. A couple of minutes ago. He's on his way."

I breathe a sigh of relief. "Thank goodness. She needs him right now. And it certainly can't hurt to have another doctor in the house. What about your parents?"

"I didn't want to worry them. I'll call when we have news."

I nod. "That's probably for the best."

Megan moans again and Cooper flinches. "Is she okay?" he asks.

"Her heart rate is normal, her water hasn't broken yet and labor seems to be progressing as smoothly as can be hoped for."

I pretend that this is a term birth, and Cooper seems grateful for it.

"Good."

"Dylan," Megan screams from the other room. Cooper and I rush toward the bathroom where Megan is hunched over the side of the tub, panting.

"What's wrong?" I ask. I kick off my shoes, ready to get in if I have to.

"Don't…know. Rushing…between…my legs."

"Her water," I mumble to Cooper, and with a quick check, it's confirmed. Also, that she's at nine centimeters. No more backup plans. The baby is coming.

"Listen," I say, squatting in front of Megan so we're face-to-face. "I know this isn't what we planned, but I promise you, everything is going to be fine. People have home births all the time. I know you can do this."

"But the baby," she says. "What if its lungs aren't developed? What if it can't breathe?"

She must have read in one of her books that the lungs are the last organs to develop. It's my fear, too.

"The ambulance will have oxygen," I assure her. "And you know what, sweetie? You have one of the best pediatricians in the city here."

Megan nods. "Best in the country," she says.

"Best in the world." I laugh, and she smiles weakly.

When another contraction grips her, I find a scrub brush and offer her the handle to squeeze. I direct Cooper to grab a rag and wet it with fresh water to place on her forehead. I shush her and push her hair away from her face, struggling to keep my expression relaxed. My palms sweat.

Once the contraction passes, I excuse myself to grab my bag.

"She's having the baby here," I say to Cooper as he follows me out. Even I can hear the quiver in my voice. I pace the bedroom.

"What can I do to help?" he asks.

"I don't know. I don't know, Cooper." I rub my hand over my forehead to bring my training to the surface. "I don't have anything. I don't have a heart rate monitor. I don't have a contraction monitor. Heaven forbid she needs a C-section. I have one glove," I shout hysterically.

Cooper stops me with a hand on each shoulder. He puts his face close to mine. That helps. Breathing in his scent helps.

"Dylan, you can do this. You've done this hundreds of times."

"But you don't know what's happened—" I start to say.

"Yes, I do. Stephen told me." Of course Stephen told him. "But that had nothing to do with your ability. People have been giving birth without all that equipment for thousands of years with a lot less training. Let's get creative."

I nod, exhale, run through the list in my head. "I'll just have to keep my hands as clean as possible. Can you find some scissors and sterilize them the best you can to cut the umbilical cord? And…a rubber band to tie it off?"

If he smiles, he hides it quickly. "See. You've got this."

"What if I screw this up? She'll never forgive me. You'll never forgive me."

I'll never forgive myself.

"Dylan, you are not going to screw this up."

"If that baby needs a NICU—"

"Dylan," he says more sternly. "I'm here." I can hear in his voice that he doesn't only mean as a pediatrician.

"Okay," I say. I grab my bag off the dresser and walk to the bathroom, but turn back. "Coop," I say.

He stops, already to the hallway. I want to thank him for his support, for making me feel like I can do this. He's always made me feel like I could do anything I set my mind to, even when I was just a young, heartbroken med student trying to find my place in the world.

"I…"

His lips twitch into a smile. There's not enough time to

express what he's done for me over the years, but he under-stands. He nods and falls into the darkness.

"How are you feeling?" I ask Megan in the bathroom. Her elbows are hooked over the side of the tub, her eyes are closed. The contractions are so close together that she keeps up a steady stream of controlled moans, like she's fallen into a meditative state.

"I have to…start pushing."

"Let me check you again," I say. But before I can reach between her legs, another contraction hits, and I can tell from her cry that this one is different. This one is pushing the baby down with or without her help.

"I have to push," she says through gritted teeth. "I have to push."

"Okay," I say, channeling my own peace because proce-dure will do me no good here in this bathroom. It's me and her. "I trust you. Trust your body. I'm right here."

"Where's Stephen?" she asks.

"I'm sorry, Megan. Right now it's about you and your baby. Let's focus on that."

Her face crumples and tears leak from her eyes, but after a moment, she pulls herself together and breathes deeply.

"It's coming," she says in a whisper. She takes control of her breathing, and I know she's found that place. She's ready.

"Need an extra hand?" Cooper says, slipping into the room.

He sets out supplies on the bathroom sink. Megan nods and holds her hand out to him. He lowers himself onto the floor and takes both her hands in his, holding them tightly. Then he looks at me and smiles, and in this awful situation, when so many things could go wrong, his optimism makes me believe that just maybe, things will go right.

I take a deep breath and utter my favorite words.

"It's time."

★ ★ ★

"Everything is going to change," Abby said the night she told me she was pregnant. We were in my bed, and, unable to sleep, I'd pulled my blinds all the way open to let the moonlight shine in, brightening all the clean, organized surfaces in my room. It was one of the rare times Abby had sneaked into my room instead of me sneaking into hers. She had tucked her head into the nook under my arm, like a toddler, and in that moment I felt like the older sister. I felt like I was the strong one—strong enough to get both of us through this.

"Not everything," I said. "You'll still be you. I'll still be me. We'll still have each other."

She looked up at me and smiled. It faded quickly, and she turned her head back down again.

"I won't be able to go to college," she said. "I won't be able to travel. How can I be a good journalist if I can't travel?"

"Maybe not at first. But you know Mom will help with the baby. And when he or she gets older, you'll find a way to make it work."

"I hope it's a she," Abby whispered.

I grinned. "Me, too."

Abby sighed. "I'm going to end up stuck here, Dylan. People have a small window of opportunity to break out and create a life of their own away from their parents, and I'm going to miss it." She was less than a month away from graduating high school. She'd been planning on fleeing like a baby bird from its mother's nest the moment the rolled-up certificate landed on her palm.

"Ab—"

"I don't want to be comforted right now. Please. I just want to be realistic, okay? No one is going to want to date a single teenage mom. No one is going to hire a journalist without a degree who can't travel. All the adventures I've wanted to have, all the places I've wanted to see...they're just a sad dream now."

Abby sniffed, and a small patch of moisture bled through my shirt onto my shoulder. I wanted to say something to encourage her, but what did I know about life? If my older, more experienced, more courageous sister couldn't see a way out of this, what advice could I offer?

"Maybe you can come up with a new dream?" I asked her.

"You can't just come up with a new dream, Dylan," she said, like I'd suggested she grow a third arm. "Each of us is born to do something important with our lives. You can't just pick something different out of a hat."

I thought she was probably right, but I couldn't bring myself to tell her that maybe most people didn't actually know what that important thing was at eighteen years old. Maybe what she thought was important now would change.

"What's your dream, Dylan? Basketball?"

"No," I was quick to say. I liked basketball. I was good at it. But if I had only one important thing to do with my life, I didn't think basketball was it. "I don't know. If I figure out anything to do that could be considered 'important,' I'd be happy."

Abby shifted so she could look up at me. Today, I felt like I was already doing something important.

"That's a cop-out answer," she said. "There has to be something you want to do."

I sighed, thinking. "There was this one time last year when one of the girls on the team was having trouble in math—"

"Who?" Abby asked.

I laughed. "Uh-uh. No gossip tonight. So she was having trouble with math, and her parents had threatened to take her off the team if she didn't get her grades up. We were talking about it in the locker room after practice one day, and I offered to help her with it. I didn't mean for it to be a big deal, but she was really grateful. We met at lunch for a few weeks, and I helped her with her homework and showed her how I calculated the problems. Sometimes the way teachers explain things is just stupid—" Abby hummed her agreement "—but the way I approached it seemed to work for her. Before two weeks was up, she was doing it on her own, and she finished the year with straight As. And she hasn't even needed my help at all this year." I shrug. "It felt good to help her feel like she could handle it."

"So you want to be, like, a teacher or something?"

"Maybe," I said. "Maybe not. I just like helping people."

I said it quietly and waited for her to laugh, to tell me I hated people. It was a common misconception. In truth, I hated small talk, gossip, petty arguments. I loved being with people when we could break through all that and get to the heart of things. That's how Abby and I had always talked, and I never understood why I couldn't find a friend like that. Maybe I never worked hard enough to get past the getting-to-know-you phase.

Instead, Abby said, "I think you have a lot to offer people. You've always been there to help me."

I couldn't help it. I laughed. What could I have possibly done to help Abby—the one who had everything figured out?

"I'm serious, Dylan," she said. "I know I give you a lot of crap about not getting out more and meeting new people, but you're the only person I've ever been able to truly count on. You're always there when I need you, even when I don't deserve it. That'll get you a lot further in life than chasing adventure. Speaking from experience."

The sullen mood fell over the room again, but her compliment fanned the spark of hope in my belly. Maybe I had a dream after all—even if it wasn't fully formed yet.

"Promise me you're not going to give up," I said. I rolled onto my side and scooted down until we were face-to-face. I was already taller than her. "We'll find a way to make this work. I'll help you."

"See, you're doing it already." I pushed her shoulder and we both laughed. When we fell silent, she said, "I'll tell you what. I promise not to give up if you don't."

"Give up on what?" I asked.

"Whatever your dream turns out to be. And…a little bit of adventure." She held her thumb and forefinger half an inch apart in the space between us. I smiled and stuck out my pinky finger. It was what we'd always done to seal a promise, and I wanted Abby's word that she would never stop being the girl I looked up to, the kind of woman I hoped to one day be. Abby stuck out her pinky, too, and locked it with mine.

"Promise," she said.

I held her pinky tight and kissed my thumbnail for extra assurance.

"Promise," I said.

As the overcast sky begins to brighten with the morning sun, the red ambulance lights flash color onto every wall in the house. Megan and Stephen both lie on the bed, the baby in Stephen's arms, as medics look over mother and child to make sure they're fit for travel. Megan has changed into a long nightgown and looks tired but more happy than I've ever seen her. Stephen is still in awe.

Cooper checked out the baby immediately after birth, and he's shown no signs of being anything but healthy, aside from a little jaundice, though doctors will probably want to keep him at the hospital for a couple days for observation. It's unbelievable. With Erika's baby, the scene was set for the best possible delivery, and the worst happened. This time everything went wrong, and yet, it all turned out fine. Great, even.

"I don't want to go to the hospital," Megan says. She reaches across the bed and runs the back of her finger over the baby's head. The black woman examining her raises an eyebrow at me, questioning whether or not we're going to have a problem getting Megan into the ambulance. I smile and give her a discreet shake of the head.

"I know," I say. "But I need to make sure you don't need any stitches, and I'd feel better knowing the baby has been checked over by a clocked-in pediatrician, just to be sure."

"This little boy is perfect," she says to her son in baby talk.

"Yes, he is."

A knock on the door frame makes us all look up. Cooper stands at the threshold.

"See," Megan says, "there's our pediatrician."

Cooper grins and takes a seat at the edge of the bed, admiring the sleeping boy. He runs a finger over the baby's toes as a young male medic crouched next to Stephen listens to his little heartbeat.

"You know," Cooper says, "I see babies all the time...but this one just feels different."

Megan laughs. "That's what Dylan has said at all of our prenatal appointments."

Cooper grins at me. "It's because he's family."

A smile plays at my lips, but I look away.

"Do you want to hold him?" Megan asks Cooper.

"If he's finished," he says, nodding to the medic. "I don't want to interrupt."

"I'm done here," the medic says. "We're going to grab the stretcher." He stands and leaves the room, his colleague right behind him.

Stephen passes the baby over to Cooper like he's made

of paper, and Cooper takes him just as gingerly. He pulls the baby close, and even though the little one is fast asleep, Cooper rocks him and shushes him naturally. He has years of experience as a pediatrician, but something tells me this movement is more instinctive.

"You want to hold him?" Cooper asks, turning to me like he's ready to hand the baby off before he accidentally shows his sensitive side. I stifle a laugh.

"No. That's okay."

"Go on," Megan says. "He's still your nephew. And god-child...I hope."

I take a step back and put my hands up, my cheeks warm with emotion. It's overwhelming, this gesture of uncondi-tional love.

Stephen rises from the bed and places an arm around me.

"C'mon," he says. "This isn't a moment you're going to want to miss." He guides me forward. Cooper holds the baby out and places him in my hands. He's so warm and soft and can't weigh more than six pounds. His skin really does feel like paper against my lips as I lean down to place a kiss on his forehead. I leave a tear there, as well.

"He's beautiful," I say. "He has Stephen's nose."

Stephen and Megan both laugh through their happy tears. "He does, doesn't he?" Stephen says. "It's a good nose."

"It's a good nose," I agree.

Cooper comes to stand next to me and brushes my hair behind my shoulder. He places his cheek against mine, and my heart melts. In spite of myself, I lean into him to ease the mutual ache for the future we could have had.

Ten minutes later, Cooper and I wave to Megan and Ste-phen as the paramedics close the ambulance doors. We stand with our hands shielding our eyes from the drizzle still coming down and watch them disappear around the corner. It's eerily quiet.

Cooper looks at me, a tilted grin on his face. It's the last expression I expected from him after what he witnessed at his office, but it's so Cooper.

"What?" I ask.

"Nothing. Just, tonight…watching you work. You're amazing at what you do."

I roll my eyes but can't help the smile that creeps across my face. "You've seen me work before."

"Yeah, but it's been a while. I forgot. And you've gotten better. A lot better. It was like you didn't believe in yourself before." He takes a step closer. "But once you relaxed and gave in to the situation, you were completely in control in there. It's incredible what you do. You don't just deliver a baby—you're, like, the Pregnant Woman Whisperer."

"Pregnant Woman Whisperer, huh?"

He chuckles. "I don't know. It was the first thing that came to mind."

Cooper steps closer and reaches for my hands. I hesitate, then take them and lean my head back to let the rain kiss my face. When I look to Cooper, he appears awestruck. When I ask him what he's thinking this time, he shakes his head, looking at me with something that looks like adoration. His tired smile makes my heart skip a beat.

"I have to tell you something," I say.

"Okay."

I'm not sure why it's important to tell Cooper about my sister—it means nothing to him now—or why it feels like the right time to finally get it off my chest. Maybe because it's important he understands I'm not any kind of whisperer. I'm just a woman and a doctor with the best intentions. Or maybe because I need him to know that I understand how I used it to distance myself from him, and I accept my part for what went wrong between us. Either way, he's been there for me all these years. He deserves to know.

"You were right. I have been keeping a secret from you."

"What is it?" he asks. He doesn't look nervous, no sense of foreboding, like he once had whenever I tried to open up to him about my past. At first I think it's something in him that has changed, but then I realize it's me. There's no fear in my heart when I begin to speak the words. There's no urge to flee for him to pick up on. There's just me, and the truth.

"There's more to my sister's death than I've told you."

And then I tell him everything. About how she confided in me. About how I kept her secret when I felt like I shouldn't. About our hospital trip the night she died.

"And then *my* sister asked you to keep her secret, too," he says.

"It's okay," I say. "I'm okay. She's worth it. Besides, it all worked out perfectly."

I go on to tell him about how my guilt put a rift in my relationship with my mom, and how we've begun to repair it. I confess my father's adultery, how it ruined my parents, and what I've learned from it. I tell him all the dark parts of my life that I was once ashamed to tell anyone, especially the man I am—still, inexplicably and completely—in love with.

When he's heard it all, he frowns as he tries to process it. Finally, he says, "Oh, babe," and pulls me into his arms. He holds me so close we could melt into one, and I revel in his embrace. I need it. "I can't believe you never told me this. I can't believe you've been living with it all this time, thinking it was your fault." He takes me by the arms and holds me in front of him so he can pointedly say, "You do know it wasn't your fault, right? It wasn't your fault, Dylan."

I nod, my lips pursed. "It took me a long time to realize it, but I think I finally believe it."

He fills his cheeks with air and blows it out, like it hurt him to hear the story more than it hurt me to tell it.

"I wish you'd trusted me enough to tell me before," he says. "It could have changed so much."

"I know," I say. "Believe me, I know. But sometimes it takes going through something big to finally face what we're afraid of."

Cooper frowns. *Something big.* The end of us.

"It wasn't only losing you," I say. "There are a lot of things I've been too afraid to deal with. But I couldn't have done that last one without you." I nod toward the house.

He puts his thumb to my cheek and grazes his skin over mine. "You can do anything without me. The question is whether or not you want to."

"I don't think I want to," I whisper.

His gaze flickers over my face, from my eyes to my lips and back again, as if he doesn't dare believe the words. I don't know if this counts as an adventure—trusting a man who could break my heart again—but it's a risk I'm willing to take. Looking into his eyes and knowing his heart, it doesn't seem like a very big risk to me.

"Can I take you home?" he asks me, reminding me of the night we met, when we fell in love, whether I wanted to admit it or not. I bite my lip and bite back the overwhelming happiness that fills my chest.

I nod.

When we walk into the house, the energy is different with Cooper here again. I take Spencer out while he gets a drink in the kitchen. I take my time outside, letting it all sink in.

When I go back inside, Cooper is leaning against the

couch, waiting for me. I stop a few feet from him, watching him, watching me. I've never wanted so badly to know what he was thinking. He takes one long, deep breath as if preparing for what we both know will come, then he rushes over to me and takes me in his arms. And I want more. I want all of him. My lips search for his, and when they find them, he hesitates for only a moment before he kisses me back—the soft, loving, familiar kiss that is all I've ever wanted. He pushes my hair back from my face, kisses away the tears on my cheeks. My lips wait for his to return, and when they do, I convey everything I've been feeling, everything I've been wanting, everything I've been needing for months and years. I show him how I feel with every touch until we're grasping at each other with a hunger I've never felt before—love, with no barriers between us.

"I love you, Dylan," Cooper gasps, and I realize he's crying, too. "I can't live without you." I cry harder.

Cooper carefully sweeps me off my feet and carries me to the bed. The early morning light brightens the room just enough to see him in shadows. He sets me down in front of the bed and looks into my eyes. Everything I've needed to know is there. It always was.

Cooper peels off my clothes. I take his off in a rush. I crave the feel of his skin on mine. I wrap myself around him, and we fall together.

Cooper and I lose track of time and space as we make love for hours, caressing one another, reintroducing each other to how our desires have changed over the years—changes we've missed in our old routine that fulfilled only physical needs. The only time we speak is to say "I love you" over and over again. Eventually we reach a point somewhere between exhaustion and an altered state of consciousness, and we curl up next to each other as easily as everything else has come today.

"God, I missed you," Cooper says. He pulls me closer and kisses my hair. I smile and nod, trace lazy circles on his chest. I could stay like this forever. But there's still so much to figure out. If Cooper and I are going to make it this time, we have to learn to talk to each other again.

"Why did you fall in love with me, Cooper?" I ask as a place to start.

He turns to face me. He's wearing a reminiscent smile, and his eyes are bright with happiness. I'm sure mine are, too.

"Well, you came home with me that first night."

I roll my eyes.

"No, I'm not talking about *that*. I mean, that sure didn't hurt—"

I cut him off with a playful smack on the arm. He laughs and kisses me. He won't stop kissing me.

"Do you remember what you told me when I asked you why you wanted to be a doctor?"

I shake my head. "That was a long time ago. I'm not even sure I would give you the same answer."

He traces his thumb across my chin. "You said it was because people are afraid and lonely...especially when they're hurt or sick or about to do the scariest thing they can imagine. You told me all they want is someone who will tell them it's going to be okay and mean it. And you wanted to be that person."

A coy grin creeps across my face. "Boy, I sure was naive back then, wasn't I?"

"Yes, you were."

But the answer still holds true. I still feel that way. I still love to help people.

"And when I told you that you wouldn't be able to do that for everyone," he says, "you said you could try. Right then

I knew no one else would make me happier or more proud than you. And I was right."

I swallow hard, and tears leak from my eyes. I can't believe he remembers so much from that night when I assumed, while it was happening, it would be a night I'd want to forget. He knew all along our conversations would mean something some day, and he memorized them. What I would give for that kind of faith.

"Do you remember what you told me when I asked you why you wanted to be a doctor?" I ask.

He shakes his head.

"Because you wanted people to have to call you Dr. Caldwell."

We laugh and kiss and fall into silence again. Cooper combs my hair away from my face with his fingers.

"I do love delivering babies," I say. "But I still can't help but feel I'm meant to do more."

"You are, Dylan. I should never have forgotten that."

"And I should never have forgotten that being able to live a long life with the ones you love is why doctors exist. Or that you're the one I want to live mine with."

He's smiling from ear to ear.

"What?" I ask.

"I just can't remember the last time I've seen you so happy. You're really beautiful, you know that?"

My cheeks warm, and I bury my face in his shoulder.

He leans down, and I come out from hiding for a kiss. When he pulls back, I look away. There's one more thing to discuss, and I hope it won't ruin the progress we've made in the last few hours. I feel no shame for what happened with Reese. Maybe it's wrong of me to forgive myself so easily when it was nearly impossible for me to forgive Cooper, but when the foundation of a relationship is shattered, sometimes it takes time away from the wreckage to see if it's worth re-building. Still, the omission would hang over my head for-ever. Cooper and I can't start a future based on lies. It's what almost broke us the first time.

"There's one other thing I feel like I should tell you," I say in a whisper. His body tenses, and I know he knows what I'm about to say. He takes a deep breath and runs his finger across my collarbone.

"Is it going to affect us from this day forward?" he asks me.

"No," I say. A month ago, I might not have had the same answer, but now I know, without a doubt, where my home is.

"Then don't tell me," he says.

"Are you sure?" I ask. It would be easy to tell him. Nothing happened. But the fact that he trusts me without having to say it means so much more.

"I'm sure."

18

The day is cool, but the sun is bright with no clouds to hide behind. Autumn is here. I sit at my mother's vanity in her room, inserting one of her pearl earrings into my ear. White, to match everything else. I look up when I hear the door open behind me, and Megan comes into the room. She stops just inside the door. Her hair is twisted into an elegant knot, revealing the warm glow of motherhood on her face.

"You look breathtaking," she says.

"I should. You picked the dress."

"I always wanted a sister to dress up. Cooper wouldn't let me."

I laugh and she comes over to adjust my veil, and it feels like the most natural thing in the world, almost as if she really is my sister. Within the hour she will be, and though she'll never replace Abby, she'll be a part of a new family that starts today.

"Is that dirt under your fingernails?" I ask.

She looks at her hand and smirks. "Stephen and I took Benjamin for a hike this morning."

"A hike?"

"Well, you know, compromise and all that. You'll learn soon." She winks.

I stand, pulling the train of my dress behind me, and I wrap my arms around her. She laughs and extends her neck to avoid smudging her pink lipstick on the face my mother spent all afternoon putting together.

"Maybe we'll all go next time," I say.

"That would be great. Stephen would love that."

We're interrupted by another creak of the door. Mom sticks her head in, and her smile is so vibrant my breath hitches. *There's my mom*, I think. The pizzeria owner's wife.

"Sorry to interrupt, ladies," she says. "It's time."

I smile at the familiar words.

Yes. It is.

When I asked my mom to plan the wedding, I assured her I wanted something simple—just close friends and family. And soon. We'd put it off long enough, and at this point it's more for them than it is for us. I pledged my commitment to Cooper the night he moved back in, when I finally said *yes*.

Giving Mom something to do helped her through the roughest days after Dad left, and it gave us something to bond over. After I sent in my grant application, Vanessa cut my new patient appointments in half. I thought I would feel lost, unsure of what to do with myself, but since I no longer carry the burden of trying to save everyone, I've been able to relax and enjoy the patients I have, knowing I can't protect them from everything, but that I can give them my best. Finding more balance in my life has made that easier to do. I should hear an answer about the grant in the next few weeks, and I'm hopeful.

In the meantime, I used my free time to come over a few afternoons each week and let Mom tell me about the progress she'd made on my wedding over iced teas. She was so happy to have something productive to put her focus into, I didn't make a fuss when she suggested making cookies and cakes that were entirely too fancy for the occasion, or when she ordered even more flowers to decorate the backyard. In fact, she loved it all so much, she got a job at the local florist.

Together, we pruned her garden in preparation for winter.

With Megan on one side and my mom on the other, I make my way down the staircase to the main floor, where pastries and food platters line the kitchen counters. In the dining room, my dad waits for me, wearing a sharp black suit and a smile. At the sight of him, Mom gracefully disappears into the backyard, taking Megan with her. It's still hard for my parents to be in the same room with each other, but I have faith that over time, we will be a family again—a different kind of family. Maybe one that works better.

"I've dreamed of this day since you were a little girl," Dad says with a tear in his eye. He runs a hand lightly over my hair. His face can hardly contain his smile. I lean forward and kiss his cheek.

There is no string quartet when I step out onto the patio, no doves released into the air, only a still silence of the people I love watching me glide down the steps, and the lapping of the waves at the shore. My brother is here, of course, along with Stephen and Megan, and my godson, Benjamin, already a month old. Cooper's parents are huddled together near the front, both of them crying. My aunt made it, as well as a few of the doctors and nurses from the hospital and Cooper's practice.

And there, at the end of the aisle created by the people who have seen us at our best and at our worst, stands Cooper in white pants and a loose white button-up, looking out at the water. Once again, I wish I knew what he was thinking, waiting for me with his hands clasped in front of him. I hope he's thinking of our future, the way I am as I walk toward him. Maybe our honeymoon—a trip to Hawaii. Maybe lazy nights around the house or tending the garden together—our new favorite hobby. I hope he's thinking about our future children, and watching them grow. Watching each other grow, and the adventure our life will be.

★ ★ ★ ★ ★

Acknowledgments

First, I want to thank my agent, Claire Anderson-Wheeler, for seeing in me and my story what I hadn't yet seen myself. This book would not be what it is without you. This is OUR win.

Thanks to my editor, Allison Carroll. Your love of my story has "stuck with me in my bones" and will be what I return to whenever I doubt my purpose. Thank you, and everyone in the Graydon House/Harlequin team, for believing in my book and bringing it to life.

Thanks to those who provided invaluable information on the medical front, namely Peggy and Salena. Any narrative liberties are mine.

To my Soul Sisters: Shawna, for being my first fan and the best midnight storyteller. Deborah, for being the kind of woman I model heroines after and for being my other half. Bubble, for always asking about the book and checking in to see if I was surviving this whole writer-mom thing. Erika, your awesomeness showed up in my book before I even met you—the Universe must have known. And Victoria, from MySpace to IRL. You all keep me going and believing.

I have so many writer friends to thank: Selena Laurence,

for always keeping my head on straight and for promising we'll be crazy old ladies at the coffee shop together. Alyson, for reading this book almost as many times as me and loving it every time. Aimie, for being my conference wife and the best road trip copilot. The Badasses, who kept me laughing when it so wasn't funny anymore—especially Kate Moretti, who provided invaluable feedback on the story and who always inspires me to be more badass. The Motivated Writers, both online and in real life—there are no words for how much you mean to me. You are my people. And the Women's Fiction Writers Association, where I've found my home.

I want to thank my family: Dad, you are the reason I can't help but write the most lovable father characters, the reason I'm strong and the reason I believe I can do anything. Mom, thank you for being there when you didn't have to, and for making me proud to turn out just like my mother. Sarah, my seester, my almost-twin, helloooo! I love you to the ends of the earth. James, Peggy and Theresa, you are my family, no "in"s about it. I could not live this dream without you. Thank you for absolutely everything. And lastly, to Aunt Charlotte, for believing I'd grow up to be a star. Here's hoping.

Most important, thank you to my husband, without whom I could not have done this. Thank you for our beautiful life and beautiful family. Thank you for believing in me and supporting me unwaveringly, in every way possible. And to my girls: thank you for giving me the greatest privilege of a lifetime of watching you grow. I'll always love you the best.

PERFECTLY

UNDONE

JAMIE RAINTREE

Reader's Guide

GRAYDON
HOUSE

QUESTIONS FOR DISCUSSION

1. The balance between relationships, family and career is a common struggle for women in the 21st century. How do you feel about the balance Dylan strikes at various points throughout the book? Do you think her choices make her unlikable or relatable (or both)? In what ways do you struggle with finding balance in your own life?

2. Discuss the effects Abby's death had on Dylan's career path. What line of work do you think Dylan might have chosen if Abby had lived?

3. The unconditional love of family is a deep desire for Dylan, and she feels as much a part of Cooper's family as her own—maybe more. Compare and contrast the two families and the effect their dynamics had on Dylan, Charlie, Cooper and Megan. Which family do you most identify with?

4. Dylan has spent her young adulthood fearing she would become like her mother—distant and too overcome with grief to connect with those around her. In what ways have they been alike all along? In what ways are they different?

5. When Cooper admits to being unfaithful, Dylan asks him to move out immediately. Do you think this was the right choice or do you think Dylan should have tried to work through the transgression with Cooper first? In the same situation, which decision would you have made?

6. While Dylan helps Reese plant flowers in her garden, Reese does not allow Dylan to correct what she views as mistakes. What role do you think Reese plays in widening Dylan's perspective? In what other ways are Dylan's actions different in the garden versus the other areas of her life? How does that change over the course of the story?

7. When Dylan decides not to sleep with Reese, it becomes a catalyst for change and she begins to turn her life around. Why do you think this is her breakthrough moment and what realizations do you think she comes to? Do you think she should have pursued a relationship with Reese? Why or why not?

8. When Erika's baby dies during childbirth, Dylan grieves the loss in much the same way she did Abby's death. A common coping strategy for dealing with the loss of a loved one is to wonder what those around them could have done differently—if an alternative choice could have saved them. How much responsibility do you think Dylan should accept in each situation? Do you think she should have gone against her sister's wishes and told her parents that Abby was pregnant? What risks does Dylan take when she agrees to keep Megan's pregnancy a secret?

9. Dylan discovers a packet of daisy seeds and plants them at the beginning of the story, but they never sprout. What do you think the seeds are meant to symbolize? How do they relate to Dylan's emotional growth?

10. There are parallels between the relationships of Dylan and Cooper, Stephen and Megan, and Dylan's parents. Why do you think Dylan and Cooper, and Stephen and Megan are able to overcome their conflicts while Dylan's parents are not?

11. Dylan decides to continue pursuing her research grant, reducing her hours at the clinic. Do you think this was the best choice for Dylan or do you think giving up the grant altogether would have been the ultimate act of moving on from Abby's death? Do you hope Dylan gets the grant? Why or why not?

12. Do you think Dylan was right to forgive Cooper for his infidelity? Do you think she was right to accept any responsibility for Cooper's decision to cheat? Has the story changed your perspective at all on the subject of infidelity?

13. Forgiveness is a common theme throughout the book. Which was your favorite moment of forgiveness? Who do you think it was most important for Dylan to forgive to find happiness?

14. The title, *Perfectly Undone*, seems to pair contradictory ideas. How do you think it captures the tone of the story and Dylan's emotional journey?

For a sneak peek at Jamie Raintree's next unforgettable novel, turn the page…

Is home a place or a person? A season or a time of day? A sound, a song, a feeling? For me, the memories are so woven together, it's hard to separate them from one another—to pinpoint what I long for when I'm gone, or what I feel welcoming me when I return.

I sense it now—its unique gravity—at eleven minutes before midnight as I take the final right turn onto the dirt road that leads to The Perfect White Vineyard.

My home.

I snap off the radio in the little four-door rental car and sit up straighter in my seat. With a knee on the steering wheel, I twist the elastic out of my thick hair and shake it out in preparation for the greeting I've looked forward to all day, and for the five years since my last visit. Then, so I don't disturb anyone, I switch off my headlights, drowning the car and the expansive property in darkness. The car continues to jostle down the long drive and I wait for the house to come into view. It's been five years since I moved to New York but the scents, the sounds and the feeling that wash over me are the same. Home never changes.

I roll down the windows to let in the warm spring night as I drive beneath the arching sign that welcomes me and past the refurbished barn turned tasting room, the paint still as fresh as the day I helped roll it on. Then, up on the hill, there it is—the house I grew up in, a single light on in the kitchen like a beacon. I smile.

Farther up, the outbuildings come into view. The stables. *The guesthouse.* My breath hitches. Still.

I swallow back the memories of the last summer I spent here, not allowing them to steal this moment from me. I focus on the stables, where I know who will be waiting for me.

I creep my way up the parking lot, dust and gravel betraying my arrival, and park next to my dad's old pickup. When I turn off the engine, it's deathly silent. So silent I feel the pressure on my eardrums. I'd forgotten how quiet it is this far from the city. Silence doesn't exist in New York City.

I tiptoe down the path to the stables. The barn door clicks as I lift the latch and pull it open. I leave the lights off. I can walk the path to Midnight's stall with my eyes closed, but enough moonlight shines through the high windows that I don't have to. A full moon. A sign, maybe.

"Midnight," I call into the open space. There's the rustle of live animals but no other sound.

I call again, and when her nose pokes into the breezeway, I let loose a laugh, no longer caring about waking anyone. I close the space between us and open my palm to her silky lips.

"Hey, girl," I coo. "I've missed you so much." I rub my fingers over the length of her nose and rest my cheek against hers. I've lived without her sweet comfort for far too long, and I can't wait a second longer.

I grab Midnight's halter from the wall and lift the stall door latch. With the quick motion of a practiced movement, I slide the halter on her and lead her out of the stall. Her dark color blends into the night, aside from her white haunches, which practically glow.

"Want to go for a run, girl?" I ask.

"Not even gonna say 'hi' first, are you?" a rough voice responds. I start, my hair whipping over my shoulder as I look behind me. The light in the stable office flicks on, and in the doorway stands my dad. He leans against the frame with his hands in the pockets of his jeans, holes in the knees. All his jeans have holes in the knees. But his jaw is smooth and his plaid button-down is one of the two he saves for holidays. He dressed up for my homecoming.

"Dad," I say, breathless. I run to him and throw my arms around his neck, allow myself to be enveloped in his earthy scent, his subtle strength and his love.

"You are in big trouble, Mallory Victoria. You are not allowed to leave your room for the next twenty years. No, make that thirty."

"I missed you, too," I whisper in his ear, grinning.

"Could've fooled me," he says with a gruff laugh and a nod toward Midnight.

I shrug. "She's prettier than you."

"Can't argue with you there."

Dad takes my shoulders and holds me back. He looks me over and shakes his head, tears brimming his eyes.

"How did you get so grown-up?" he asks. "You were still a little girl when you left."

"I saw you last Christmas."

"Is that what you call handing each other gifts over the salt and pepper shakers at a restaurant I can't even remember the name of?"

I frown. "Sorry, Dad. But any apartment this girl can afford isn't even big enough to hold the necklace you gave me, let alone houseguests. I appreciated you coming, though. And I love the necklace."

I dig the pendant out from beneath my shirt—an abstract outline of a horse, its mane blowing in the wind of my breath.

Dad rubs his calloused thumb across the white gold surface and his smile saddens.

"Hey, none of that," I say, nudging his shoulder. "Save that for when I leave."

"You just got here and you're already talking about leaving?" He groans and feigns stabbing himself in the heart.

"Dad."

"Oh, go on," he says, shooing me toward Midnight.

"Are you sure?" I ask, even as I'm stepping toward her.

"Go on."

I smile, plant a kiss on Dad's cheek, then grab hold of Midnight's mane. I throw my leg over her bare back, send one last glance toward Dad and then, with the quick hitch of my heel, Midnight trots out of the stables into the night.

When I wake in the morning, the sun is high in the sky, lighting up my childhood room in a soft orange glow. I stare straight up at a poster taped to my ceiling that says, "Today is the first day of the rest of your life." I snort a laugh. I was a lot more optimistic when I put that up there. These days, I call it naive.

My phone chimes on the nightstand next to me. I grab it and hold it over my face as I blink my eyes into focus. It's a text from Denise, my boss from the marketing firm where I've interned for the last year. My *ex*-boss as of yesterday, unless I accept the permanent position she offered me a few weeks ago as my internship was coming to an end.

Are you bored yet? she asks. Don't forget that I need an answer by next Friday!

The smile on my face is involuntary. Denise is New York, born and raised, and she never misses the opportunity to remind me of how different our personalities are. When I told her I was coming home for a couple of weeks after my internship ended, she curled her lip and asked, *But what will you do?*

I text her back.

Slept til 7 am. Jealous?

I return my phone to the nightstand and as I stare back up at the poster on my ceiling, the smile slides off my face. Underneath the humor, I recognize her message for what it is: a reminder that I have a big decision to make and very little time to make it in.

Downstairs half an hour later, Mom is humming in the kitchen, flipping pancakes and frying bacon. She's in sweatpants and a tank, her dark hair messy down her back, no bra. This is her small rebellion against the nine-to-five life. Dad's rebellion was to give up a job in manufacturing, move us halfway across the country and deplete my parents' entire savings to follow his dream of opening a vineyard. My mom forgoes bras on the weekend.

"Hey, Mom," I say. She squeals when she sees me and pads barefoot across the Mexican tile to wrap me in a hug. She kisses me all over my face like I'm still four years old and I laugh, allowing her this indulgence. In the time I've been gone, we've only seen each other a handful of times and it's been as painful for me as it has, no doubt, been for her.

"I just sort of made...everything," she says and motions toward the breakfast bar on the kitchen island. I pull my hair back into a ponytail and pull up a stool.

"Dad out *loving on* the vines?" I ask, finger quotes on the "loving on." Mom's smirk says it all. She sets a plate in front of me, stacked high with pancakes, bacon, scrambled eggs, half a grapefruit and some strawberries.

"Of course he is. He *loves on* those grapes more than he *loves on* me."

"TMI, Mom."

She waves my comment away but her cheeks turn pink beneath her glowing olive skin and her dark brown freckles. My dad says those freckles are the only thing keeping us from looking like twins. He leaves out the twenty-three-year age difference and she loves him more for it.

"I missed you," I say, suddenly overwhelmed by the emotion. In New York, my life is so busy, there are no cracks for reflection or emotions to creep into. But already, after a single morning here, I feel them sneaking up on me.

Mom pinches the bridge of my nose and says, "I missed you, too, kiddo."

I clear my throat and sit up straighter. I pretend for her, and for myself, that it's in preparation to tackle my breakfast. "So you're going to put me to work, right?"

"I don't have much of a choice," she teases. "You probably picked the wrong time to make an extended visit."

She pulls up the stool next to me and takes a bite of her bacon. We both know this is the first time since I left that I have no commitments holding me in the city, between getting my degree from Columbia, the job I worked to pay for it and my internship this last year. When my parents came to visit for Christmas, Dad casually mentioned he was thinking of having a planting party this spring—assuming, of course, that I wouldn't be able to make it, but ever hoping anyway. I was grateful that, to his surprise, I could finally give him the answer he was looking for. The guilt of being away from my family had long since been weighing on my shoulders and, if I was being honest with myself, I'd been thinking about home more and more often in the few minutes before I fell asleep alone each night.

"I wouldn't have missed this for anything," I say with the luxurious confidence of already being here.

Mom takes my hand and squeezes it, looking me purposefully in the eye. "It means everything to your dad that you're here."

This planting party means much more than a few acres of new grapes. Most people romanticize the life of a vintner as all affluence and glamour, but in reality, my dad is a farmer through and through. He has struggled to make the vineyard a success for nearly two decades and for the first time in the history of The Perfect White Vineyard, the business is profiting. The planting party is an expansion and a celebration. It's an affirmation that my parents' hard work over the years has finally paid off.

I squeeze her hand in return. "It means everything to me to be here," I say.

After breakfast, I return to my room and rummage through my suitcase for more running clothes. They're the only outfits I own that aren't tailored for the office. I settle on a pair of black capri yoga pants and a loose white T-shirt. I catch a glimpse of my riding boots sitting in the corner of my room where I left them five years ago, worn in and dusty. I pause, frown and then lace up my tennis shoes.

Outside, the weather is cool but with the undercurrent of warmth that seeps up from the dry ground, promising that spring is finally here. There's a hint of moisture in the air, too, which we only get in Paso Robles when the heavens are smiling down on us. I send a prayer to the sky—the new vines will need a healthy amount of water to acclimate to the new soil.

When I reach the stables, Tiramisu's stall is open and I hear the clanking of a bucket on the horse feeder. I already know who it is. I stop in my tracks, put my hands on my hips and say, "Hey, cowboy."

The bucket clatters to the ground and I cover my ears with my hands, laughing. When Tyler peers around the corner, his eyes light up and his jaw hangs open.

"No way," he says. I laugh as he jogs to me, wraps his arms around my waist and spins me around. "Your dad told me you were coming back but I didn't believe him. But shit, you're actually here."

His mouth is still slack as he looks me over, gauging how much I've changed. I haven't seen him since my last summer here when, according to Dad, he also went in search of greener pastures. And yet, here we both are again.

"Look at you," he says. "You're, like, a woman." He stumbles on the last word like it's explicit. Tyler and I have always had a sibling-type relationship, especially since I don't have any of my own. But we haven't seen each other since I was eighteen and he was twenty-one. I *am* a woman now.

"Look at you," I counter. He's changed, too. His face isn't as soft as it used to be, having grown into its angles. His cheeks are scruffy with strawberry stubble where it was once as smooth as a freshly polished saddle. I swipe his baseball cap and run my fingers through his cropped red hair. It's darkened over the years. "You've grown up quite a bit yourself."

"And still no cowboy hat," he says, snatching his cap back from me and pulling it onto his head.

"I'll get you one for your birthday."

"You wouldn't dare."

I shrug. "Part of being a woman. I'm more stubborn than ever."

"As if that's possible."

I smack him on the arm playfully and he laughs. Gratitude for the intimacy of a true friendship stirs inside me and I'm surprised at the stinging I feel at the corners of my eyes.

Tyler doesn't seem to notice.

"Want to go for a ride?" he asks. "I was just about to saddle up Rocket."

I blink a few times and nod. "I thought you'd never ask."

"Five years. Geez, Mal." Tyler draws out the words as he sits atop Rocket, a large American Warmblood—Dad's horse—who stands two hands above Midnight and me. His coat is a splotched dark brown and white, like chocolate milk, not fully mixed together. The horses saunter side by side through the rows of my dad's grapevines that spread as far as the eye can see. Dad moved us here seventeen years ago when the Paso Robles wine country was just up, not so much coming. Having been gone for so long, I appreciate its growth anew. Looking out to the east, I see the plot of land that has been prepared for the new vines, the trellises currently standing empty, waiting.

"Has it gotten quieter since I was here last?" I ask.

Tyler laughs. "No. Your tolerance has just lessened."

"I couldn't even sleep last night. I swear, I could feel it pressing in on me."

"You went and turned into a city girl on us, didn't you?"

I narrow my eyes at him, assaulting him with a long pause. "Never."

"When was the last time you even rode a horse?"

I hesitate. "Yesterday?"

He laughs.

"Well, how many stables do you think there are in New York City?"

"Fair enough."

Tyler and I point the horses up the trail that leads to the

top of the hill overlooking the vineyard. Tyler lets me lead, and I close my eyes, tilting my head toward the sun. It thaws the northeastern winter from my bones. Midnight rocks back and forth beneath me with every step, and the sensation is so familiar, I could be a teenager again, full of possibilities and confusion...love and a broken heart.

"So, your boss finally let you take a vacation?" he asks.

I come back to the present. "Something like that," I say.

"What's it actually like?"

I laugh. Leave it to Tyler to not let me off the hook. He hasn't changed at all.

"Actually..." I twist my fingers into Midnight's mane. "I don't really have a job at the moment."

I look over my shoulder at him. His brow is furrowed. He urges me on with his eyes.

"My paid internship ended yesterday. I have to decide whether or not I'm going to take a permanent position there. Or, I guess, somewhere else. Or something else."

"That's a lot of decisions to make," he notes.

A humorless laugh escapes my lips. "Yeah, it is."

We're quiet as we finish climbing the hill, instead focusing on avoiding the sharp, dry tree limbs overhead. I used to be able to avoid every branch that jutted out, thirsty for blood. Now they're everywhere, the path less trodden.

We reach the top and Tyler brings Rocket to a trot next to me. We lead the horses to the break in the trees, stopping at the edge where we can see the entire property. I could sit here and memorize the horizon for hours.

"So what's it going to be?" Tyler asks, not missing a step. It's the question I've asked myself a thousand times over the last few weeks.

"I don't know. I was kind of hoping coming home would help me decide."

Tyler looks at me but doesn't respond right away. His expression is studious as he tries to apply this new information to the Mallory he used to know. That Mallory didn't think through decisions like this. She made one and let the cards fall where they may.

"What?" I finally ask.

"I don't know. It's just…you usually run headlong into any opportunity that presents itself. That's kind of your thing."

I find a tear in the leather on Midnight's saddle and pick at it. "Well, I'm not a teenager anymore. Everyone is a little reckless when they're teenagers."

"Some things don't change."

"Some things do."

"Maybe. Maybe not." He winks, taking some of the pressure off the conversation. I grin.

"You talk a lot for a cowboy."

"I'm not a cowboy."

Tyler moves Rocket sideways until he can hook his arm around my neck, pulling me into a rough hug.

"It's good to have you back," he says.

I slip my arm around his waist. The way his T-shirt sticks to his back hints at the sheen of sweat beneath that reminds me of many summer days spent washing horses and polishing saddles with him.

"It's good to be here," I say.

"You see Kelly yet?" he asks.

I purse my lips and let my arm fall away from him.

"No. I haven't."